TROUBLET

BOOK THREE

THE MYSTERY

GARTH NIX

AND

SEAN WILLIAMS

SCHOLASTIC INC.

This book was originally published in hardcover by Scholastic Press in 2013.

ISBN 978-0-545-25905-7

12 11 10 9 8 7 6 5 4 3 2 1 14 15 16 17 18 19/0

Printed in the U.S.A. 40
First paperback printing, April 2014

The text was set in Sabon.
Book design by Christopher Stengel

*To Anna, Thomas, and Edward
and all my family and friends
— Garth*

*For my grandmothers, Isobel
Jean Williams and Evelyn
Mary Schiller — Sean*

Table of Contents

PROLOGUE

OUT OF THE RAIN

Young Master Rourke sat upright in his armchair, startled awake by a sudden noise. Despite his name, he was actually an old man, only a few days short of his eighty-fifth birthday. He was known as "Young Master Rourke" because his father had been the one and only "Mister Rourke" in the area for many, many years. Old Mister Rourke had built Rourke Castle and had bought up all the railways, shipping lines, and the whaling stations for miles around. In doing so, he'd become one of the richest and most influential men of his time.

Most of the riches were now gone, but Young Master Rourke still owned Rourke Castle. A vast, rambling palace that extended across two sides of a hill, it had towers, stables, three ballrooms, a Greek temple, a Venetian canal, and a scale copy of an Egyptian pyramid that was a hundred feet high. (The pyramid looked like stone on the outside but was in fact hollow, made of concrete slabs over a steel skeleton.)

Rourke Castle was so big that it was spread across two towns. Half was within the bounds of a small town called Portland, the other half in the neighboring town. When the castle had still had staff, they'd used to joke about going to Portland or going to Dogton when crossing from one side of the castle to the other.

Over the years more and more of the castle had been locked up and left, as it was too expensive to maintain. Young Master Rourke kept moving from larger rooms to smaller ones as his needs shrank. Finally he left the main castle entirely and moved to the old porter's lodge near the front gates, past the lake that had once boasted real icebergs and penguins, even in summer. Now the giant ice machine was broken and the penguins had been sent to a proper zoo. The lake was just a dark expanse of water, choked by rotten lilies.

The lodge and the land around it were half a mile outside the boundary of Portland. Rourke had not thought this important when he moved. He had forgotten that someone had once told him that he should take care to stay on the Portland side of the boundary at all times.

The sound that had woken him came again. Young Master Rourke tilted his head back as he tried to work out what it was. The grandfather clock in the corner of the room ticked slowly and melancholically, but that wasn't it. The time was five minutes short of midnight and the clock far from striking.

The night was quiet for a few seconds. Then the noise came a third time — a quick rush of beats that swept across the roof and were gone.

"Is that . . . rain?" muttered Young Master Rourke, blinking the sleep from his eyes.

He took off his half-moon reading glasses and consulted the ornate, gilded barometer that stood next to the grandfather clock.

The barometer's needle was sitting at FAIR.

"Stupid thing," Young Master Rourke mumbled.

He struggled out of his deep leather armchair and crossed the room to tap the face of the barometer, firmly.

The needle quivered, then moved, but not toward STORMY. It kept insisting the weather should be fair.

Another round of what sounded like heavy raindrops crossed the roof. Rourke went to the window and looked out. There were still a few working lampposts on the broad avenue that went up toward the castle, alongside the lake. Above, the sky was cloudy and utterly empty of stars, but Rourke couldn't see any actual rain.

"Just a shower, you daft old fool," he told himself. "Forget about it and go to bed."

He bent down and picked up the book he'd been reading, his mood improving instantly. Rourke had read *Gorillas vs The Fist* before, but it was one of many favorites that he often revisited. Reading pulpy old detective stories was one of his two main activities. The other one was looking after the only legacy of his father's that he actually treasured: the animals of the old Rourke Menagerie.

In his father's time, the menagerie had contained elephants, lions, tigers, and other kinds of exotic animals. Now there were only two chimpanzees, a warthog, three lemurs, a zebra, a jackal, two wolves, and a macaw named Cornelia, who was at least a hundred years old. (When Young Master Rourke had been much younger, he'd believed that Cornelia had been stolen from a pirate.)

In old Mister Rourke's day all the animals had been housed in a complete zoo, up past the eastern wing of the castle. But that area was a weedy wasteland now. The remaining animals lived in a much smaller collection of cages and enclosures built on the old polo field right next to the lodge where Young Master Rourke lived. It was nowhere near as impressive as the grand old menagerie had been, but it was closer and much easier to deal with.

The new cages were also outside Portland's boundary.

Rattling rain fell on the roof again as Rourke shuffled out of his study into the lodge's main corridor. This time, when the heavy beat of the drops ceased, a sudden, loud bang immediately followed, then a much heavier thudding along the roof.

"That's not rain. . . ." whispered Rourke, looking up to follow the sound as it traveled toward the back of the lodge. His heart was suddenly thumping in his chest, faster than was good for him. "That's footsteps."

The sound stopped. Rourke's head snapped back down as a man-shaped shadow passed across the narrow stained-glass window to the left of the back door.

There was someone out there — someone who had apparently come down with the rain.

It was only then that Rourke remembered the warning about staying inside the Portland town limits, and what might happen if he didn't. . . .

The book was still in his hand. He raised it, gnarled old fingers moving faster than anyone might expect, and flipped it open to the back page, where there was a simple white sticker with a phone number and address of a business in Portland.

Rourke stumbled to the ancient phone that sat on a seventeenth-century chestnut table in the corridor and put one shaking finger into the rotary dial.

At that moment he heard Cornelia the macaw, who had a free run of the new menagerie but most often slept in a custom-made box under the eaves at the back door of the lodge. Cornelia normally never said anything but "Who's a pretty girl?" and "Nellie wants a nut." Now she started shrieking.

"To the boats! Abandon ship!"

The other animals started braying and screaming and kicking, making noises that Rourke had never heard, not in all his long lifetime spent looking after them. They were hooting and howling, barking and biting, shaking their cages and filling the night with unnatural terror.

Frantically, Rourke dialed the number.

As the dial whirred in its final rotation, the noise of the animals suddenly stopped, as if a conductor had snapped down his arms for a sudden finish.

Rourke held the phone to his ear, hardly hearing the sound of ringing at the other end. All his senses were focused toward the back door and the menagerie beyond.

The animals were quiet now, but there were other noises. Cages were swinging open, one by one. These sounds were familiar to Rourke, who opened them every day. There was the screech of the chimps' door, the one he had been meaning to oil for weeks. There was the scrape of steel on concrete, the bent door in the fence that surrounded the wolves' enclosure. . . .

The phone kept ringing, and now Rourke could hear animals moving. Much more quietly than normal, though he still heard the soft pads of the jackal, the hooves of the zebra, and the shuffling gait of the warthog. The wolves, he assumed, remained stealthy, moving with their characteristic silence.

"What?" asked a tired voice on the phone. A man, grumpy at being woken up so late.

Rourke's mouth opened and closed. He struggled to speak but couldn't get any air into his lungs. The uncaged animals were at the back door now — he could see their shadows against the stained glass.

"No!" he tried to say, the word emerging as little more than a croak. "No!"

The handle of the back door slowly turned. The door edged open.

"Who is this?" asked the voice on the phone.

The back door swung open. A man stood there, a man wearing a hat and a trench coat just like the one on the cover of Rourke's book, except both were thoroughly wet. Water dripped from the brim of the hat that shadowed this man's face.

The animals were gathered around the stranger, silent companions pressing in as close as they could as he eased through the doorway.

"David?" the old man gasped.

There was something very odd about the animals. It took Rourke a second to process exactly what it was.

"Their eyes . . ." gasped Rourke. "Their eyes are white!"

The phone fell from his hand as the man in the door lifted his head to stare at him. The shadow of the man's hat brim rose and light fell on his face, reflecting from his eyes — eyes that, just like the animals' eyes, were utterly white, without pupil or iris.

++Where is it, old fool?++ asked the intruder. No sound came from his mouth, and his lips did not move, but the voice was clear in Rourke's mind. **++Where is it?++**

Rourke opened his mouth but only a choking rattle came out. His hand flew to his head, as if he could ward off the stabbing, awful communication that was going straight into his brain.

++Answer the question!++

Rourke suddenly clawed at his chest with both hands. *Gorillas vs The Fist* fluttered forgotten to the floor.

++No!++ shouted the stranger. He dashed forward and caught Rourke as he fell.

White began to swirl in Rourke's eyes, too, but it could not outpace the other change that gripped the old man.

Young Master Rourke went limp. The life ebbed from his eyes, leaving them open and unseeing.

The stranger lowered the heavy body to the floor. He grabbed the phone and pulled it from the wall, the cord coming out with a piece of plaster the size of a dinner plate. Then he bent down and searched through the pockets of Rourke's dressing gown.

Without any sign or gesture from the stranger, the two white-eyed chimpanzees went into the study, while the other animals silently roamed the study as though looking for something.

The stranger flicked through the pages of Young Master Rourke's book. As he did so, a thick, gray mist formed above him and several heavy drops of rain fell onto his back. He paused and looked up, and made an angry dismissive gesture that caused the mist and rain to immediately disappear.

In the study, the chimpanzees began to move books out of the bookcases, carefully opening each one before dropping it disinterestedly onto the floor. The wolves circled Rourke's fallen body, sniffing his pockets.

"It *must* be here," whispered the stranger, using his voice this time. It sounded strangely like a growl, at first neither man nor animal, but then shifted to being fully human. "But if it's not, there's always Plan B."

Behind the chimps, the clock shook. Springs whirred inside its cavernous casing, cogs grated, and a chime sounded the first of twelve strokes of midnight.

The sound echoed through the lodge and, faintly but clearly, outside. The ancient macaw, hiding in the topmost branches of one of the great elms that lined the castle avenue, heard the clock and lowered her proud-beaked head.

"Every parrot for herself," she muttered, and launched herself into the air, beginning a slow but steady flight to the east, toward the shimmering lights of Portland.

CHAPTER ONE
THE ACCIDENT

The twins were doing math questions when they heard the first siren scream past the school, heading north, and then stop not much farther on. Back in their old home in the city, they wouldn't have paid it any attention at all. But in the small town of Portland, even a single siren was unusual. When it was followed by another, as was the current case, it became almost interesting.

"That's the ambulance," said curly-haired Kyle, one of those kids who could recognize the slight individual variations in the sirens of the local emergency service vehicles. "And the second one is the fire engine. . . ."

His voice trailed off as another, more distant siren joined the mix, getting louder as it raced toward the town.

"And that's the rescue rig from Scarborough!" he exclaimed. "Something big must be going on!"

He jumped up and rushed to the window, followed by most of the class.

"Children, children!" admonished Mr. Carver, but as he didn't actually raise his voice, only the front row heard him and stayed in place.

Jack and Jaide looked at each other and didn't immediately follow, having already experienced quite a lot of disasters and emergencies in the last few weeks. Also, they were from the city and had a reputation to hold up as not being impressed by something that probably wouldn't rate a mention on the news back home.

Over the cacophony of all the sirens, there came a deep, fast beat that the twins knew very well. The *wokka-wokka-wokka* of an approaching helicopter.

"Airswift Aeromedical 339, twin-engine," said Jaide, jumping up and angling quickly between a couple of kids to get to the window. Her brother, Jack, followed in her wake.

"How do *you* know?" asked Kyle.

"That's our mother's helicopter," said Jack. "This *must* be serious. Can you see anything?"

"Not really, but the helicopter looks like it's going to land near the iron bridge." Kyle craned up on tiptoe, trying to get a better view. "Yeah, there it goes — must be right in the middle of the road!"

"Class, I would particularly appreciate it if you would return to your seats," said Mr. Carver, still in his normal conversational voice, "while I endeavor to ascertain if this emergency affects the school."

His students didn't even turn around. The kids in back kept jostling to get to the window, while the kids in front pushed back with their elbows to stay in place.

"CHILDREN! Back to your seats!"

No one had ever heard Mr. Carver shout before. There was a moment of shock, followed by a sudden cascade of students rushing back to their desks, several of them tripping over the beanbags that were used during Mr. Carver's "meditation time." They didn't so much sit back down as do controlled crashes into their chairs.

"Continue with your math problems." Mr. Carver wasn't shouting now, but his voice was still louder than usual, clear even over the noise of the sirens and the helicopter winding down. "I am going to see what's going on. I expect everyone to stay in their places unless requested otherwise, by me or another teacher."

He took his phone out of his pocket as he strode out of the class, dialing with one hand as he pushed the door open with the other.

"Wow! I've never seen him like that before," said Tara, the newest student in the school. "I mean, I thought he was nothing but peace and light all the time."

"Nah, old Heath loses it occasionally," said Kyle, using Mr. Carver's first name, as he preferred his students to do, although few of them could ever bring themselves to do it. "Three years ago he freaked out when that tree branch fell down in the parking lot just before the bus left for the whale-watching excursion."

"That wasn't three years ago, Kyle," said Miralda King, daughter of the mayor.

"Yes, it was," Kyle snapped back.

"We went fossil-hunting on Mermaid Point three years ago," retorted Miralda. "Whale-watching was *four* years ago."

"Actually, it *was* three years ago," said one of the other kids, and then all the locals who'd been at the school long enough started arguing about whether they had gone whale-watching four or three years ago, and whether or not the branch had fallen that year, or in fact some other year, when the bus was leaving for some different excursion.

"I guess you have to find your own excitement in a small town," Tara whispered to Jaide.

"Whatever's happening on the bridge is enough for me," said Jaide. "I wish we could see what's happening."

"Can't be too big, or we'd have to evacuate," said Jack. "I mean, if it was a gas tanker that was going to explode or something."

"There's a lot of sirens," said Jaide. "And Mom's helicopter, so someone must be badly hurt. Maybe lots of people."

"You know, I thought I heard something before the sirens," said Tara. "A kind of thudding noise, like when a big truck goes past and shakes everything a bit. Just for a second."

"I didn't hear anything," said Jack. "I was totally concentrating on the math questions."

"Yeah, sure," said Jaide. "You were practically asleep. I saw you."

Jack shrugged. His twin knew him too well. He had finished the problems ages ago and had been daydreaming, imagining himself using his Gift, merging into the shadow by the wall and escaping from school.

"I suppose we had better do these questions," said Tara to Jaide. "They won't go away on their own."

The students were bent over their papers — all except Jack, who had moved on to imagining increasingly unlikely accidents to explain the unusual events in Portland that morning — when Mr. Carver came back into the room a few minutes later. He was talking on his phone.

"So there is no danger to the school? Good, good. What exactly . . . ? Into the river? Yes, of course I know . . . oh my . . . oh my . . . oh dear!"

Jack and Jaide were not looking up, or they would have seen Mr. Carver suddenly stare at them with an expression they all knew well. His forehead had wrinkled and his mouth flattened into a straight, sincere line.

Tara saw it. She nudged Jaide.

"You just got the Caring Sharing Face from Heath."

"What?" asked Jaide. All of a sudden she felt a stab of fear. The helicopter . . . her mother! But the helicopter had landed fine. Why would they be the object of Mr. Carver's Caring Sharing Face?

Mr. Carver put his phone away and carefully walked among the desks, over to where Jack and Jaide sat.

"Class, continue with your work," he said brightly. "Jack and Jaide, could you please come with me to the office? There's something I'd like you to help me with."

Jack and Jaide stood up and started to gather their books.

"No, no, leave everything and come along," said Mr. Carver.

He opened the door and gestured to them to go in front of him. Out in the corridor, Jack stopped and said, "What's going on? Is Mom all right?"

"Yes, I'm sure she's fine," said Mr. Carver quickly. He made some tentative gestures again, as if he was trying to herd ducklings into his office. "Just step inside and I'll tell you when you're sitting down."

"We were sitting down before," said Jaide, as she and her brother sat uneasily on the shiny orange-and-yellow couch.

Mr. Carver perched himself on the corner of his desk and fiddled with a small Tibetan prayer wheel, flicking it till the bells began to jangle.

"Yes, but this is . . . what I have to tell you . . . it's best not in class. No, I think more suitable that you be sitting together . . . you may even want to, in fact I think it's a good idea if you hold your brother's hand, Jaide —"

"Just tell us!" both twins said at once.

"I'm not sure, I don't have all the details, but it seems that about twenty minutes ago, a car was forced off the road just before the iron bridge, into the river. . . ."

He spun the prayer wheel more forcefully.

"So?" asked Jack, now extremely puzzled. "*What* car went into the river . . . ?"

"A yellow car, an old yellow car," whispered Mr. Carver.

It felt as if time froze for the twins, as if everything stopped. For a long second, neither of them could move, or think, or speak, and then everything started again, and Mr. Carver was gabbling about "your wonderful grandmother" but it was meaningless. All they could think about was Grandma X's old yellow car going into the river, taking Grandma X down with it, down into the muddy depths. . . .

"But . . . but it couldn't . . . it couldn't happen," Jaide said finally.

"No," agreed Jack. "No way."

"I know it is difficult to comprehend," said Mr. Carver. "Fate is fickle, and in accidents such as these, anything can occur —"

"No," said Jaide. "You don't understand. Grandma X is . . . is *special*."

She couldn't say what she really wanted to say. That Grandma X had magical Gifts, and wisdom, and . . .

There was the clatter of boots in the hall, and then all of a sudden, the twins' mother was in the doorway. Mr. Carver stood up nervously, but she ignored him and dashed to the children.

"Jack, Jaide!"

The twins moved into Susan's hug as if she was a life preserver thrown to them at sea. She hugged them just as tightly for a moment, then eased them back.

"Is . . . is she dead?" asked Jaide. She could hardly get the words out, or keep back the tears that were suddenly welling up in her eyes.

"No," said Susan. "But the car was in the river for some time, and they've just got it out and she's still inside. She *is* conscious, which is a very good sign. We'll be flying her to the hospital as soon as they can . . . get her free. I just ran over to tell you that Rodeo Dave is on his way, and he'll drive you to the hospital. I'll be there, of course."

"Which hospital?" asked Jack. He looked at Jaide, and she knew what he was thinking. Grandma X might have to be taken beyond the wards, and neither of them knew what effect that might have.

Grandma X was the Warden of Portland, charged with secretly protecting the world from The Evil, a terrible force from another dimension. If it hadn't been for the Wardens, the world would have been taken over long ago. Jack and Jaide were going to be Wardens one day, but for now they were troubletwisters, young Wardens whose Gifts were unreliable and occasionally dangerous, despite the best efforts of their grandmother to teach them how to use them. The first time their Gifts had appeared, the twins had accidentally blown up their house in the city and they had been forced to move away from the life they had always known.

Their grandmother was strict and knew a lot more about everything than she ever let on, including her name. They just called her Grandma X while everyone else mumbled when they had to call her anything. The twins had been in Portland for months now, constantly learning about their Gifts and their new responsibilities, but sometimes it seemed as though they had barely begun. There was still so much they didn't understand.

Would the four wards of Portland, which kept The Evil from breaking into the world, still work if the Warden in charge of them left?

What would happen if she died?

"She'll go to Scarborough, of course," said Susan, ignorant of their concerns. She didn't like being reminded of the legacy the twins had inherited from their father, and Grandma X had "encouraged" her ability to forget. "Better facilities. Not to demean Portland Hospital, but —"

Her walkie-talkie crackled and a voice said, "Sue! Almost there. Three minutes."

"On my way!" Susan replied. She hugged the twins again. "I have to go. She'll be okay, I'm sure of it. She's the toughest person I know!"

She turned quickly to Mr. Carver. "Dave Smeaton from the Book Herd is authorized to pick the children up. He'll be here in a moment."

With one last hug and one last look to the twins, she was gone.

The next five minutes were very long. Mr. Carver spun the prayer wheel one more time, then put it down and picked up his nose flute, but he put that down again without playing anything. He opened his mouth to say something, and nothing came out. Finally, he got up and slid through the door, pausing to mutter something about "leaving you to your thoughts" and "must get back to class."

As soon as he was gone, Jack and Jaide started whispering furiously to each other.

"She'll be okay," said Jack. "She probably wasn't even really hurt. Right?"

"But a *hospital*, Jack. What if they fly her to Scarborough? Shouldn't we do something?"

"We should call Dad," they said together.

"But we don't know where he is," Jack pointed out.

"Custer!" said Jaide, thinking of their father's old friend. "Custer will know."

"We don't know how to get in touch with him, either. Or the other Wardens. Grandma X did all that."

"Mom must have a number for Dad," said Jaide, but she didn't sound very convinced.

"He always loses his phone," said Jack glumly. "And he's usually somewhere weird anyway, where nothing works. But he might have, you know, secret Warden ways of knowing stuff. Maybe Grandma X sent him a . . . a thought message . . . or something."

"I cannot reach your father," said a faint voice behind the twins, apparently emanating from the wall. Jack and Jaide leaped off the couch as if it was suddenly red-hot.

Behind them, on the wall, was a faint image of their grandmother. She didn't look young like she usually did when her spirit form appeared, and it didn't look three-dimensional. This was more like a blurry photo being projected onto the wallpaper. Her white hair was even messier than it was every morning. Her eyelids fluttered.

"I am somewhat injured," said Grandma X. "But I will be all right, so you don't need to worry."

"But they're taking you to Scarborough!" exclaimed Jaide. "What will that do to the wards?"

"They are *not* taking me to Scarborough," said the blurry image with familiar stubbornness. "Shortly, they will decide that it is better to take me somewhere closer, even if the facilities are not so advanced. Portland Hospital will fit the bill perfectly."

Her eyelids closed completely, but not before the twins saw her eyes roll back upward, into her head.

"Are you really okay?" asked Jack anxiously.

"I have a concussion . . . and my body was affected by the cold of the river," said Grandma X, her eyes opening again. "I don't have much time. Custer will monitor the wards. I don't expect trouble, but if anything does come up, and Custer is not available, you can . . . ow! . . . be careful —"

Grandma X's voice was cut off, and the image disappeared.

"Hello, you two," said Rodeo Dave from the doorway behind them. The twins spun around again, uncertain how long he'd been there. He bobbed his head and said, "All ready to go? Scarborough Hospital, your mother said."

"Uh, yeah, thanks," said Jack. "Only maybe, we should check first —"

Dave's phone rang.

"Hang on, Jack. Dave here . . . oh, right . . . no problem. We're on our way."

He put the phone away and said to the twins, "Not Scarborough General. Portland Hospital. We'll be there in a jiffy. Come on!"

The helicopter lifted off as they got to Dave's white van, which he used to pick up and deliver books. They all piled in the front and, after reminding Dave about his seat belt, they drove out onto River Road.

"We'll have to go the long way," said Dave. "The bridge will be closed for a while."

The twins peered past the willows to the bridge, which was surrounded by emergency vehicles. At the southern end, the crane truck that usually worked at the marina was up on its supports, with a chain going down to the battered, mud-strewn wreck of a yellow Hillman Minx that had been pulled out of the river.

Seeing the car made it all seem more horribly real. Jack had to look away, and Jaide found herself the victim of a sudden attack of the shivers.

“Your grandmother will be fine,” said Dave, noting both of these events. He leaned across and opened the glove compartment. “Grab a couple of the sweets, there. You’ve both had a nasty shock.”

The sweets were nothing the twins had ever seen before, old-fashioned boiled things wrapped in paper that was hard to remove. Concentrating on getting the paper off took up most of the trip to the hospital.

Susan was waiting for them in the lobby.

“Grandma is okay,” she said. “We were worried for a moment, but she rallied as soon as we got her here. That’s amazing for someone who’s been through a major accident.”

“Can we see her?” asked Jaide, as Jack said, “Is she awake?”

“The doctors are with her now,” said Susan. “They’re going to keep her in Critical Care until tomorrow morning, probably. They may still have to move her to Scarborough. As for what happened . . . it’s not that clear. She told Officer Haigh a truck or a van came up fast behind her, tried to overtake her before the bridge, and then cut back in unexpectedly, forcing her off the road and into the river.”

“And the truck didn’t stop?” asked Jack. “Wow, that’s mean.”

“More than mean,” said Susan. “It’s criminal. The police will be looking for it. But don’t worry about that. I’m going to need your help. Things are going to be a bit complicated at home for a while. I can’t get someone to cover me immediately — you know how we’re always shorthanded, so you’ll be by yourselves a bit more than usual. I will be home tonight, though. Maybe we can find someone to check in on you until my shift is over.”

"What about Tara?" asked Jaide. "We could hang out with her."

"Yes, good idea. I'll give her father a call . . . but we can't rely on them every night."

Rodeo Dave, who had until that moment been occupied with grooming his thick mustache, cleared his throat.

"Renita Daniels — that is, Rennie — has been helping me out at the shop," he said. "I've let her have the small apartment up top, and I'm sure she'd be happy to . . . uh . . . babysit, if you pardon the term, Jaide, Jack. . . ."

Susan nodded with relief. "Thank you, Dave. And thanks for bringing the twins here. Can I ask you to take them back to school as well? I hope you don't mind."

"Of course not." He winked at them. "It's a pleasure."

"Oh, and I should have said before how sorry I was to hear about Young Master Rourke. He was a friend of yours, wasn't he?"

"He was," said Dave, his face falling. "He bought a lot of books from me over the years. In fact, I'm heading up there the day after tomorrow, to catalog his collection for the executors."

"Young Master who?" asked Jack.

"What happened to him?" added Jaide.

"We'll talk about it later," said Susan. "Now, remember, Grandma X is very fit and strong . . . for someone her age. So don't worry . . . honest —"

She was interrupted by three quick bursts of sound from her walkie-talkie. Not words, just the crackle.

"Got to go! Love you!"

There was a whirlwind embrace, then she was off.

"Okay," said Dave. His smile returned as though it had never vanished. "Your chariot awaits."

CHAPTER TWO

AN UNEXPECTED ENCOUNTER

Four hours later, water was dripping from the edge of the umbrella Jack Shield held and trickling right down the back of his sister's neck. Jaide shuddered and tugged her collar tight up to her throat, pulling her head in as best she could. She could see nothing outside the umbrella but sods of disturbed earth, the mud-spattered feet of the adults walking around them, and the base of a heavy, gray stone wall three yards away. The rain continued to stream down on them, far heavier than it had been back in the town.

"Remind me what we're doing here?" she grumbled.

"You suggested it," said Jack. "You asked Mom if we could hang out with Tara."

"But this wasn't what I was expecting!"

They were standing next to a life-size castle — a real one, to all appearances, with turrets and a portcullis, even a deep moat filled with murky brown water. Nearby were a number of smaller buildings scattered on the edge of a large and even murkier lake. A squat pyramid peeked around the shoulder of a low hill.

"Dad says this is one of the most important landmarks in Portland," Tara said, coming up behind them. She had her own umbrella, a purple-spotted thing that looked brand-new, vastly different to the moth-eaten black antique the twins had found in the back of Tara's car. It leaked and two people couldn't quite fit under it, but Jaide told herself it was better than nothing. "He knew you'd love to see it since you're interested in old buildings and stuff."

"Er, right."

It was Jaide's turn to want to kick her brother, this time for the ridiculous lie he had come up with to explain their former interest in Tara's father, a property developer. It meant long lectures on the renovation potential of old warehouses and barracks and being dragged about in all manner of weather, whether they asked to go or not.

"You know, Jaide, it *is* pretty cool," said Jack, peering out and up at the castle wall, tipping the umbrella in the process and sending another wave of water straight into Jaide's right ear. "There was nothing like this in the city."

Jaide braved the rain to take another look. The side of the castle seemed to go up forever, broken every now and again only by a narrow, slitlike window, for archers to fire from. Jaide didn't think there had ever been a need for archers in Portland, but there probably hadn't been any need for a moat, either.

"Young Master Rourke lived here?" she asked.

"Not here exactly. He was in that little building we passed, by the gates."

"And he really just died?" Jack asked, thinking of the sadness in Rodeo Dave's eyes and the weirdness of their present position. They had only just heard about him, and now here they were, exploring where he had used to live.

"Saturday night," Tara said. Her eyes gleamed with gruesome relish. "Dad doesn't know who found him."

"Maybe his butler," said Jaide.

"He didn't have a butler. He cooked and cleaned for himself, and lived here completely alone."

Jack peered curiously around, at the little they could see through the sheets of heavy rain. He could make out people striding about in boots and raincoats, some of them holding nets and odd mechanical lassoes.

"I can't believe Portland has a *castle*," he said, wondering if it was cool for a grown-up to want to live in one, or a bit weird. He had thought Grandma X was the strangest person in Portland, but now it seemed she had some competition.

Used to have competition, he reminded himself. That thought, combined with the thought of her all alone in the hospital, made him worry about her even more.

"I can't believe Portland has a castle, either," exclaimed Tara's dad, sticking his head into their huddle of umbrellas with a wide, white-toothed smile. He was, as always, wearing a cap with the name of his company on it, MMM Holdings. "And it's prime real estate, just perfect for redevelopment. When the will is sorted out, we could be sitting on a gold mine! Do you know, the main building has thirty-seven bedrooms and hasn't been lived in for twenty years? Think how many apartments we could fit in there!"

"Dad!" protested Tara. "The old guy only just died! And you're already moving in on the property?"

"Officially, the council asked for a valuation, in case Rourke left it to the state," he said, ruffling her black hair before she could flinch away. "But it doesn't hurt to speculate. I mean, imagine the possibilities. There's a lot of work to be done. We'd have to get that bridge fixed, first of all. . . ."

He hurried off to oversee four council workers who were trying to shift a footbridge that had fallen into the stream that fed the castle's moat. A sheet of water was building up behind it and spreading like a gleaming, translucent pancake across the muddy lawn. Everyone's footprints were being submerged, human and animal alike. On the far side of the lake, two more council workers were struggling to catch something that looked very much like a zebra.

"Do you think he had a pet platypus?" Tara asked. "I've always wanted to see one of those."

"Really?" said Jack. "They'd creep me out, I reckon."

"Why?"

"Well, it's like they're made from bits of lots of animals, all mixed together."

"Like Frankenstein's monster?"

"Yeah, I guess."

Tara was quiet for a moment, then she said in a distant voice, "I had a dream like that . . . I think. There was a monster . . . or something . . . made of lots of smaller things. You were in the dream, Jack. And you, too, Jaide. But I can't quite remember it."

Jaide sought some way to change the subject. Tara wasn't remembering a dream, but something that had really happened to all of them. Four weeks ago, they had been attacked by The Evil, which had a nasty habit of taking over living things and mixing them together, creating very real monsters that could in turn attack people. After The Evil had been vanquished, one of Grandma X's fellow Wardens, a big-haired man named Aleksandr, had used his Gift to cloud Tara's memory of everything that had happened to her. Sometimes the memory poked up again, though, before returning to the depths. What would happen if it ever came right out, Jaide didn't like to imagine.

"Look down there," Jack said. "Are they statues down by the creek? Let's check them out."

Tara shook herself, sending droplets of water tumbling down her green overcoat. "They don't look like anything special."

"Come on," said Jaide, relieved to hear Tara's voice returning to normal. "We're going to get washed away if we stay here."

The pool of water was spreading rapidly toward them, backed up from where the bridge had fallen into the creek. Tara's dad was waving his arms imperiously, to the annoyance of all, and the sound of raised voices was getting steadily louder as the problem showed no sign of being fixed.

Jack, Jaide, and Tara gave the puddle a wide berth and headed past the impromptu dam to where a much-reduced trickle ran along the slimy creek bed. The ground was slippery underfoot and the rain showed no sign of letting up.

It was weird, Jack thought, how Portland had been sunny when they had set out after school. The clouds had only gathered when they'd reached the estate. And it was odder still how it seemed to be raining *only* on the estate, not anywhere else. It was so heavy and set in. . . .

"There you go!" Tara called back to them from the line of statues. "Men in sheets and women without any arms. What's with these old guys? Don't they have any taste?"

Jack opened his mouth to say that being rich meant you didn't have to have any taste, but Jaide pulled him to a sudden halt.

"Look," she whispered, pointing into an untidy copse at the far edge of the estate. "There's someone in those trees, waving at us."

"Where?"

"There!"

Jack peered into the shadows under the trees, using his Gift to see details Jaide could only guess at. His Gift was strongest at night, but the sun was so hidden right now behind heavy rain clouds that his sight was clear. There *was* someone in the copse, a lone man in a coat and hat, his eyes invisible behind dark glasses. It was hard to make out more than that, but he was definitely staring right at Jack and his sister, and his right hand was above his head, waving back and forth.

"That looks like Dad," said Jaide.

Jack squinted. "It couldn't be him, could it? He isn't supposed to come anywhere near us."

"What if he's here because of Grandma's accident?"

Jack raised a hand, tentatively, and waved back.

The shadowy figure raised both hands in a triumphant thumbs-up.

"It *is* Dad!" exclaimed Jaide.

The twins hadn't been this close to their father since their Gifts had woken, apart from once, when the protection supplied by the four wards of Portland had broken. He wasn't allowed to be near them because it made their Gifts go crazy.

There was, however, no denying the relief they felt upon seeing him. Someone must have told him about what had happened, and perhaps he had come back to check on them from a distance.

Jaide waved, too, and suddenly, with long energetic strides, their father moved toward them, stepping out from under the trees and across the sodden lawn. Jack and Jaide were torn between being pleased to see him and freaking out.

"What's he *doing* here?" hissed Jaide. "If someone sees . . ."

Jack looked frantically around. Tara was busy poking her finger into the eye socket of a statue. The council workers were hard at work shifting the bridge and chasing the escaped animals — but all it would take was one of them to look around and recognize their father.

"We need a distraction!" Jaide said. Their father had already crossed half the distance between them.

Jack thought fast.

"Use your Gift," he said, glancing up at the clouds. Jaide's Gift was mostly tied to the sun. "It should be kind of damped down right now. I'll go talk to him while you keep everyone busy — just keep your distance while you're doing it."

"I'm not sure that's a good idea," said Jaide. "Besides, I want to talk to him, too!"

"Can you think of anything else?"

"Not right away —"

"There's no time. Just do it!"

"All right, all right!" said Jaide, giving him the umbrella. "I'll do my best — but don't use your Gift when you're near him. Who knows what might happen?"

Jack could easily imagine. When he could control it properly, his Gift gave him power over light and shade, allowing him to shadow-walk, among other useful skills. When he couldn't control it, it had the power to black out the sun.

"Be careful," he said to Jaide.

"I will. You, too."

Jack hurried toward the bank of the creek, practically vanishing into the thick, gray sheets of rain.

Jaide shielded her eyes with her hand and turned to look up the slight rise past the dammed creek to the castle, where Tara's dad was still arguing with the council workers.

"A distraction," she whispered to herself.

She felt for her Gift, and embraced the slight breeze, collecting it around her, building it up so that she could use it. A gust escaped her hold for a moment, pirouetting around her like an invisible dancer, sending her damp hair flying.

"That's right," she whispered, gesturing with her free hand to usher the wind away from her. Strands of wet red hair lashed her face, but she ignored them. "You can do it."

The gust grew stronger, whisked twice more around her, then shot off up the slope, where it capered around the arguing men, snatching up Tara's dad's hat. He clutched at it and missed, knocking the man closest to him onto his backside. The hat smacked the face of a third man, and everything dissolved into chaos.

Jack heard sudden shouts behind him, but he didn't turn around to see. His attention was fixed on his father, who was approaching rapidly across the muddy field. The rain seemed to fall even more heavily around him, so much so that it came down in visible sheets, beating on the umbrella so hard it sounded as if it might collapse under the impact.

Hector Shield raised his hat and waved it in one hand. He shouted something that Jack couldn't make out. They were close enough now that Jack could clearly see locks of curly brown hair plastered to his father's high forehead, so like Jack's own. His glasses were completely smeared with rain. Even with the characteristic welcoming smile on his face, he looked strained and worried.

"It's not deep!" Jack called out, as Hector suddenly stopped on the other side of the creek.

Hector didn't move. He had stopped as suddenly as if he'd run into a wall, and now he backed up a few feet, taking off his glasses and wiping them on his sleeve. He squinted at Jack with eyes that were a perfect match for his son's, apart from being desperately myopic.

"It's not deep!" Jack shouted again. "Come over!" The rain was so loud now it drowned his words. He could hardly hear himself.

All of a sudden, one side of his umbrella collapsed, and a great deluge washed down Jack's back. He cried out and threw the umbrella down in disgust.

His father shouted something in return, but Jack couldn't hear him. The rain was amazingly loud. Jack pointed at his ears, then at the sky, and shrugged.

Hector Shield nodded, and pointed urgently at something behind Jack, stabbing the air with his finger.

Jack whipped around, squinting against the rain. Even through the downpour he could see what his father was pointing at so emphatically.

A thick, black twister was rising up over the castle like a supernatural cobra gathering its strength to strike.

A tornado.

Jaide's Gift had gone out of control.

"No, no," she hissed into the wind. She'd forgotten about trying to be unobtrusive, and was making wild hauling-in motions with her hands. "That's way too much!"

The twister didn't listen to her. It sucked in the rain and blew it out sideways like a fire hose, knocking a council worker upside down and sending him sliding across the mud with the speed of an ice hockey puck. Then it swooped down and picked up the bridge, raising it high up above the heads of the cowering workers.

"No!" shrieked Jaide. "*Listen* to me! Obey me!"

The twister slowed and bent forward, toward Jaide, the bridge still spinning thirty feet up in the air. The huddle of council workers suddenly split, everyone running in different directions.

Jaide felt the tension in the tornado, the built-up energy that just had to go somewhere. It needed to do *something.*

"All right," said Jaide sternly. "Just don't hurt anyone, and then you really have to go back to normal."

The tornado spun faster still, crouched down like a discus thrower about to throw, and then the bridge suddenly flew out of it, sailing across the field and smashing into the distant pyramid, broken pieces of timber sliding down the reinforced concrete slope.

Downstream, Jack watched openmouthed as the twister reared up even higher, got thinner, and then winked out of existence.

He had to shut his mouth as he suffered a massive raindrop straight down his throat. Coughing, he turned back toward his father, shrouded in rain on the other side of the creek. The water level had suddenly risen now that the fallen bridge was no longer blocking the creek upstream, so there was no chance for either of them to get across.

"Jack! Mmmm the mmmmm."

"What?" shouted Jack, as loudly as he could.

"Catch — the — phone!"

The twins' father pulled back his left arm and threw something small and black high across the creek bed. Jack stepped back, stretched, and caught the object. In the next instant his feet slid in the mud and he went over backward, landing with a jarring thud.

"Ow," said Jack. "Major ow."

He looked at the cell phone clutched tightly in his hand. It was in a plastic bag, with a charger. The screen was lit up, showing a message.

I heard about Grandma. Will call you later. Don't tell your mother I was here!

Jack looked across the stream. His father was backing away, disappearing into the darkness of the torrential rain.

"Wait! Don't go!"

A hand tugged at his shoulder.

"Jack? Are you all right? Did the tornado get you?"

It was Tara.

"Yeah, no, I just slipped."

"Well, come *on*. Don't just stand there! You'll drown."

The creek was rising with incredible speed. The rain was phenomenal — it had to be some kind of cloudburst. Jack staggered to his feet, slipping the phone and charger into his pocket as Tara helped him up. She tried to hold her umbrella over him, but one last, errant remnant of the twister blew past, smashing the umbrella's ribs and turning it inside out.

"Oh no!" exclaimed Tara. "That was Mom's! This weather is *crazy*!"

"You can say that again," said Jaide, who had just run up. She looked apologetically at Jack, but there wasn't time to say anything more before Tara's father bore down on them.

"Are you all right?"

He pulled Tara into a hug. Tara's dad had been much more protective of her since The Evil's last attack, when she'd been caught up in the train wreck. Tara had told the twins she both liked and disliked this new attention. This time, she let him keep his arm around her.

"Do you three want to go home?" he asked. "I can come back later by myself. You're soaked, and this rain, this amazing wind . . ."

"I think it's easing," said Tara. "I'm not cold. And I don't mind being soaked. I want to see the rest of the estate."

The rain *was* easing, at least near the castle. Farther off, toward the woods where the twins' father had gone, it was still bucketing down.

"What about you two?"

"We're fine," said Jaide. "Lead on, Lin!"

She fell back a few paces as they headed for the pyramid.

"Did you speak to Dad?" she whispered to her brother. "What did he say?"

Jack retrieved the message and held the phone out to her, keeping it cradled in his palm.

Jaide stared at it, her pale brow creased, the rain trickling down her face like tears.

"Is that all?"

"He didn't have time for more. Someone might have seen him."

"But still —"

"We can ask him when he calls us. Besides, look, Jaide — he gave us a *phone*."

The upside of their brief encounter with their father only occurred to her then. The twins had been hankering for a cell phone for months, but neither their mother nor their grandmother had given in. It was hard to play them off against each other when they agreed so absolutely, if only on that single point. But now their father had given them one, and they hadn't even had to ask!

Despite the circumstances, it was a welcome development.

"Let's call him," Jaide said.

"The number he texted us from is blocked. . . ."

Tara glanced over her shoulder to hurry them up, and Jack hastily put the phone away again. Whatever their father had to say to them would have to wait a little while longer.

CHAPTER THREE
THE MISSION

The phone burned a hole in Jack's pocket all the while they were on the castle grounds, following Tara's father from place to place as he inspected the other structures for their market potential. None of it was all that interesting because a lot of the rooms were locked. Even the pyramid was a letdown, although Jack was kind of impressed that the bridge hadn't even dented the outer face.

Ordinarily, the twins would have been interested in the makeshift menagerie and its unhappy occupants, but by that stage they just wanted to get home and find out how Grandma X was.

Most of the animals were being patched up by Portland's vet after being recaptured. The vet was a slender woman with surprisingly big hair, even with the rain weighing it down. She explained that several animals were still missing, including a gray wolf and both chimpanzees.

"There's a macaw, too," she said. "If you see it, leave it well alone. Parrots can have a nasty bite."

"No problem," said Tara. "All I want to do now is get out of the rain."

"Agreed," said Jack. "Can we go?"

Tara's father was staring at the porter's lodge, no doubt thinking about how it could be redeveloped or knocked down.

"What? Oh, sure. I've seen enough."

Susan was waiting for them when they got home. Dinner was on the stove, a stir-fry whose vegetables had been cooked so long it was hard to tell the chicken from the carrots. Neither twin cared about that, though. The appearance of their father at the estate had thoroughly rattled them. His presence suggested that Grandma X was sicker than anyone was telling them.

"She had a brain scan this afternoon," Susan reported. "They're waiting for the results. It's perfectly routine, so you don't need to worry about it. Just go get changed and then we'll eat, okay?"

"Have you spoken to Dad?" asked Jack.

"I tried calling him while I was in the hospital. He didn't pick up, but then he called an hour ago. I could hardly hear him, but I think he got the message about Grandma before the call dropped. I have no idea where he is, the middle of nowhere, probably. Now, go! You're dripping all over the floor."

Jack bit his tongue to stop himself from telling her that Hector wasn't on the other side of the world, but practically on Portland's doorstep. Only the message on the phone stopped him: *Don't tell your mother.* Whatever was going on, it was strictly Warden business.

By the time the twins were dried and warm in fresh clothes, the vegetables were even gloopier and their anxieties hardly quelled. Jaide barely tasted her mother's cooking, which was probably for the best, and Jack did little more than push his food around the plate.

"Tell me what you did with Tara today," Susan said in an attempt to bring them out of their thoughts.

"We went to the Rourke Estate," said Jaide, but instead of distracting her, the topic only made her think of her father again. She kept one hand on her jeans pocket at all times.

The phone their father had given them was an old-fashioned model that sent text messages and took calls but unfortunately did little else. Jack had worked out how to turn it to vibrate, and the twins were taking turns keeping it in their pockets.

"I was talking to Doctor Peters in the hospital," said Susan. "He told me people only knew that something had happened to Young Master Rourke when his animals started showing up in town."

"Why's he called Young Master Rourke?" asked Jack.

"Mister Rourke was his father, so he was 'Young Master' even when he was old. That's what everyone called them, anyway."

"Did you ever meet him?" asked Jaide.

"No, but your grandfather did. He serviced the clocks on the estate while he was alive."

Jack's ears pricked up. They knew very little about Grandma X's husband. "Dad's dad?"

Susan nodded, but had nothing else to add. He had died years before Hector and Susan had met. "There's a Rourke Road. I guess that's named after either Mister or Young Master Rourke. The swamp, too, and the park."

"How did he die?" asked Jack.

"Doctor Peters said he had a heart attack. Although there were some suspicious circumstances. Apparently the lodge, where they found him, had been turned inside out. Officer Haigh said it looked like a break-in, but nothing obvious had been taken."

"Why weren't you called out?" Jaide asked.

"Because I wasn't on duty. Besides, a ground crew could get there easily enough."

"Could you have done anything if you were there?"

"I don't think so, Jaide. He was an old man. There's nothing anyone could've done."

With a soft thud, Ari, a ginger tomcat who frequently put in an appearance at mealtimes, jumped through the open kitchen window. His whiskers twitched as he surveyed the meal from the vantage point of the windowsill.

"I disagree," he said. "Something needs to be done immediately. All the noise on the old man's estate has scared the mice away."

"Always hungry," said Susan, almost as though she could hear what Ari was saying. "Don't feed him, Jack. You'll only encourage him."

Ari looked less than impressed by the broccoli Jack had surreptitiously offered him. Turning up his nose, the cat looked pointedly at the chicken, but Susan shooed him away.

Ari jumped down and sat at Jaide's feet, rubbing his head against her ankle. Jaide put her hand on the phone for the thousandth time. It felt just like an inert lump of plastic. Cell phones were very unreliable in Grandma X's home, losing reception and power for no reason. What if their father was calling at that very second but couldn't get through?

"Have they found the person who drove Grandma off the road yet?" Jack asked.

"No, but I promise you they're looking," Susan said. "In a small town like this, nobody gets away with anything for long."

Across the table, Jaide jumped as though Ari had bitten her on the leg. She stared at Jack wide-eyed for an instant, then jumped again.

"Can I be excused?" she asked.

Without waiting for an answer, she ran from the table. Jack fought the impulse to run after her. It was hard, since he knew that the only reason Jaide would act like that was if the phone was ringing. If only *he* had had it at that moment. He might be the one talking their father, hearing his familiar voice in his ear.

He was so distracted thinking about the call that he ate two whole pieces of broccoli without having to be asked, all the while watching the door for Jaide's return.

A minute later she peered around the kitchen doorway, her eyes bright and the phone safely tucked behind her back. She jerked her head, indicating that he should join her.

"Can I be excused, too?" he asked.

"What's going on with you two?" Susan said as Jack hurried from the table. "I'll start dessert without you if you take too long!"

Jack held his breath until he and Jaide were up in their room, well out of earshot.

"It's him," she whispered, taking the phone out of her pocket and putting it on speaker so they could both hear.

"I'm back," she said. "And I have Jack with me."

"Hello, Dad," said Jack.

"Hello, son," came the familiar voice over the phone. Hector Shield was almost inaudible, thanks to a roaring noise in the background that Jack realized was more heavy rain. "I'm sorry it took me so long to get through to you. The house makes it very difficult. . . ."

His voice disappeared under the drumbeat of the rain for a second. When it came back, he was still speaking.

". . . must all be very frustrating to you, but you surely understand by now why I can't come any closer."

"Our Gifts," said Jack, hoping his wouldn't suddenly go crazy and ruin everything.

". . . saw what happened today at the estate. With your grandmother incapacitated, your Gifts are even more dangerous than usual . . . can't set foot in Portland without risking a disaster."

The twins understood but couldn't help but be disappointed.

"Do you know how Grandma is doing?" asked Jaide. "Mom tells us not to worry —"

"But she *would* say that," put in Jack. "Can you tell us what's really going on?"

"I know as much as you do," said Hector. ". . . waiting for the results of the scan . . ."

The twins leaned closer to the phone, straining for every word.

". . . called me just before she was hit by that van . . . was on the way to retrieve a powerful artifact, hidden from The Evil long ago . . ."

Hector's voice was lost again. He sounded as if he was talking in front of a waterfall.

"Dad, speak up!" said Jaide into the phone, as loud as she dared.

"Did The Evil cause the crash?" asked Jack, the thought sending gooseflesh spreading in a wave up his arms.

". . . not possible . . . wards still intact . . . no danger to her or to you . . ."

Jaide breathed a sigh of relief. That was one less thing to worry about. But it was still odd, the accident happening just as Grandma X was on such a mission.

"She was planning to meet me afterward," Hector Shield said. His voice was a bit clearer now, as if he'd found somewhere out of the rain. ". . . near where I saw you at the Rourke Estate, where the artifact was hidden. *Is* hidden. It must still be there, since she didn't make it that far. It's critical we find the artifact quickly, before it's sold off and lost forever . . . might even fall into The Evil's hands . . . I've searched every inch of the estate outside the wards and it's not there . . . must be inside the castle, inside the wards . . ."

Once again a roaring, gushing sound drowned out his voice. The twins looked at each other, thinking exactly the same thought.

"We could help you, Dad!" exclaimed Jaide. It wasn't the same as being with him, but it was close. "There's nothing stopping *us* from going back."

"I was going to ask Custer. . . ."

"He's busy minding the wards for Grandma," said Jack.

"Or a Warden from out of town . . ."

"Why, Dad?" Jaide persisted. "We're right here — and we were right there on the estate today. If we'd known, we could've looked for you then!"

"I'm not sure," their father said, but they could tell he was thinking about it. "The artifact is very powerful. It could be dangerous in the hands of a troubletwister."

"We'll be very careful," Jaide promised. "Please let us help."

"*Please*," Jack added. "I know we can do it."

The noise of the rain redoubled, smothering their father's voice. They could still hear him, speaking slowly and firmly, as though fighting to be heard, but his words were unrecognizable.

"Stupid house," said Jaide, staring up at the ceiling and shaking her fist. "Let him through! It's not going to do any harm, just *talking* to him!"

As though the house heard her, the rushing noise faded, and the words became clear.

"All right, but . . . call later, hard to talk now . . . ask the *Compendium*."

"What do we ask it?" Jack leaned close to the phone to hear as best as he could.

"The Card of Translocation . . . but remember, be careful!"

With that final word, the call cut out completely, and Hector Shield was gone.

The twins sat staring at the phone for a long minute, considering everything their father had told them.

"The Card of Translocation," said Jaide, rolling the words around her mouth as though that might tell her what they meant. What did *translocation* mean? What kind of card? And why was it hidden at the Rourke Estate?

"It doesn't sound like much," said Jaide. "What's so special about a card?"

"Is there someone else up here?" asked Ari from the door to their room.

Jack snatched up the phone and shoved it deep into his pocket. Their father may have given it to them, but not with their mother's or grandmother's permission.

"No," he said. "We're just, uh, talking about homework."

The cat narrowed his eyes for a moment. "I thought I heard someone else."

"You couldn't have," Jack insisted, "because there's no one else here."

Ari's eyes closed down to menacing slits, as if he was stalking a mouse. Jack and Jaide shifted uncomfortably, even though they weren't lying to him. They *were* the only people in the house apart from him and their mother.

"You're sure you didn't hear anything?" asked Ari.

Jack and Jaide slowly shook their heads.

"Ah, well." Ari's eyes opened wider and he yawned, revealing every one of his very sharp teeth. "Perhaps I imagined it."

"You must have, I guess," said Jaide weakly.

"But I have been hearing an odd voice all evening," mused the cat. "Hard to pinpoint . . ."

Ari suddenly shook his head once, then shook it a second time more violently, as if he was trying to dislodge something from his ear.

"Have you seen Kleo, by any chance?" he asked.

Kleopatra was the second of Grandma X's Warden Companions, a Russian blue who was also Protector of the Portland "catdom."

"I haven't seen her since yesterday," said Jaide, only realizing that fact as she said the words. Kleo was normally close at hand, keeping an eye on the troubletwisters in case they got into trouble.

"Sorry," said Jack.

With a worried look, Ari thanked them and padded from the room.

"Oh," he added at the top of the stairs. "There's chocolate pudding."

"Homemade or from the store?" asked Jack.

"The store. And if you're not there in a minute, your mother's going to give it all to me."

The twins bolted past the cat to the kitchen, where Susan had just served up two bowlfuls of Jack's favorite dessert and was in the process of adding dollops of thick, farm-fresh cream to both. She placed a smaller bowl of cream on the floor for Ari, with a wink at the twins as though to say, "Don't tell your grandmother."

Even as they ate, thoughts of their father, mysterious cards, and their mission were far from forgotten. They couldn't raise any of those subjects, but Young Master Rourke, who had a mysterious Warden artifact hidden somewhere on his estate, was still fair game.

"He can't have been *completely* isolated up there, can he?" said Jaide. "Surely he had friends, family, the occasional visitor. . . ."

"There was a groundskeeper, I believe," said Susan. "But no one else. He was an only child who never married and didn't leave any heirs. Sorting out what happens to his estate will be a terrible exercise, I'm sure."

"I wonder what he did all day?" asked Jack, thinking of how easily a single card could get lost among so much stuff.

"I guess he read his books," she said. "He was a great collector, apparently, and his library was very extensive."

"Wasn't he lonely?" asked Jaide.

"Some people like the quiet, Jaide. Remember, your grandmother was alone until we came to live with her. Apart from the cats, of course."

She reached down to pat Ari, who had finished his cream and looked up hopefully for more.

"It's funny," she said, more to herself than her children. "I thought it'd be quiet here, but there always seems to be something going on. Giant storms, trains coming off the rails, rich old men dying, car crashes." She shook herself and smiled brightly. "Well, at least it's not boring. Now, when you've finished, I believe it's your turn to do the dishes."

"It's *always* our turn to clean up," said Jaide.

"That's because you're so good at it."

Jack and Jaide polished off the last of their dessert and

reluctantly took the dishes to the sink, where after a short argument Jack washed and Jaide dried. Susan wandered off to another room to do her own thing on the computer, Ari hopped back out the window, and the twins were able to whisper between themselves.

"How are we going to get at the *Compendium*?" asked Jack.

"Later, when she's asleep. I'll set the alarm on the phone." Jaide blew soapy foam off the back of a plate. "I'm more worried about how we get back into the estate. I mean, we can't keep going with Tara's dad, can we?"

"I don't know," said Jack. "Maybe we can. Besides, there might be another way. Remember what Mom said about Young Master Rourke and his books?"

"He collected them. So?"

"Rodeo Dave said that he was going back to the estate to catalog the collection for the . . . what do you call them? Not executioners."

"Executors. Of course! We'll ask tomorrow."

The twins finished the dishes and the rest of their chores, and went to bed satisfied that they had at least the beginning of a plan.

CHAPTER FOUR
FORGOTTEN THINGS

An earsplitting beeping woke Jack at two a.m. He lurched bolt upright in bed, heart pounding. He had turned the phone's volume up to high because he hadn't wanted to sleep through the alarm. Now the whole house would be woken up for sure! How could he have known it would be so *loud*?

The beeping appeared to have stopped, however, and only slowly did he realize that it had only *seemed* loud to him. As well as turning the volume up, he had put it under his pillow next to his right ear. Once his head was off the pillow, he could hardly hear it at all.

The flashing screen was bright to his eyes, enhanced by his Gift. He switched the alarm off and slipped out of bed, tiptoeing across the room to wake up Jaide. It took him two attempts, and even when her eyes were open he suspected she was still mostly asleep.

"Is the Monster back?" she asked, blearily.

"No, that was last time. And it wasn't a monster, anyway, remember? It was the Living Ward."

"Oh, right." She slowly put the pieces together. The four wards of Portland came in different "flavors," memorialized in a poem every troubletwister was taught:

SOMETHING GROWING
SOMETHING READ

SOMETHING LIVING
SOMEONE DEAD

The first time The Evil had attacked, it had been through the "Something Read" ward, formerly a brass sign on top of Portland's lighthouse. The twins had made some romantic graffiti their parents had written the new ward, and The Evil had been repelled. But a part of The Evil had been caught inside the boundary established by the wards, and it had attacked the Living Ward next. This was a former axolotl that had mutated into a hideous creature Portland's citizens had occasionally glimpsed, thinking it a monster. When the giant axolotl was killed, the new Living Ward was Rennie, a woman who had once been absorbed by The Evil but who had managed to free herself, though she was horribly injured. Now she lived in the attic above Rodeo Dave's bookshop, recuperating and doing whatever it was the Living Ward was supposed to do, which the twins suspected was basically just staying alive.

The Evil had been quiet since then, and there had been no signs of it stirring. The weather vane on top of Grandma X's house had only pointed in the direction of the wind for weeks now, and none of the other magical items that she had deployed showed any signs of activity.

Jaide got out of bed and put on her father's old dressing gown. Even though there was a slight risk that it might interfere with her Gift, since anything a Warden interacted with for a long time absorbed a little of their powers, Grandma X had admitted that the chance in this case was very slight and had allowed her to keep it.

Jack took his sister's arm and guided her through the house and up the stairs to the top floor, both of them carefully avoiding the creaky floorboards that they had memorized from frequent practice.

They paused on the uppermost step, listening automatically for the sound of Grandma X's snoring. But that night there was only silence. Grandma X was in a hospital bed on the other side of town — they wouldn't be up in the middle of the night were she otherwise. The top floor of the house was empty.

Even as they took the final step, however, they heard a faint voice calling, "Rourke!"

"Did you hear that?" hissed Jaide.

"Yes," whispered Jack. "I wish I hadn't."

"Rourke!"

Jaide felt her brother's hand tighten on her arm.

"Maybe it's the old man's ghost?"

"Why . . . why would he be calling his own name?"

"I don't know."

"Rooooourke!"

"Where's it coming from?"

Jaide pointed at the door on the top landing. It looked like an ordinary door, but it wasn't. Although it should have opened onto a north-facing bedroom, against all laws of geometry and space, it actually led to the house's basement, where Grandma X maintained the secret workshop that was the heart of her mission in Portland.

Called the blue room, it contained talking skulls, silver swords, living chess sets, and a thousand other things that defied easy description. There was also a huge mahogany writing desk that had no obvious special powers, but was the home of *A Compendium of The Evil*, the repository of knowledge collected by Wardens down through the centuries. A thick folder full of notes, drawings, and often incomprehensible essays, it was kept safely away from Susan while she was in the house. They saved their true education for the three days of every normal week when their mother was stationed in Scarborough.

The only other entrance to the basement was from the front of the house, through a blue door that was hidden from the eyes of non-Wardens. The lock on that door could only be opened from the inside, and although the twins had worked out how to manage that during their first days in Portland, it was much easier to take the stairs.

"Rooooourke!"

The distant cry came again.

"I suppose we should check it out," said Jaide, but she didn't move.

"Maybe we should wake up Mom?"

"We'll never get the *Compendium* if we do that," said Jaide. She took a deep breath and then forced herself to step forward.

Nervously, one synchronized step at a time, they crossed the landing and opened the door.

"Rooooourke!" cried the voice again as they stepped through the door. It was much louder than before, and Jaide jumped, rising six feet off the ground and almost colliding with the ceiling before she got her Gift under control.

Jack felt an urge to run back to their bedroom, but instead he pulled Jaide down and led the way onward.

The blue room was dimly lit by the eternal candle flames of two crystal chandeliers. Little was visible in the gloom, even to Jack's night vision. There were so many competing shadows, a few of them quite dissimilar to the objects that cast them. A hat rack cast a shadow that bent into a right angle in the middle. The broken grandfather clock cast no shadow at all.

Atop a coffee table balanced on one slender leg sat something new: a cloth-covered shape that was round about the middle, like a barrel, and domed at the top. The silken cloth shone in the candlelight, patterned with red and gold hibiscus flowers. Tassels along the bottom swayed gently, as though in a breeze.

"Rourke! Rourke! Rourke!" shouted the voice, startlingly loud in the gloom, and this time both twins nearly hit the ceiling.

"Who's there?" asked a stern voice from the other side of the cloth-covered shape, which was now rocking furiously from side to side. "Come forward, where I can see you!"

The twins knew that voice, and they obeyed it instantly.

Sitting in a chair shaped like a dragon's mouth was a regal, blue-gray cat.

"Jack and Jaide," Kleo said with the slow decision of a judge. "What are you two doing down here?"

"Oh, Kleo," said Jaide, "we came to look something up in the *Compendium*, and then —"

"Rourke! Rourke!" shrieked the voice.

"What *is* that?" asked Jack.

Kleo nodded at the cloth-covered thing. "Take a look. She won't hurt you."

Jaide reached out with one tentative hand, grabbed the cloth by a dangling corner, and swept it aside.

Both twins stepped back in surprise.

Beneath the cloth was a big, brass cage. Inside the cage, running back and forth on a thick, wooden perch, was a very grouchy-looking parrot.

"Rourke!" it said, fixing them with first one baleful eye, then the other, swiveling its head from side to side as it did so. Its curved beak was black and sharp tipped. Even in the gloom, the coloring of its feathers was magnificent, a deep royal blue, apart from a dash of bright yellow around each eye and another on either side of its beak. It was easily the largest bird Jack had ever seen, its tail feathers so long and pointed they stuck out the side of the cage.

"Rourke!" it said, and Jaide suddenly felt like giggling. Was it saying "Rourke" or just squawking?

"*Rawk*?" she said back at it.

The bird took a step away from her.

"Cut and run," it said in a hoarse but clear voice. "Parrots and children first!"

"What is it?" asked Jack, coming around to look at it from the other side.

"*She* is a Hyacinth Macaw," said Kleo, licking a paw and smoothing down the fur behind her ears.

"What's she doing down here?" asked Jaide.

The macaw clicked loudly with a thumblike tongue and glared at her again.

"Cornelia is here because I am guarding her."

"Guarding her from what?"

"Ari, partly," said the cat. "Can you imagine what he'd do with a giant bird in a cage? He has no self-control with food. Begging your pardon, Cornelia."

Jack could imagine Ari eating Cornelia for sure, even if the cat felt really bad about it afterward. But the parrot also had a very large beak and a wicked eye. Jack smiled. Perhaps the protection was for Ari as well.

A series of sudden understandings had come to Jaide, too, along with a suspicion or two. Ari had been hearing the macaw's voice long before they had, which meant the bird had been in the blue room for some time, perhaps all weekend — and the town vet had mentioned a macaw that had escaped from the old man's menagerie and was still on the loose. . . .

"What else are you guarding her from?" Jaide asked.

"I'm not entirely sure. Cornelia doesn't want to talk about it yet. But she was at the estate the night the old man died, and it's possible she saw something."

This was a juicy revelation.

"So you think he didn't just die of a heart attack?" Jaide asked. "You think it might be murder?"

"Which means Cornelia's under witness protection until Grandma comes back?" added Jack excitedly.

Kleo raised a calming paw.

"Don't jump to conclusions, troubletwisters. We don't know that she saw anything at all. She arrived here Saturday, just after midnight, in a terrible state. She won't talk to me because I'm a cat, no matter how much I try to persuade her that I am no ordinary cat, and she won't talk to Custer, either, because he turns into a cat. She just gets agitated and shouts the old man's name over and over. All I know is that something frightened her, and frightened her very badly."

"Custer was here?" asked Jaide.

"After the accident," Kleo explained. "He came by to collect some of your grandmother's things, and he set up the cage for Cornelia while he was here."

"Did he say anything about Grandma?"

Kleo's ears flattened in regret. "Only to keep an eye on everyone in this house, and to keep Ari away."

Cornelia was watching them with her big black eyes, rimmed with yellow so they looked permanently startled.

"Rourke," she chirruped quietly.

Jack felt sorry for her. He didn't know much about parrots, but he knew they lived for a long time. Cornelia might have been in Young Master Rourke's menagerie for decades. Maybe they had been friends. Now he was gone.

"Perhaps *we* could try talking to her," he said, edging closer to the cage.

Kleo stood up on all four legs, as though about to intervene, but all she said was, "Perhaps, Jack, but be careful."

"I know," he said. "I read once how a parrot bit the leg off an eagle."

Jaide watched curiously as Jack bent over so he was eye to eye with Cornelia. The macaw studied him warily, too, leaning with her weight mainly on her left clawed foot. It had a metal ring around it, he noticed for the first time, as though she had once been tagged by a scientist. Her head bobbed up and down, not encouragingly, more as though she was reassuring herself of something.

"Rourke?"

"I'm not Young Master Rourke," Jack said, "but I'd like to be your friend, if you'll let me."

Cornelia tilted her head one way, then the other.

"There's a bag of seeds and nuts by the cage door," said Kleo. "Try offering her one."

Jack fished around in the paper bag until he found a Brazil nut. He held it by one end and slid it between the bars.

The macaw's tongue appeared again, tapping against its beak as though tasting the treat already.

Cornelia took one step closer.

"That's it," said Jack. "You can trust me."

The sharp-tipped beak reached out as though to take the nut, but then she suddenly stopped, turned her head sideways, and glared at Jack's fingers before suddenly jerking back and flapping her wide blue wings, the cage rocking violently.

"Enemy in sight!" she cried. "Rourke! Rourke!"

Jack jerked away, so startled by her sudden violence that he dropped the nut onto the floor. He hadn't done anything except talk kindly to her and offer her something to eat. What had gotten her so upset?

"She was fine until she got close to me," he said.

"Maybe you smell bad," said Jaide.

"How could I?!" protested Jack. "I've had the equivalent of ten showers today."

"Put the cloth over the cage," said Kleo. "That calms her down, eventually."

Jaide did as instructed, sweeping the silk up and over the brass bars. Cornelia watched her with avian wariness and flapped her wings, making the cover puff out like a curtain in front of a window on a windy day.

Then with a few softer "Rourke"s and one final, plaintive "All at sea," she settled down into silence.

"Poor thing," Jack said, almost to himself. "I feel sorry for you."

"I wouldn't feel too sorry if I were you," said Jaide. "I reckon you almost lost a finger a minute ago."

"How would you feel if your master had just died?" asked Jack angrily. "She must've come here for help and wound up stuck in a cage — can't you imagine how that must *feel*?"

Jack wasn't angry at his sister very often. He was by nature an even-tempered boy who shied away from serious conflict. Perhaps because he was tired and worried about Grandma X, or because he had always wanted a pet of his own, this was suddenly one of those times. Anger flared up in him like a wild thing, and his Gift responded instinctively. The candles flickered, and a deep dark shade fell across the room, as though the air was suddenly full of black smoke.

"Jackaran Shield, listen to me."

A soft but insistent bump against his left calf muscle brought him back to himself. He blinked and looked down at Kleo, who carefully put one paw on his leg and slowly extended her claws. She didn't do anything else, but it got his full attention.

"The cage isn't locked," she said. "Cornelia can let herself out anytime she wants. I think she's in there because it makes her feel safe. That's why she came here in the first place."

"Oh," he said, feeling foolish. "Sorry, Jaide."

"It's okay, little brother," she said, punching him lightly on the shoulder. She rarely called him that because the distance between them was only four minutes, and because he hated it when she did. "I cracked a stupid joke and we're both tired."

"I'm not surprised," said Kleo, glancing at the nearest working clock. "What did you say you were doing down here at this hour?"

"We came to look at the *Compendium*," Jaide said.

"What for? It's very late to be doing homework."

"I know, but it's about what happened to Grandma. Did she say anything to you before she left this morning?"

"Anything about a card of some kind?" added Jack, putting the matter of Cornelia behind him.

"Not that I recall." Kleo looked from one twin to the other. "Should she have?"

"That's okay, Kleo." Jaide wondered if she should try to look disappointed. If Grandma X hadn't mentioned the missing card to her own Warden Companion, there must have been a reason. Or Kleo had been instructed to keep it a secret from them. Perhaps it was best not to push too hard. If Kleo found out they knew, she might try to talk their father out of letting them help.

"We understand," said Jack. "But it would make us feel better if we could just take a quick look."

Kleo looked more amused than suspicious. "All right, troubletwisters. You know where the *Compendium* is kept. But don't stay up too late or you'll be tired tomorrow and get into trouble at school."

"We won't!" they promised, heading around the cage to go up the steps to the landing where the great mahogany desk sat. There, between two other large folders, rested the enormous blue folder that now contained brief records of their own encounters with the Wardens' ancient foe, along with everyone else's. A small card stuck into its plastic sleeve said *A Compendium of The Evil*.

Jaide pulled the folder free and laid it open on the desk. A great mass of different sorts of papers rustled and shifted, sounding uncannily as though the *Compendium* itself was waking up, as she had, from a very deep sleep.

"Remember what Dad told us to look for," she whispered to Jack, closing the folder again and putting her hands on the cover. Jack did the same, and faintly, barely audible at all, she heard him whisper.

"The Card of Translocation . . . the Card of Translocation."

Jaide closed her eyes and repeated the name with him three times more, then she opened her eyes and together they opened the *Compendium* to see what it would show them. She could never tell in advance what that might be. A picture, sometimes, more often on thick parchment than photocopied; or an essay, typed or written in the crabbed hand of a long-dead Warden. Once, after asking who the first Warden was, they opened the folder to find a collage made from feathers, shells, and ochre. Neither of them knew what to make of the answer.

What they saw that night were numerous pages that appeared to have been printed on a modern laser-jet printer, held together with a thick metal clasp.

"What does it say?" asked Jaide.

The type was very small, and Jack had to lean close to read it.

Along the top of the first page, underlined, was a title. Below that were names, and to the right of each name were two columns, one for *Use*, the other for *Location.*

<u>The Register of Lost and/or Forgotten Things.</u>
#1 The Sundered Map
#2 The Sound of Meredith's Horn
#3 Edgwick Bartle's Shoes
#4 The Silver Card of Oblivion

"What is it?" asked Jaide.

"It's a list."

"I can see *that*. A list of what?"

"Lost and/or Forgotten Things, of course."

Jack put his finger on the page and scrolled down, then turned to the next page when the name he was looking for hadn't appeared. He found a lot of Cards — and, oddly, reading glasses — but not all of the cards were made of metal. Some were ivory, while others were plastic or even crystal. He wondered what sort this one might be.

It was on the fourth page, halfway down:

#261 The Golden Card of Translocation

Gold.

"Jaide, you know those decks of cards that Custer and Grandma have?"

Jaide nodded. Of course she did. Grandma X had used a deck of large, incredibly heavy cards of gold to try to evaluate their Gifts when they'd first come to Portland. Custer had done the same more recently. Their cards started off blank and changed to reveal a symbol when touched by someone with a Gift. No one had ever told them who made the cards or what powers they might possess.

"It's one of those cards, do you think?" she asked.

"It must be."

"But what makes a card so powerful and dangerous?"

"Maybe the Register will tell us."

He scanned across the page, reading as he went.

"This is weird. It says 'at this time forgotten, best so, and lost to us, if not to the world.'"

"That's not very helpful."

Jack leaned back and rubbed his eyes.

"Well, at least we know it exists."

"Fat lot of help *that* is," Jaide said. "I wonder what Grandma and Dad want it for?"

"What would happen if we ask about gold cards in general?" Jack asked.

"Let's try it."

They closed the *Compendium* and concentrated on an image of the two decks of gold cards they had seen so far. When they opened the folder again, there was a picture of a blank card on the page and a brief explanation beneath written in a looping, old-fashioned script.

For the Divination of Potential Powers and Safekeeping Thereof.

"By *Powers*, do you think it means *Gifts*?" asked Jaide.

"I guess so," said Jack. "But what does it mean by *Safekeeping*?"

"I don't know. Maybe Wardens use the cards to store their Gifts when they're not using them."

"Why *wouldn't* they use them?"

Kleo leaped onto the desk next to them, making them both jump.

"Did you find what you were looking for?"

Jaide slammed the *Compendium* shut, but the cat had seen the page they'd been staring at.

"No, we didn't," she said.

"Your grandmother's deck is securely hidden and I won't tell you where," Kleo said with feline smugness. "Back to bed, now. Troubletwisters aren't supposed to be nocturnal creatures, like cats."

The twins let her lead them back past Cornelia's cage, to the elephant tapestry that hid the door to the upper floor. Jack listened for any sign of life from the macaw, but heard only a faint, stealthy shuffling of feathers.

"Promise me you won't tell Ari about Cornelia," said Kleo. "You can come back to say hello, but no other visitors are allowed. Not until she's settled, anyway."

"All right," Jack promised. He *would* come back as often as he could. Cornelia must be lonely, he thought, without Young Master Rourke. Surely she would get used to him, and wouldn't bite his finger off.

"Good night, Kleo," said Jaide, scratching the cat under the chin. Kleo leaned in with a purr. The two of them had had their differences in the past, but they were now firm friends again, even if they were keeping small secrets from each other. Jaide imagined how surprised Kleo would be when the twins completed Grandma X's mission on their own. The thought made her smile.

"At least now we know what the card looks like," she whispered when they were back in bed. "That'll make it easier to find."

Jack's eyes were heavy. "It must be especially well hidden if no one's found it before now," he observed.

That sobering thought followed Jaide into sleep.

There were no answers waiting for her in her dreams.

CHAPTER FIVE

MONSTERS OLD AND NEW

There was no time to ask Rodeo Dave about the Rourke library that morning because the twins slept late and had barely enough time to scoff down some toast and hot chocolate before riding their bikes to school. They had hoped to visit Grandma X on the way, but Susan explained that it wasn't possible that morning.

"I rang as early as I could," she said. "The results of the scan were inconclusive. Someone's coming in from Scarborough today to look at them, a specialist in brain trauma."

The twins looked at each other with concern. "Brain trauma" sounded like something to worry seriously about.

"Will you go see her?" asked Jaide. "Will you make sure she's okay?"

"I promise I will," their mother said, giving them a squeeze. "The nurse said they're keeping her in strict isolation so she's forced to rest. You can imagine it, can't you? I bet she's bossing them around at every opportunity, when the sedatives wear off."

Jack could imagine it very well, but he didn't find the thought amusing or reassuring. It worried him that she hadn't tried to contact them since the brief vision yesterday. He was afraid that, once again, all the important goings-on in Portland were being kept from them because they were too young.

Mr. Carver's "Happy Song of Beginning" was already under way when they ran through the front door of school. It sounded like a flute being tortured.

"I thought you weren't going to make it," whispered Tara as they slipped into their seats at the desk they shared. "What's that?"

The phone had slipped from Jack's bag and slid across the desk. He snatched it up.

"Uh, it's a phone," he said.

"I thought you weren't allowed to have one!"

"Dad thought we should," said Jaide, which was true enough.

"Great! What's your number? I'll put it into my phone and we can text each other."

Jack and Jaide stared helplessly at each other.

"We've forgotten it," said Jack.

"That's okay. I'll give you mine, and then you can text me."

She wrote down her number and Jack put it into his phone's memory. He texted "testing testing" and waited. A second later, Tara's phone buzzed.

"Got it," she said. "But your dad must've blocked your number. Why would he do that?"

"Maybe to stop us wasting all our minutes," improvised Jaide. "If people can't text us, we can't text them back."

"What's the point of a phone if you can't text?"

"Phones away, please," said Mr. Carver as he came into the room, massaging his nostrils after a long session playing his welcome music on the nose pipes. "Today, we're going to start with a short discussion. As many of you will be aware, Portland lost one of its most venerable citizens over the weekend: George Archibald Mattheus Rourke the Third. He was a very rich man, and a recluse, but I expect he touched all of our lives in one way or another. What can anyone here tell me about him?"

"Is he really dead or just missing?" muttered a voice at the back.

There was a small amount of laughter, but less than Jaide might have expected. The boy was referring to Rennie, who had, for a week or so, been presumed drowned before revealing herself to be very much alive.

"He's really dead," said Miralda, who fancied she knew everything about everyone in Portland. "Under mysterious circumstances, too. They say his face was awful, like he was scared to death."

"That's not true," said Kyle.

"Oh yeah? How do you know?"

"Because my dad . . ." He stopped and looked down, as though he wished he hadn't spoken up.

"That's right," said Miralda with a smirk. "Your dad worked for him, didn't he? What was he, again — a gardener or something?"

"Groundskeeper," said Kyle with a flash of anger. "And there's nothing wrong with that. He was the second person to see Young Master Rourke . . . Young Master Rourke's body . . . so he knows what he's talking about."

"Not much call for *groundskeepers* around here," Miralda said. "Not anymore, anyway."

"Now, now, children," said Mr. Carver, trying weakly to forestall another argument. "Let's stick to Mr. Rourke."

"Not *Mister* Rourke," said Miralda, voice dripping with scorn. "That was the father. Young *Master* Rourke didn't do anything. Without *Mister* Rourke, Portland wouldn't even be here. He built the railway line and the town hall. He brought all the fishermen here —"

"Whalers, not fishermen," said Mr. Carver.

"Fish, whales — what's the difference? It got the town going properly, didn't it? Young Master Rourke never did anything with his money except sit on it. That's what my dad says, and he would know, because the old guy never gave *him* any."

"He sponsored the library," said a girl at the back. "His name's on a plaque there."

"And the cactus gardens," said another.

"And he paid for the costumes for the annual musical, even though he never went himself."

"What about the Peregrinators?" asked someone else. "Didn't he build their clubhouse or something?"

"The what?" asked Jack.

"A bunch of crazy guys chasing UFOs," said Miralda with a sniff. "And besides, it's not a clubhouse — it's the sport shed on the oval. The Portland Peregrinators only use it once a month."

"Yeah, but he paid for it, didn't he?" said Kyle.

"Anyone can *buy* stuff," said Miralda. "It takes leadership to do something with it. That's what Dad says —"

"Who cares what your dad says? My mom says he's just a guy who wears an ugly necklace and likes the sound of his own voice."

Again, Mr. Carver was forced to intervene, banging on a drum until he had everyone's attention.

"The important thing," he said, "as I think this all proves, is that no man is an island. Or woman, either. Everything we do affects someone else, even if no one notices at the time."

For once, Jack thought Mr. Carver had a point. Young Master Rourke might as well not have existed for all he and Jaide had known. But now that he was gone, it was apparent that everyone was involved to some degree, either because of things he had done while alive, or because of jobs they might lose now that he was dead.

Kyle simmered silently all through that morning, as the class moved on to various states and countries and the names of their capital cities. Memorizing them wasn't compulsory — nothing at the Stormhaven Innovative School of Portland was compulsory — but Jack didn't mind paying attention. Thinking about geography distracted him from worrying about Grandma X, and made him think of all the places his father must have been in his long career searching for such Lost and/or Forgotten Things as the Card of Translocation. Maybe one day, Jack thought, he, too, would travel like that when he became a Warden.

When the lunch bells chimed, this time without Mr. Carver's nose flute accompaniment, Jaide took the opportunity to put the next stage of their plan into action.

"Let's go see Rodeo Dave," she whispered to Jack, just a little too loudly.

"Can I come with you?" asked Tara. "It's boring around here when you guys sneak off at lunchtime."

"Er," said Jack, glancing at Jaide, "I guess so?"

Jaide thought fast. Although they had nothing secret to discuss with Rodeo Dave, involving Tara in any expedition back to the estate might make searching for the Card of Translocation that much more complicated. But there was no way to put her off without sounding rude.

"Sure," Jaide said. "Come along. It's just an old bookshop, though."

"I love books," Tara said. "Maybe I'll find something I haven't already read."

"You're bound to," said Jack. "Rodeo Dave has everything."

That wasn't remotely true, Jack knew, but he had yet to be disappointed. He liked reading, too, and when he had finished the stack of childhood favorites his father had left behind in Grandma X's house, Jack had gone looking in the Book Herd for something similar. There was row after row of old Westerns. He could read for years without running out.

As they explained to Mr. Carver that they were going home for lunch, Jack felt as though he was being watched. He glanced over his shoulder and saw Kyle sitting on his own, staring hotly at them. Jack didn't know what they'd done to offend him. Maybe he was just upset because his dad might lose his job at the estate. Or maybe it was because they had each other and he had no one.

For a microsecond, Jack considered inviting Kyle along, but there were too many of them already, and Kyle had done nothing to initiate friendship before. The middle of a mission wasn't the time to start making new friends.

On the way to the bookshop, Tara spotted a carved memorial stone outside the fish markets that had been dedicated by George Archibald Mattheus Rourke the Second in 1923, commemorating the loss of a commercial ship to a storm just outside the harbor.

The Book Herd was open but empty of customers, as it always seemed to be, but Rodeo Dave wasn't alone. Rennie was there, as well. She and Dave looked up from his desk as the twins and Tara walked through the door.

"Well, hello," said Rodeo Dave, brushing imaginary sticking-out hairs back into line on his thick, proud mustache. He was in his usual jeans and cowboy boots, with a red-and-white check shirt. "I wasn't expecting you kids around these parts on a school day."

"Hello, Dave," said Jaide, echoed by Jack. "Hello, Rennie."

Tara said nothing, and neither did Rennie. The woman who was Portland's Living Ward simply nodded her head and almost smiled.

She looked pale and thin, scarred physically and mentally by her time possessed by The Evil. She was wearing a black cotton dress with very long sleeves that didn't quite hide her twisted right arm or the complete absence of her left hand. She wore a yellow silk bandanna to conceal her lack of hair, and the skin of her throat was pockmarked and scarred. The Warden healer called Phanindranath had done her best, but neither Warden Gifts nor modern surgery could correct all Rennie's injuries.

The almost-smile was new, though. It showed that Rennie was healing on the inside, where it counted.

"Renita's going to be minding the store while I'm busy on the Rourke Estate," said Rodeo Dave. "I could close the store, but with Renita living here I figured, why miss out on the custom?"

A flicker of trouble crossed Rodeo Dave's face as he said the name *Rourke*, but the twins didn't notice. This was the perfect opportunity for them to get back to the estate!

"Mom says the library is huge," said Jack. "Won't that take longer than a few days?"

"We could help you," said Jaide brightly. "Then you'd be done in no time at all."

"I'm not sure that's a good idea," said Rodeo Dave slowly, looking from one to the other.

"We won't get in the way," said Jack. "We promise."

"But it'll be very boring."

"Anything's better than homework," said Jaide.

Rodeo Dave laughed. "Well, yes, that's bound to be true. All right, then, fine with me, but I'll have to talk to your grandmother first."

"She's still in the hospital," said Jack. "Mom'll probably be grateful we're not at home alone, getting in her way."

"Sensible thinking, but I'll be sure to make sure. What about your friend here? Does she want to come, too?"

Tara was staring at Rennie with a blank look on her face. When Rodeo Dave spoke to her, she blinked and looked away, as though waking from a dream.

"Oh, hello. Do you have anything with vampires?"

"Over on the far wall," said Rodeo Dave, "next to the maps of Vanuatu."

Tara wandered off.

"She half remembers," said Rennie unexpectedly, in a voice both rough and soft.

"Remembers what, Renita?" asked Rodeo Dave.

"Nothing important," said Jaide hastily, keen to change the subject before Rennie said something that Rodeo Dave shouldn't hear. "Will you call Mom and ask her? Shall we come back here after school?"

"Unless you change your mind." His usual grin returned. "I'm sure you can think of better things to do than hang out with an old man's books. Now, who's for lunch?"

"Me!" said Jack, opening his lunch box on the desk. It was lunchtime, after all, and his stomach was complaining. Rodeo Dave joined him, unwrapping a thick ham, cheese, and mustard sandwich. Rennie didn't eat anything, even when Jaide offered her a bright red apple Susan had insisted on packing for her, even though Jaide didn't like apples. Rennie just watched them eat, perched on a high stool among the books like a solitary bird in a rookery.

"You knew him, didn't you?" Jack asked Rodeo Dave.

"Knew who?"

"Young Master Rourke."

"I suppose I did."

Rodeo Dave thought about his own answer for a moment, then added, "If anyone could say that. He was one of my best customers, always calling me up, looking for this or that. I would take him his books in person rather than use a courier, but George was never one for talking, just like his father."

"Did you meet *him*?" asked Jaide. "Mister Rourke, I mean?"

"I never really met him. But I saw him around. Always out and about the town, always talking, making his opinion known. You could see him a mile off, a tall, rakish man with an enormous nose, and you could smell him, too. Not because he never bathed. He was fussy in that regard. He used to slick his hair back with this gel — I forget what it was called, now — but it was ghastly, sticky stuff. The stink of it was enough to make you feel ill."

Rodeo Dave made a face.

"He sounds horrible," said Jack.

"Mister Rourke had faults. There's no denying that."

"What happened to him?" asked Jaide.

"He died in Africa. Some people said he was trampled trying to capture an elephant, but actually he caught malaria and wasn't treated properly. Which goes to show that money can't buy you everything."

"Nobody's perfect," whispered Rennie.

"Indeed." Rodeo Dave raised the half a sandwich he had been holding, uneaten, as though in a toast. "The dead outnumber the living. Let's not tempt fate by speaking ill of them."

Tara chose that moment to return from the shelves, clutching a scuffed, cloth-covered book in one hand.

"This is all I could find," she said. "I was looking for stories, but most of the books you have in that section seem to be nonfiction, which is weird because vampires aren't real."

"Monsters are only as real as we believe them to be, like tyrants." Rodeo Dave took the book from her and studied the spine. "Ah, *Dracula*. The original and the best."

"There was no price on it."

"That's because it belongs to you," he said, giving her back the book with some of his usual sparkle.

Tara looked confused. "You're giving it to me?"

"Books find their own owners. I just hold on to them until they meet each other. Money is often an unwelcome complication."

"But . . . I mean, won't you go out of business?"

"Have no fear on that score, Tara," Rodeo Dave said. "Not with Renita here to keep the shop open."

"There's more to living than busy-ness," said Rennie in a soft but firm voice.

"Exactly!" Rodeo Dave grinned widely, as though having someone in the store to not take money from nonexistent customers solved all his problems.

Jack and Jaide could understand Tara's puzzlement. Her mother ran a gift shop in Scarborough, and her father was relentless in his pursuit of the next business opportunity. It wasn't surprising that she found Rodeo Dave's philosophy completely alien.

Come to think of it, most people would find it pretty weird. Not for the first time, Jack wondered whether Rodeo Dave was secretly rich or something. Maybe he owned a cattle ranch somewhere.

His thoughts were interrupted by Tara suddenly leaning close to Rennie and staring at her. *Dracula* hung limp in her hand, forgotten.

"Where do I know you from?" she asked.

"We drew pictures of her," said Jaide quickly. "At school, remember? When we thought she had . . . you know?"

Mr. Carver had held a small memorial for Rennie when the town believed she had drowned in The Evil's storm, one year after her own children had drowned.

"That's right," said Jack, picking up on Jaide's quick thinking. They had to stop Tara from remembering The Evil and the old Living Ward, everything she had seen in the cave under Little Rock. "There was no one to give the pictures to, and you didn't want them to be thrown out. You had them in your backpack during the train crash. I guess you took them home afterward. That must be where you've seen her face before."

"Oh, yeah," said Tara, some of her confusion slipping away. "That's it. The pictures. I don't know why I've been keeping them. It's like I dreamt her . . . dreamt *you*. . . ."

"I would like to see those pictures," said Rennie.

"I'll bring them in," said Tara. "Tomorrow."

"Thank you."

Tara blinked and looked away. Whether the explanation made sense or not, it seemed to have helped. Rodeo Dave pulled up another chair and she sat down with the others to eat her lunch, a cold noodle salad, and a chocolate bar that she broke into five pieces and shared with everyone.

CHAPTER SIX
TREASURE HUNT

It was Jack's turn to hold the phone that afternoon, and although he waited anxiously for it to buzz, it stayed resolutely silent. Jack couldn't help but wish their father would check in again. He could, at least, have sent them a *text*. . . .

The last hour of school dragged horribly, but finally it was over, and Jack, Jaide, and Tara hurried off, hoping that they would be given permission to go with Rodeo Dave to the Rourke Estate.

Outside the Book Herd, the twins were surprised to see their mother's car. They hadn't expected to see her there. She tooted her horn as they approached, and a few moments later Rodeo Dave appeared from the store, waving at them.

"Hop in," he called out. "We're getting a lift."

"So it's okay for us to go, Mom?" Jack asked as the three kids piled into the backseat.

"Of course, Jack, as long as you're home in time for dinner. I said I'd drop you there and pick you up afterward to make sure. Your dad will collect you from our place later, Tara."

"Great!" Tara said brightly. "Thanks!"

On the way through town, Susan drove over the old iron bridge. There was no sign of the rescue crew that had been there yesterday, just a couple of skid marks on the road leading up to the bridge and some broken glass on the verge.

"Can we see Grandma?" asked Jaide. "The hospital's kind of on the way to the estate." Actually, it was in a completely different direction, but everywhere was close in Portland.

"I'm really sorry, we can't today," Susan said. "She's undergoing more tests. I spoke to the new specialist not long ago. Doctor Witworth says she needs to double-check a couple of things showing on the first scan."

"What kind of things?" asked Jack, feeling his heart beginning to race.

"She didn't say. . . . 'Abnormalities' was the exact word she used, but I wouldn't read too much into that. That's just something doctors say when they don't know what's going on."

Neither Jack nor Jaide was terribly reassured by the suggestion that something was going on that doctors didn't understand. Especially if it meant Grandma X staying in the hospital and them not visiting her.

"Your mother's right," said Rodeo Dave, turning around in the front seat to beam at them. "If they'd looked into your grandmother's head and *not* seen something out of the ordinary, that would've been cause for serious concern."

"True enough," said Tara. "There's no one in the world like her."

"And I did speak to her on the phone this morning," Susan added. "She sends her love and reminds you to do as you're told and keep up with your homework. That sounds like her, doesn't it?"

It did, and the twins were willing to let their worries on that front ebb slightly. Until they saw her with their own eyes, though, they wouldn't be completely reassured. With her suddenly absent, there was an enormous void in their lives. Jack had dreamt the previous night that he had woken to a world where no one had ever heard of Grandma X or the Wardens, and his Gift had vanished. Jaide occasionally found herself daydreaming about moving back to the city — and not in the excited way she once had. Their life was with Grandma X now. Without her, everything was at risk of turning upside down again.

The sky above was gray, mirroring their moods, but there was no sign of the rain that had saturated them the previous day, not even as they approached the high hedges and elaborate gates of the estate. Wide enough for two carriages to pass side by side, the gates rose up in a high arch over the drive, wrought-iron curlicues swirling and tangling in a pattern that Jaide hadn't been able to make out the previous day.

The right-hand gate was closed. This time, without the rain to obscure her vision, she discerned a fish's tail in its elaborate design.

Then, as the car passed onto a thickly graveled drive, Jaide realized that the open left-hand gate wasn't a mirror image of the right. Instead of a fish-like tail, there was a great, rounded head with a single metal eye. Putting the two halves together in her mind, Jaide realized that the gate, when closed, depicted not a fish but a whale.

That wasn't all. High on the corner of each gate was a ship braving the turbulent seas, crewed with men waving harpoons, hemming the whale in.

The drive curved to the left, and a stand of trees blocked her view of the gates. Rodeo Dave guided Susan along a fork leading away from the smaller building in which Young Master Rourke had been found. That stretch of drive wound around the lake and up toward the castle. The creek was now running clear, and there was no sign of council workers, just one large man in overalls tending a rose garden — Kyle's father, Jack presumed — and a young, round-faced security guard sitting half on, half off the seat of a golf cart. He stood up as the car approached and crunched to a halt in front of him.

Rodeo Dave stepped out of the car, wiped his palms on his jeans, and cleared his throat.

"David Smeaton," he said. "And these are my three helpers."

"I don't have any helpers on my list," said the guard, glancing at a clipboard.

Jaide's stomach sank. If the guard wouldn't let them in, how were they supposed to find the card? She bet that wouldn't have been a problem had Grandma X been there. She would have just bossed him into it. Jaide couldn't imagine Rodeo Dave bossing *anyone* around. He was already turning to them with a look of apology.

"Thomas Solomon, isn't it?" said Susan, getting out of the car with a sunny smile. "I used to know your mother, years ago. We bumped into each other again today, in the bakery, and she said you were working up here. It's nice to meet you."

"Ah, and very nice to . . . um, who did you say you were?"

"Susan Shield. These are my children, Jack and Jaide, and their friend Tara. I'll be back in two hours to pick them up."

"Well . . ." Thomas Solomon looked as though he might argue the point, but then he smiled and said, "What's the harm? Just don't tell anyone else, or we'll have all the kids up here." He put the clipboard facedown on the seat of the golf cart. "Two hours it is."

The twins and Tara climbed eagerly out of the car and waved as Susan drove off. Jack was impressed. He'd thought they were going to be turned back for sure, and he was amazed at how well his mother was fitting in to Portland, having never wanted to come here at all.

As Jack turned to follow Dave across the drawbridge over the moat, he caught a glimpse of a huge muscular animal running through the grounds. He immediately thought of the escaped menagerie animals. No one had mentioned a tiger! But then it raised its head to look at him, and he saw the enormous teeth.

There was only one saber-toothed tiger in the world that he knew of. It was the animal form of Custer, the Warden whose job it was to look after the wards while Grandma X was in the hospital.

Jack automatically went to wave, then turned it into a tug at his hair in case anyone had noticed. Custer winked and kept running, vanishing behind some bushes an instant later.

"You saw him, too?" Jaide whispered.

"Yes." Jack wished they could talk to him about their father. If Custer had been able to stop, he could have helped them look for the Card of Translocation. But he supposed it was hard work, minding four wards singlehandedly. Grandma X made it look easy, but that, Jack was sure, only came from years of practice.

"Come on," called Tara. "Dave's almost inside!"

They hurried after her, their feet making hollow wooden sounds on the drawbridge. The moat surrounding the castle was deep and dark, with smooth, steep sides. Jaide didn't want to imagine what it would be like to fall in. Luckily, despite the hollow sound, the planks of the drawbridge were as unmoving as solid stone.

Two high towers loomed over them. Thick chains connected the drawbridge to the castle walls. On the other side of the moat was an open gateway where Rodeo Dave was waiting.

"This way!" he said. "There's a lot of books a-waiting!"

The gateway led into a small courtyard. There were archers' notches high in the walls around them, and one solid door ahead. If it was a real castle, Jaide thought, this was where friends would be welcomed and foes stopped in their tracks.

"This is the inner passage," said Rodeo Dave, fumbling in his pocket for a ring of keys. They jingled and clinked with the deep voices of antiquity. "The inner door is always locked."

"I didn't see the guard give you those keys," said Tara.

Dave didn't quite look at her as he mumbled, "Oh, George . . . Young Master Rourke gave me a set so I could deliver books straight to the library."

He selected the largest key, and slid it into the lock. It turned with a series of heavy clunks.

He pushed the door, and it swung open with a groan. A wave of cold air rushed out over the twins. Tara went *brrr*, which startled Jack. He didn't think anyone actually made that sound in real life.

"So you've been here bef —" Jaide started to say to Rodeo Dave, but stopped at the flurry of echoes that bounced back at her from within the castle. What lay on the other side of the door was hidden in shadow.

She tried again more quietly. "So you've been here before?"

"Not for a few years," said Rodeo Dave. He took three steps inside and fumbled along the wall to the right of the door. "It's here somewhere — I'm certain of it."

There was a click, followed by a series of smaller clicks deeper within the castle. Fluorescent lights pinged on overhead, one at a time. Section by section, the covered courtyard within was revealed — dusty portraits on the walls, sheet-covered furniture on the floors, actual suits of armor guarding the corners, a tall grandfather clock on the opposite wall, and high, wooden beams above. Two particular paintings had pride of place, one of a forbidding man with receding black hair and long fingers, the other of a small, oval-faced woman with startlingly green eyes. They faced each other, unsmiling, from different sides of the hall.

Jack followed Rodeo Dave inside, struck by the thought that, although it looked like a museum, this room had once been part of someone's home. Jaide and Tara followed him, looking around in awe.

"Welcome to Rourke Castle," said Rodeo Dave, his cowboy boots sparking off the cobblestoned floor. "George's father, Mister Rourke, had this built out of real stone from the country his family came from. Some said it was an actual castle, but that wasn't true. Just the ruins of one. But the plan was based on a real castle, so there are towers, halls, and cellars, just like they would have had centuries ago. There's even a chapel and an armory, and a solar on the top floor."

"A solarium?" asked Tara.

"No, a solar. It's where the lord of the castle and his family could spend time alone, away from the staff and the soldiers. *Solar* here comes from *sole*, meaning alone, nothing to do with the sun."

Rodeo Dave was talking more quickly than normal. He seemed nervous, Jaide thought.

"Is the castle haunted?" she whispered, suddenly afraid to raise her voice too much.

He smiled at her, but there was no humor in it. "Only by memories. See that clock? Your grandfather Giles had terrible trouble with it. It kept losing time and made Mister Rourke terribly impatient."

Both twins admired its carved wooden panels and painted face, impressed by the fact that this was something Grandma X's husband had once touched.

"Now, come this way and I'll show you the library."

Rodeo Dave led them from the entrance hall into a wide corridor lined on one side with tapestries depicting hunts, dances, and feasts. One showed a whale being speared from two sides at once. Heavy wooden doors, all of them shut, lined the other side of the corridor. Cobwebs stirred above them, swaying in air that might not have moved for years. The castle was tomblike around them.

They reached a fork in the corridor.

"This way," said Rodeo Dave, turning left. Then he stopped, facing a dead end. "No, the other way. I'm sure of it."

They took the other leg of the corridor, stopping at a double door opposite a flight of spiral stone stairs. Rodeo Dave fished out another key and opened the doors. With a flourish, he opened both doors at once, and waved the twins and Tara ahead of him.

They entered a huge room with a ceiling forty feet above them, with an internal balcony running all the way around, halfway up. Electric lights in shell-like shades sent overlapping pools of illumination all across the library, banishing shadows to the farthest corners. Every vertical surface was lined with shelves, some of them protected by glass doors, all of them holding books. Big books, small books, books with gold writing on the spine, books in different languages — there were so many books that Jaide could only gasp in amazement. How did Rodeo

Dave ever imagine that he might catalog them all in just a few days!

"*You* sold him all these books?" gasped Tara.

"Good grief, no," replied Rodeo Dave. "Most of these were George's father's. That's the father there, as a young man."

He indicated a marble bust sitting on a plinth. It showed a more youthful version of the man in the portrait they had seen earlier. His nose was pointed and his lips thin, with a faint hint of a sneer. The eyes of the bust seemed to follow Jack as he walked around it, judging him and finding him wanting.

"He looks horrible," said Tara, folding her arms and turning her attention to the ceiling.

"I've seen him before," said Jaide.

"When?" asked Jack in surprise.

"I don't know." The memory was frustratingly incomplete. She definitely knew that cruel face from *somewhere*. But no matter how she scratched her head, the details weren't coming out.

Above the room's enormous, inglenook fireplace was a tall painting of a smiling blond woman in a primrose gown sitting at a table under a tree bedecked with autumnal leaves. She was playing Solitaire with a deck of old-fashioned cards, their faces yellow and white, diagonally striped. A pale clay-brick path snaked behind her, between fields of ripened wheat on one side, buttercups on the other. The overall impression was one of intense gold.

That, and the deck of cards the woman was holding, reminded Jaide of what they were supposed to be doing in the castle. The Card of Translocation lay hidden somewhere in its walls. Standing between them and finding it was only one obstacle: the hundreds and hundreds of books they had said they would help Rodeo Dave catalog.

"Do you mind . . . ?" she said. "I mean . . . do you think it'd be all right if . . . ?"

"Of course, Jaide," said Rodeo Dave with a smile. "I know why you're really here."

She blinked in surprise. "You do?"

"Yes. You want to explore the castle. And that's fine with me. Everywhere you shouldn't go will be locked and I'll be busy for at least an hour or so, just checking the general condition of the books. The actual cataloging will start once I've done that. Until then, you are free to wander. Just don't touch anything. There are a lot of fragile, precious things in here, including yourselves. Don't get lost!"

"We won't. Thanks!"

"I'll ring that when I'm ready for you," he said, pointing at an elaborate gong as big as a bass drum, suspended in a black wooden frame opposite the fireplace.

Tara and the twins ran out of the library before he could change his mind.

"Which way?" asked Jack.

"Up the stairs, of course," said Tara. "Last one to the top is a rotten egg!"

The twins raced after her, the sound of their footfalls echoing brightly off the walls and filling every corner of the castle with life. The next floor up contained a series of locked rooms with brass plaques on the doors: the Right Room, the White Room, the Pygmy Bryde Room, the Bowhead Room. Not until they came across the Humpback Room did Jack guess that they were all named after species of whale. They stopped to peer through a keyhole. Jaide and Tara could see nothing, but Jack's dark-sensitive eyesight made out a four-poster bed, a cupboard, and a tightly shuttered window.

They went back down briefly and explored several other labeled rooms: the Bakehouse, the Pantry, the Garrison, the Granary, the Blacksmith, and the Prison. Their doors were open, but they contained little of interest. The door to the Cellar was locked, so they went back upstairs and searched until they found a stairwell that led to a guardhouse in one of the corner towers. The view from the top was spectacular, right out over the lake and surrounding trees. Portland was also visible; Jaide found the Rock, and from that landmark she easily worked out where their house was located. She could just make out the weather vane, pointing resolutely south.

"This would be the perfect place to play hide-and-seek," said Tara.

"You think everywhere's a good place for hide-and-seek," said Jaide. Tara was particularly good at that game.

Jack was about to second what Jaide had said, intending to add that they had to go back to Rodeo Dave soon, but before he could speak he felt a sudden buzz in his pocket. The phone was ringing.

"I agree with Tara," he said. "And she's it!"

With that he ran from the guardhouse, down the stairs and along the corridor, trying doors at random. Most of the rooms were locked on the top floor, but some were open. A broom closet would do, just so long as he could get there before his father hung up.

He found a door that would open and flung himself through it, slamming the door shut behind him, not seeing what the room contained. He didn't even turn on the light. Jack could see perfectly well with the lights out.

He whipped the phone from his pocket and pressed the flashing green button.

"Dad?"

"Hello, Jack," came the voice on the other end of the call. "You sound out of breath. I was beginning to wonder if you were going to pick up."

"Had to hide from Tara," he gasped. "We're in the castle!"

"I know. I saw you arrive."

"You did?"

"From the trees. I've been waiting for you."

Jack imagined Hector Shield stretched out on a branch with a pair of binoculars.

"Did you see Custer go by?"

"I did, and I'm glad you didn't interrupt his work. You mustn't interfere with his concentration. I saw your mother as well — you didn't tell her about me being here, did you? It would only upset her, and I've done enough of that already. Unfortunately Warden business must take priority over our feelings."

"No, we haven't told her."

"Good. I know it's difficult, but it won't be for long, I promise. Everything will be the way it's supposed to be once the card is found."

"And Grandma's better."

"Yes . . . that, too."

Jack's father sounded distracted and very serious. There wasn't even a hint of his usual jokey friendliness, reminding Jack that the war against The Evil was far from a game.

"I don't have much time," Hector said. "Tell me what progress you've made."

"Well, we've only just started exploring. The castle is huge. It has hundreds of rooms. Most of them are locked."

"You'll have to find a way into them."

"We're helping Rodeo Dave clear out the library. He has keys. . . ."

"Best to keep him out of Warden affairs. Don't ask for the keys — or even think about stealing them from him. You don't want to raise his suspicions."

The thought had crossed Jack's mind. He suppressed it with reluctance, although what Rodeo Dave had to be suspicious of, exactly, he didn't know. But he didn't want to attract his attention. Rodeo Dave wasn't a Warden, but he did seem close to Grandma X, and he hadn't freaked out when the whirlwind had carried him up the drive when they'd first arrived in Portland, so maybe he did know about Warden stuff and The Evil.

"If it's not in one of the open rooms, you'll have to find another way into those locked rooms, one that doesn't involve David Smeaton or his keys. Perhaps there's some way you could use your Gifts."

Jack suddenly remembered something. "Of course! It's just like in *The Second Spiral Staircase*."

"The what?"

"One of your old books. Don't you remember? There was a locked room that no one could get into. The keys had been lost. But they found a skeleton key that would work on lots of doors. That's how they got it open."

"Good thinking, Jack. Skeleton keys . . . hmmm. Father . . . your grandfather . . . wasn't a Warden, but he used to have a key for opening clock cases. It's probably in the blue room."

"We'll look for it as soon as we can."

"Tonight, Jack. It's vital you find the Card of Translocation as soon as possible."

"We will, Dad. Don't worry. We'll find it soon, I promise."

Jack spun around in surprise as a voice suddenly spoke from behind him.

"Well, you won't find anything in *here*, I can assure you of that!"

CHAPTER SEVEN

SEEKING AND HIDING

The voice had come from inside the room in which Jack was hiding, but it belonged to neither Jaide nor Tara. It wasn't Rodeo Dave, either. It sounded like a grouchy old man.

"Who's there?" Jack scanned the room, an ordinary attic by the look of it, with boxes stacked up against one wall and lumpy furniture covered in sheets along the other. Even with his sensitive night vision, there was no one to be seen. "Who said that?"

"Ignore me and I'll go away. It won't be the first time."

Jack reached out to the nearest sheet and whipped it off the stuffed armchair it covered. No one.

"Why can't I find you?"

"Nobody ever wanted to before."

"Are you a ghost?"

"Of course not!" Now the voice sounded offended. "Although I *am* dead."

Jack nerved himself to whip away another sheet, revealing a chest of drawers.

"Where are you?"

"If I could see, perhaps I could tell you. It's so dark in here . . . so very dark."

Jack reached behind him to turn on the light. It dazzled him for a second, before his eyes adjusted.

"How's that?"

"I can see a white blur, a considerable improvement on my former state, but still far from ideal."

Jack began tearing at the sheets at random, raising a thick cloud of dust and revealing more armchairs, a selection of tea chests, and one broken hat stand.

"Don't trouble yourself, sir," said the voice. "Just turn the light off and leave. That's what I would do in your shoes. I was rather unpopular even when I was alive."

The second-to-last sheet revealed a table. On the table was a selection of oddments: candlesticks, chipped plates, a tarnished silver service, and something that Jack mistook for a scuffed plaster bust similar to the one of Mister Rourke in the library . . . until it moved.

"Gadzooks!" it said, blinking up at him. "Are you a child or has everyone evolved into midgets during my absence?"

Jack stared at the plaster head in amazement, or the half head, since it was really only the face with the back past the ears just a flat surface. It wasn't a very flattering head at that. The nose was too large and the cheeks too fleshy. The head had no hair, and its chin receded sharply, giving its expression a look of permanent disapproval. It didn't seem like the kind of a thing an artist would make to flatter a rich patron. It looked entirely too . . . authentic.

"What are you?" Jack asked.

"Don't you mean who *was* I? Professor Jasper Frederik Olafsson, at your service. Forgive me for not bowing. You haven't answered *my* question, remember."

"I'm not a midget," said Jack, although he did wonder sometimes if he was growing too slowly. "I just came in here to talk to . . . whoops, hang on."

Jack had forgotten the phone and his father. He turned away and raised it to his ear. Nothing but silence. Hector Shield had hung up.

He had sent a text message, though: *Call you tonight 9pm. Keep looking.*

"What is that contraption?" asked the head calling itself Professor Jasper Frederik Olafsson. "The last time I was uncovered, people still spoke face-to-face. Is this the way people communicate in your world — via machine?"

"What do you mean *in my world*? It's the same as your world, surely."

"Most likely, but your present is my future. Everything changes: That is the only certainty. I must therefore take nothing for granted."

Jack put the phone away. "We still talk face-to-face, mainly, but there are lots of other ways, too. How long have you been down here?"

"I have no way to tell," Professor Olafsson said. "There is no clock in this room. I cannot see the daylight coming or going, so I cannot count the days. I have no pulse, even. Just the sensation that a vast epoch of time has passed — large enough that young men such as yourself are not startled by the apparition of a talking death mask. Are you considered normal for your kind?"

Jack was beginning to feel confused under the barrage. "Yes. That is, no, not really. What's a death mask?"

In the hallway outside, Jaide could hear voices. She knew Jack must have felt the phone buzz and run off somewhere to take the call, so Tara wouldn't overhear. She had left Tara searching fruitlessly on the other side of the castle, figuring that Jack wouldn't have gone far from where they had started. But if that was him talking on the phone in the room ahead, why could she hear a *second* voice, answering his questions?

She inched up to the door and put her ear against it.

". . . a wax impression of my face as I lay on my deathbed, then cast in plaster. It was a common custom in my time. For loved ones, you see, so they could gaze upon the countenance of their dearly departed and think fond thoughts. Except I had no loved ones. . . ."

"But this is what you looked like . . . when you died?"

That *was* Jack. Jaide turned the handle and wrenched the door open, not liking the idea of dead things talking to her brother, even if he didn't sound terribly frightened himself.

"What's going on?" she asked.

"Oh, hi, Jaide." Jack was sitting on the edge of an upholstered chair, facing a head on a plinth resting on a cluttered table. "This is Professor Olafsson. He *was* a professor, anyway, before he died."

"Oh, right," said Jaide. The white face wasn't the weirdest thing she'd seen since becoming a troubletwister and it looked harmless enough. At least it couldn't move about.

"What about Dad?" she said, not yet accepting the idea of talking to someone dead, but prepared to let it go for the moment in order to concentrate on more important things. "I thought you were talking to him."

"I was, but we got interrupted."

From behind her came the sound of Tara's footsteps. Jaide ducked into the room and shut the door behind her, motioning for quiet.

"We don't have long, Jack," she said. "Tara's too good at this game. What did Dad say?"

"Not much. Just to keep looking."

"We already knew that."

"Yes, but now we know he's still nearby, watching."

"He is?" Frustration rose up in her. "I wish he could come closer."

"I wish so, too, Jaide, but he said he'll call us later."

"What is it you seek?" asked the plaster head. "I have lived in this castle a long time. Perhaps I can help you find it."

"How?" asked Jack. "You've been under a dust sheet practically forever."

"Actually, I haven't been under a sheet the whole time. Death masks are collector's items, you know, and I have often been on display."

"Why would someone put a talking death mask on display? Shouldn't you be in a museum?"

"Oh, I can't talk to *everyone*. Imagine the fuss that would cause!"

"But you talked to me."

"There's something special about you," mused Professor Olafsson, "and your sister. Tell me what you're looking for, before your friend arrives, and I will help you if I can."

Jaide looked at Jack. It was clear he wasn't afraid of Professor Olafsson, which meant something. Besides, a plaster head couldn't be Evil, not within the Portland wards, as the castle most definitely was.

"We're looking for something gold," she said, choosing her words carefully. "Like a gold brick but flatter — about this big." She mimed the size with her hands. "It will probably be blank."

"But it might not be either," added Jack.

"A gold card," Professor Olafsson said. "Why didn't you say? *For the Divination of Potential Powers and Safekeeping Thereof*, I presume."

She gaped at him. They were the exact words the *Compendium* had used. "How did you know that?"

"Ah, I know what you are now! Troubletwisters! I was a Warden when I was alive, and a very good one, too, if I can be so bold. My death mask was imbued with my Gift, and so it has in effect become me . . . or I have become it, rather . . . and here I am, Professor Jasper Fredrik Olafsson, formerly of Uppsala, and currently of . . . wherever this is."

Jaide was amazed that such a thing was possible, but she wasn't about to look a gift horse — or a gift head — in the mouth.

"Do you know of any gold cards in the castle?"

"Not specifically, I'm afraid, but there are many places one *might* be hidden. I will give it some thought. Perhaps —"

"Shhhh!" said Jack. He had heard a noise from the other side of the door, as though someone had stopped just outside. The handle twitched.

Jaide acted without thinking. The nearest sheet was out of her reach, so she used her Gift to sweep one up off the floor and hastily drop it over the table and Professor Olafsson's head.

Before he could protest, the door burst in.

"Aha!" Tara cried. "I thought I heard you in here. But you know you're not supposed to hide *together*, right?"

Jack and Jaide feigned innocence. Professor Olafsson stayed quiet, although the sheet did move as he wrinkled his nose. Jaide tried to flatten it back down with a swift blast of air, but her Gift rebelled, making the sheet flap.

"What's that?" cried Tara, backing away with her hands at her mouth. "It better not be a rat! I hate rats!"

"I think it *is* a rat," said Jack, hurrying her out of the door before a full-on tornado could erupt. After his first encounter with The Evil, he was wary of rats, too, so it wasn't hard to fake. "Run!"

Jack and Tara fled up the corridor while Jaide did her best to get her Gift under control. The sheet whipped up into the air and flew around the room, trailing a hurricane of dust. The door slammed shut behind her. Coughing, she gathered the wind up in her hands and crushed it down into a ball, where it evaporated.

"Finely done," said Professor Olafsson. The sheet had fallen back over the bust but he could still see her with one eye. "You had best run after them or suspicions will be raised."

"Yes, but we'll be back," she said, brushing her hair back into its usual place and blinking dust from her eyes. "I don't know how or when, but we will."

"Naturally. Gold cards don't find themselves. Until next time, Jaide the troubletwister, sister of Jack."

She stopped with her hand on the door.

"How did you know our names?"

"You used them right in front of me." Professor Olafsson looked smug.

She exited the room, hurrying along the corridor to catch up with Jack and Tara. If they could talk Tara into another game, this time Tara would hide and the twins could search, pretending to find her choice of hiding place too difficult.

Echoes of a very real sound immediately dispelled that plan.

"That's the gong from the library," said Jack as Jaide ran up to him. "Rodeo Dave wants us."

"Then I guess we'd better go," said Tara. "The thought that this place has rats just makes me shiver."

Jaide consoled herself with the thought that the card might actually *be* in the library, in which case they would be poking around exactly the right place. The trick then would be to locate it before Tara or Rodeo Dave did. If they didn't, there would go their father's chance of ever using it to fight The Evil.

It took them three tries to find the right corridor. Rodeo Dave looked frustrated when they finally reached the library, which was a surprise because normally he never looked anything other than cheerful. He had the gong's padded mallet in one hand as though he'd been about to ring it again, but when he saw them, he put it down. They quickly realized that he wasn't frustrated with them, but with the job at hand.

"It's going to be a much bigger task than I thought," he said, wiping one hand across his forehead and leaving a gray smear behind. "The books used to be in alphabetical order by author, but they've been all mixed up since I was last here. Tara, do you think you could steady the ladder while I check the topmost shelves? Jack and Jaide, I'd be grateful if you could wipe all the shelves you can reach, using these cloths — they don't need to be dampened. We should have enough time to finish this part of the job before your mother arrives to take you home."

The twins put their back into their job willingly enough, peering into every corner of every shelf in the hope of seeing a telltale flash of gold. The air was soon thick with dust, and Rodeo Dave gave them masks to put over their mouths to filter out the worst of it. That made talking difficult, let alone whispering, so the twins had to be content with searching alone. The matter of their father's phone call and the professor's death mask would have to wait until later.

Mister Rourke's stony statue watched them as they worked, still maddeningly familiar to Jaide. Every time she looked at it, it seemed to be looking right back at her tauntingly, as though daring her to remember.

Finally, Rodeo Dave climbed down from the ladder and declared that it was time to go. They took off their masks and brushed themselves and each other down. The twins were covered with cobwebs, even though they hadn't seen a single living spider.

"No rats, at least," said Tara. "I think I'd die if I saw another one."

"You'll find lots of them here," said Rodeo Dave. "Mice, too. George hated cats."

Tara put her arms around herself and went *brrr* again. "Why?"

"George thought they talked about him behind his back. So did his father."

Jaide hid a smile. Knowing Kleo and Ari, the Rourkes might well have been right.

They filed through the corridors to the entrance hall, then outside. The sun was hanging low on the horizon over the countryside, unprotected by the wards of Portland. Jack wondered if his father was still watching them and resisted the urge to wave.

Susan was already winding up the drive toward them, while Thomas Solomon's security cart whirred into view from around the moat. The two vehicles converged on the waiting pedestrians where they stood by the drawbridge, readjusting their eyes to the natural light. Dusk shadows stretched everywhere, making Jack's feet itch.

This time it was Jaide who glimpsed the long, feline figure of Custer prowling through the estate's bushes and trees. The Warden didn't acknowledge her, and neither did the smaller feline shape following at his heels. Ari kept up with Custer only by running at full-pelt. Even as Jaide watched, he fell back into a winded lope and wiped his face with a paw, giving up the chase.

"All finished?" asked Thomas Solomon. Jaide turned. The security cart had been the first to arrive.

"Far from it, I'm afraid," said Rodeo Dave. "I'll be back tomorrow first thing."

"No rest for the wicked, eh?"

Rodeo Dave didn't smile. "It appears not."

"Guess I'd better do my rounds," he said self-importantly. "Can't stand around talking here all day."

The golf cart whizzed off and Jaide suppressed a smile, imagining what would happen if he bumped into Custer.

Susan's car swept to a halt in front of them.

"Right on time," she said as they clambered inside. "How was your afternoon?"

"Very educational, I think," said Rodeo Dave. "The children learned that a castle's solar has nothing to do with a solarium, and that being a secondhand bookseller is more about dust and cobwebs than actual books."

Jack got in last. An orange shape slipped in with him, almost getting tangled in his feet along the way. He bent down and skriched the hair between Ari's ears to cover him, whispering, "What are you doing here?"

"I've been patrolling with Custer," the cat said. "He's been restless all day, like he's sensing something suspicious. I thought he could use my help."

"*Your* help?"

"On Kleo's orders." The cat's eyes narrowed. "What are you trying to say?"

"Nothing. I'm sure Kleo knows what she's doing."

Tara reached down and pulled Ari up into her lap.

"Oh, hello there," she said. "You look hungry. I wish I had something to give you."

"I *like* this girl," said Ari, though all Tara heard was a purr. "She should come round more often. Tell her to pack lunch next time."

"He's always hungry," said Jaide, only half concentrating on the conversation. Susan was accelerating back along the drive. Soon the castle would vanish behind them. They *had* to find a way back to complete the search.

"Rodeo Dave is coming back tomorrow, Mom," she said. "The library is really enormous. He could be there for weeks and *weeks*."

"Hmm? Oh, not *quite* that long," said Rodeo Dave. He seemed distracted, as if his mind was elsewhere.

"It doesn't seem fair that Dave should have to do it all alone," said Jack, following Jaide's lead. "He's got his bookshop to run. What's going to happen if he's not there?"

"I thought Rennie was helping out," said Susan.

"That's true," Rodeo Dave started to say.

"Yes, but it's not the same," said Jaide. "*Can* we help, Mom? It would only take a couple of days. And it's not as if we do anything interesting at school, anyway. We'll learn many more interesting things in a castle than Mr. Carver's classroom."

Susan glanced at them in the rearview mirror.

"You're as persuasive as your father," she said. "Both of you. What about you, Tara? Are you trying to skip school as well?"

"No . . ." said Tara. "I don't think my parents would let me, and anyway, that place has lots of rats and mice. I hate rats. Even Mr. Carver's nose-flute music is better than rats."

"So it hasn't been all fun and games, then," said Susan. "And you certainly look like you've been put to good use."

"We have," said Jaide. "We're exhausted."

Susan's gaze shifted to Rodeo Dave. "Have they really been helpful?"

Rodeo Dave didn't answer for a moment, as if the question had to travel a long way to reach wherever he had gone.

"What? Oh, yes, I'd have to say —"

"I guess it's okay, then. They're all yours."

The twins cheered. Ari put his paws over his ears, and Susan raised a hand for silence.

"Just for tomorrow," she said. "After that, you must return to school."

"We will, Mom," said Jack.

Jaide promised, too. "Thanks, Mom!"

Tara looked as though she might be regretting her decision, and surprisingly Rodeo Dave didn't look entirely relieved, either. Jaide had thought he would be glad for the help, but instead he said nothing, his posture tense and unmoving, even as Tara got carried away with a story about the "giant killer rat" that had leaped out at them in an attic.

As they came into town, Susan said, "Now, Dave, I'll drop you home first, then I'll take the kids to see their grandmother."

The twins sat up straighter, excited by the thought, and Rodeo Dave started out of his daze, too.

"She's well enough for visitors?" he asked.

"I hope so. Doctor Witworth said we should swing by on the way through, just in case."

"May I come with you?"

"Family only, I'm afraid. Tara will have to stay in the waiting room. You don't mind, do you?" she asked Tara. "They won't be long."

"No problemo." She cupped Ari's face in her hands and gave it a smoosh. "Ari will keep me company."

"Kill — me — now," the cat forced out.

"I don't think Ari will be allowed in the hospital, Tara," said Susan.

"Cats and booksellers," said Rodeo Dave, reaching around from the front seat to save Ari. "We've got to stick together, eh? Never mind. I'll give you a snack when we get back to the shop. Maybe Kleo will be there to keep us company."

"If she's not," Ari said, "can I have her snack, too?"

Rodeo Dave, perhaps understanding without hearing the actual words, smiled and tickled him under the chin.

CHAPTER EIGHT
THE SLEEPER

Susan dropped off Rodeo Dave and Ari at the Book Herd, then turned the car around and drove across town to the hospital, where she parked under a chestnut tree whose spreading arms easily covered the car, and several others besides. The hospital was an uninspiring single-story building with none of the glamour and excitement hospitals sometimes had in movies. It seemed completely full of old people. Even the nurses were old.

Susan walked up to the nurses' station. "Is she . . . ?"

"Very restless this afternoon, Sue," said a stout RN with a beard that looked far from sanitary. "Doctor Witworth prescribed a stronger sedative. It's probably taking effect now, but you can go through and see how she is."

Susan nodded and led the children deeper into the hospital until she reached a closed door with a low bench outside.

"Wait here," she told them. "I'll just check."

She ducked through the door, leaving Tara and the twins standing awkwardly outside. None of them said anything. Jack and Jaide strained to hear what was going on inside the room, but could hear only mumbled voices.

Susan returned. "Go on," she told the twins. "She's a bit groggy but awake."

Jaide took a deep breath and walked through the door. Jack followed more hesitantly. He didn't know what to expect. Would Grandma X look as she usually did, or would her head be bandaged? Would there be horrible bruises . . . or worse?

In the end, she looked unchanged, apart from the fact that she was in a hospital gown and was lying propped up in a hospital bed, with her pure white hair spread out on her pillow. She looked much smaller than usual — and that, somehow, was far worse than anything Jack had imagined. The room was dimly lit and smelled of antiseptic. It looked like a place someone went to die, not get better.

"Come here, dear troubletwisters," Grandma X said, waving them closer, one each on either side of the bed. She hugged them tightly, her arms just as strong as ever. "The doctors, blast them with a thousand curses, insist on keeping me *calm* and *relaxed*, not realizing that keeping me *here* is having the exact opposite effect. I'm sorry your studies have been interrupted. I hope there have been no" — she glanced at the door — "unexpected catastrophes?"

They assured her there hadn't been. And apart from the matter of one small bridge, that was the entire truth.

"We've been out at the Rourke Estate with Rodeo Dave," Jaide started to say.

"Really?" Grandma X said. "Kleo sneaked in earlier but she didn't say anything about that. She tells me you've been in the blue room, helping our feathery guest to sleep."

Jack hadn't thought of it that way, but he supposed it had been exactly like that.

"I like her," he said. "Can we keep her?"

"I don't think so, Jackaran. Technically she belongs to the estate, and when the lawyers agree on who will inherit what, we should really let her go." She went to pat his hand, but missed. "I hope you'll understand."

"Have you spoken to Dad?" Jaide asked.

"Yes, of course, dear." A nurse they hadn't seen before entered the room and fussed about, tightening the sheets and adjusting the pillows whether Grandma X wanted them so or not. "He's very busy."

"So it's okay if we . . . go back tomorrow?" Jack persisted. It was impossible to talk openly with someone else in the room, but they had to try. There was no way of knowing how long they had before Susan took them home again.

"I don't see why not," she said. "David will look after you. You can trust him completely."

"He doesn't seem very happy about us being there," said Jaide, remembering Rodeo Dave's moody silences on the way back from the estate.

"I think he's just sad about Young Master Rourke," Grandma X said. "David was the closest friend he had — perhaps George's only friend. At the funeral on Friday, he'll be delivering the eulogy, and that's a very hard thing to do. Particularly because it would have been George's birthday."

She looked sad, too, for a moment, and then brightened when the nurse left the room, as though consciously willing herself to do so.

"Kleo says the weather has been odd," she said. "Storm clouds and rain and yet no lightning, all confined to one area. It strikes me as altogether strange."

"Could it be The Evil?" asked Jaide, still wondering if the car crash had been the work of their grandmother's ancient enemy. "Like that storm, the first time?"

"I don't think so. Wardens are trained to recognize The Evil in many forms. This doesn't feel like any of them. It does have a familiar flavor, though — one I haven't felt for some time. If I could only remember what it was. . . ."

Her voice trailed off and her eyelids drooped closed. The silver ring she wore on her right hand, with the moonstone tucked safely into her palm, looked dull and tarnished in the room's yellow electric light.

"Is she asleep?" Jack whispered after a minute's silence.

"If she is, she's not snoring." They sometimes heard their grandmother at night, even though separated from her by several walls and an entire floor. On a quiet night she sounded like a medium-size jet aircraft having trouble starting up.

"What do we do now?"

Jaide sneaked a look at the hand-scrawled sign above the end of the bed, but instead of a name there was just a Patient Number with seventeen digits.

"Beats me. Leave her, I guess?"

The twins went to step back from the bed, but suddenly Grandma X's eyes flew open. She lunged for them, catching their forearms in an alarmingly tight grip.

"Something is going on, troubletwisters," she said, in a voice that lost none of its power for being barely a whisper. "I don't know what it is, but it started the night Young Master Rourke died. The wards will protect you, as they have these last weeks, but I want you to be . . . to be . . . very . . . care . . ."

Her fight to stay conscious was taking its toll. The grip on their arms was already weakening when a lab-coated doctor entered the room, followed by the same nurse who had fussed with the bed before.

"I think that's enough excitement for one night," said the doctor, a woman in her fifties with gray hair pulled back into a tight bun. Her name tag said WITWORTH. Her voice brooked no dissent. "If you'll step outside, please."

The twins retreated, dismayed by the sight of their grandmother in such a confused state. Or *was* she confused? What if everything she said was right? The twins had never had reason to mistrust her judgment before. If she was worried about something going on in Portland, maybe something *was* going on in Portland.

But what?

Susan and Tara were waiting for them outside. The doctor followed them, and took Susan by the arm to talk to her privately for a moment. Tara surprised both Jack and Jaide by taking their hands and giving them a squeeze.

"I remember when my Po Po was sick," she said. "There was a lot of hanging around hospitals as well, watching grown-ups talk in whispers."

"What happened to her?" asked Jack. "Did she . . . get better?"

"Oh yeah. She comes to visit every year and makes my life miserable."

Her grin was infectious, and it made Jaide feel a little better.

"Off we go," said Susan, indicating that it was time to leave. Doctor Witworth nodded as they passed, not smiling, as though glad to see the back of anyone under forty.

"She'll be okay," said Susan in the car. "She's had a nasty knock on the head that would leave anyone a bit muddled for a while. We'll have to take it slowly. And so does she. Some people just don't have the patience to be a patient."

"How long until she can come home?" asked Jack.

"Doctor Witworth doesn't know. A couple of days, maybe. Longer, if the swelling doesn't go down."

"*Swelling?*" said Jaide, alarmed.

"Don't fret about the details. The important thing is that she's getting better."

They swept up Watchward Lane with a rattle of fallen leaves. Susan parked in the Hillman's usual spot. Susan had dinner ready to roll: homemade hamburgers and fries, which was something she could actually cook well, with chocolate ice cream to follow. That was what she usually cooked on her last night in Portland before going on shift. The twins knew she was spoiling them a little, and they were grateful for it.

Over dinner they gave their mother a more comprehensive but still edited account of their day, lavishly describing the suits of armor, the rooms full of sheet-shrouded furniture, and the apparently endless corridors, but leaving out anything to do with Professor Jasper Frederik Olafsson.

"I'm a little jealous," said Susan with a smile. "I'd love to take time off work and explore a haunted old castle."

"I don't think it's haunted, Mom," said Jaide, wondering if a talking death mask counted. "And most of the rooms are locked."

"Still, it's good of you to help out," she said. "Mr. Smeaton might even pay you, if you do a good job."

"He could pay you in books," said Tara. "He has enough of them."

Dinner was soon over, and so were the dishes, which it was somehow their turn to do yet again, but with two sets of hands to dry it wasn't so bad. Ordinarily the twins liked having Tara over rather than doing their mother's version of math homework, but tonight they had other things on their mind. Foremost among them was the knowledge that their father would call at nine. Luckily, Tara's father came long before then, and it was something of a relief when they waved off their friend and ran back inside.

In their room they conferred quickly and quietly. Their mother was tidying her room, just up the hallway.

"We have to get back into the blue room tonight, after Mom's asleep," said Jaide, "and search for a skeleton key."

"What does it look like, do you think?"

"I don't know. A key, I guess. Probably not much like a skeleton. Let's ask the *Compendium*."

"All right. Cornelia will still be there. Maybe she's ready to tell us something about the night Young Master Rourke died."

Jaide nodded. They froze at the sound of their mother walking past their door, then heading down the creaky stairs.

When she was gone, Jaide shut the door and checked the phone. The time was almost nine o'clock.

"Dad will call soon," she said.

"I hope so. If only we had the number of the phone he's calling from, we could call him instead of waiting."

They fidgeted in silence until the phone rang. The number was hidden, but who else could it be? Jaide pounced on it and put it close to her ear, so Hector Shield's voice was as clear as it could be.

"Hello?"

"Hello, Jaide. Is Jack there, too?"

There was the sound of heavy rain in the background again, clouding Hector's voice, but it wasn't as distracting as it had been the previous night.

"I'm here, Dad," said Jack, listening in as best he could, his head close to his sister's.

"I'm relieved," Hector said. "I thought the phone had been discovered when I hung up on you earlier."

Jack supposed it had been, technically, but not by anyone who mattered.

"We didn't find the card," Jaide confessed. She wished she had better news. "We looked in all the obvious places, but it just wasn't there."

"We're going back to the castle tomorrow," Jack said.

"Well, that's good." He sounded disappointed. "I've been thinking about what you said earlier about a skeleton key. You should definitely look for your grandfather's. But there's something else you should look for, too, something I thought of after we talked. It's a witching rod — like a divining rod for finding water, but it finds artifacts special to Wardens instead."

"Like Grandma has for The Evil, except the other way around?" said Jack. "Cool."

"What does it look like, Dad?" asked Jaide, nudging Jack away. He had gotten to talk to Hector last time, and now it was her turn.

"Use the *Compendium* like you did last night. Let it guide you. I'll call you again tomorrow to see how you got on."

"All right," she said. "But Dad . . . we could go with Tara to Scarborough for the day so you can come into the wards without affecting our Gifts. Wouldn't that be easier?"

"It would, but there's no way your mother would let you skip school just to have fun, and we can't wait as long as the weekend. If the card was lost or fell into The Evil's hands before then, that would be a disaster."

"How would The Evil get through the wards?" asked Jack.

"I saw Custer on the estate," said Jaide. "Ari said he was picking up something weird."

"Jack is right," Hector said. "The Evil would know that the wards are being closely monitored after your grandmother's accident. The slightest open attack would be noticed immediately."

"How would it know about the accident?" Jaide asked. "Would it sense it somehow?"

"Grandma says that some people work for The Evil without being taken over by it," said Jack. "There could be someone like that in town right now."

"There probably is," Hector said, "and you would never know. There's no way to tell until they act against you. The Evil has even been known to plant sleeper agents that lead an ordinary life for years, decades sometimes, before they're activated to work against the Wardens. Ideally, it would be someone who's around a lot and completely trusted by everyone. Someone harmless and easy to overlook."

That was a creepy thought.

"It could be anyone," said Jack with a shiver.

"It could be the person who drove Grandma off the bridge!" exclaimed Jaide.

For a moment there was nothing but the drumbeat of rain over the phone, and both twins feared that the call had been lost. But then Hector's voice came through.

"That's true," their father said. "Don't be frightened unnecessarily, though. All most sleeper agents do is watch and report. Just be careful who you talk to . . . and find the card as soon as possible. You'll do that for me, won't you? You'll have good news for me tomorrow?"

"We will," they promised over the thickening hiss.

"Good. And now, children, I must go."

"Already?" protested Jack. They hadn't talked about Grandma X or Professor Olafsson yet. Even over the phone, though, he could feel his Gift growing restless. The shadows were lengthening and growing darker, and Jaide's Gift was scooting dust bunnies around the floor.

"I'm afraid so," said Hector. "Be careful, both of you. You're very brave."

"We love you, Dad!" said Jaide.

But the call was already over. She lowered the phone and held it in her lap for a moment, unwilling to let go of the tenuous connection to their father it provided.

"We'd better charge it," said Jack. "The battery's getting low."

Jaide forced herself to move. The charger was in a drawer. She plugged it into an outlet near her bed and connected it to the phone.

"I wonder if Mr. Carver is a sleeper agent," she said. "That might explain the nose flutes and everything."

"That's weird but it's not actually Evil. And Dad said it would be someone easy to overlook. He's impossible to ignore."

"Someone who's been around for a long time," Jaide mused. "Someone harmless and trusted."

"The only person who sounds like that is Rodeo Dave," Jack joked, "and it can't be him because . . ."

He stopped because Jaide wasn't laughing and he couldn't think of anything to follow *because*.

"No way," he said. "He can't be. Can he?"

"Why not? He's all Dad told us to look out for."

"Yes, but . . . but . . ." Everything Jack wanted to say came back to the criteria of a sleeper agent. *But Grandma trusts him. But he's been around forever. But he's just a funny old bookseller.*

And then there were other things that occurred to him as the horrible thought took root in his brain.

"The van," said Jaide. "Grandma was knocked off the bridge road by a van. Rodeo Dave drives a van."

"And you remember at school when we found out? Grandma was cut off when she was trying to talk to us, and suddenly he was there."

"And he was surprised when Mom said that she was awake."

The twins stared at each other, shocked by the possibility. Rodeo Dave had given no signs he knew anything about the Wardens or The Evil, so could he really be a traitor, lying low in Portland and biding his time? How could he just pretend to be Grandma X's friend, and the troubletwisters' friend, too, while planning to betray them all along?

The thought was an awful one. So, too, was the thought that they would be stuck in the castle with him all day tomorrow.

"We should tell someone," said Jaide. "Custer, or Kleo —"

"What if we're wrong? We don't have any actual evidence. Remember when we thought Tara's dad was Evil, and it turned out he was just a property developer?"

Jaide did, and that cooled some of her desire to leap up and take action. Grandma was always telling them not to be so impetuous. Perhaps she should think it through, first, before making any wild accusations.

"If Grandma knew, she'd be furious," she said.

"If we were wrong, she'd be furious at us."

"I know. I guess we'll have to keep an eye on him tomorrow and see if he does anything suspicious. When we know for sure, we'll have to do something about it then."

They agreed by bumping their fists, but neither felt reassured. Worst of all, Jack thought, was the possibility that Grandma X *already* knew about him. That would explain why Kleo supposedly lived at the Book Herd, to keep an eye on him. It might also be why Rodeo Dave didn't know Rennie was the Living Ward, even though she was living and working there. But why would Grandma X put the twins into his hands so readily, without even warning them?

"It just doesn't make any sense," he muttered.

"In Portland, nothing ever seems to make sense."

The sound of footsteps outside the door interrupted them again. Jaide swung into action, throwing her backpack over the phone so their mom wouldn't see it.

The door opened and Susan leaned in.

"Time for bed."

She ushered them toward the bathroom, where they brushed their teeth. Jack cleaned his much more carefully than usual, since he thought that it might be his breath that was putting Cornelia off him.

"I've changed my shifts so I'll be around in the evenings all week," said Susan as she tucked them into bed. "That's one good thing to come out of all this," she added, brushing an errant hair out of her daughter's eyes. Both eyes and hair were the same color as her own, and although Jaide had the shape of her father's face, it would be clear that they would resemble each other closely when Jaide was grown up. "I miss you terribly while I'm away. You know that, right?"

"Yes, Mom," Jaide said. "We miss you, too." On an impulse, she added, "Do you think Dad will be able to visit Grandma soon?"

"I don't know, dear," Susan said, dropping her eyes. "You know how . . . how busy he is right now . . . how difficult it is for him to come home. It's not something I have any control over. But I wish he would come back. I wish it could be the way it was when we were all together and everything was . . . normal."

Both twins wanted to tell her that he was just outside the bounds of Portland, but even if they could have told her that, there was no way they could ever be normal again, not in the way their mother meant. That was the deep and abiding truth Susan still wrestled with, under the veil of reassurance that Grandma X had cast over her. Susan rarely thought about what had brought them to Portland — the explosion of their home in the city, the truth about her husband's work, and the legacy her children had been born into — but even with Grandma X's clouding of her mind, the facts still swam to the surface, and there was no hiding from the more painful truths of their new lives.

Susan blinked and shrugged off the dark mood that had fallen across her. She had two wonderful children and a job she enjoyed. She was even making friends, in town and at work. Life could be so much worse.

"Sweet dreams, Jack and Jaide," she said, giving them both a kiss. On the way out she only half closed the door behind her, so the room wouldn't be completely dark.

CHAPTER NINE

BETWEEN THE EVIL AND THE DEEP BLUE SEA

It took them both forever to fall asleep, and then only seconds seemed to pass before the alarm went off again. The twins tiptoed groggily past their mother's room and went upstairs a second night in a row. They had a mission: to find the skeleton key and witching rod. Without them, the Card of Translocation might vanish forever — into obscurity or into the hands of The Evil, which would, presumably, use the Gift it contained against the Wardens.

In the blue room, they found Kleo and Cornelia in exactly the same positions as before, except the silk cover of the brass cage was off.

"Hello, troubletwisters," said the cat, sitting up straight the instant they appeared. She hopped off the dragon-mouth chair and hurried to greet them. Cornelia watched her pad across the floor with one sharp yellow-rimmed eye.

"Rourke?" the macaw said, but in a way that suggested she was making wary conversation rather than looking for her dead master.

Jaide gave Kleo a pat. "Have you been in here ever since last night?"

"Yes, I'm afraid so. The life of Warden Companion isn't a constantly exciting and adventurous one, and I'm thankful for that most of the time, but I will confess to getting a little bored today."

Jack reached for the bag of seeds and offered one to Cornelia. The great macaw was crouched on its uppermost perch, about eye level with him, and she looked at him with patient curiosity.

"Has she said anything?" he asked Kleo.

"Safe harbor," the bird announced in a clear, distinct voice.

Kleo sat down and coiled her tail around her legs. "Yes, there's that," she said. "We think that's why she came here, to get away from whatever it was that scared her. All the animals around here know or at least sense that Watchward Lane is a safe haven — unless you're a mouse or a bird when Ari's around."

"You mean you don't eat mice and birds?" asked Jack.

"Not when they are seeking refuge," sniffed Kleo.

"The devil and the deep blue sea," said Cornelia, waddling over to inspect the nut Jack held. She sniffed him first, as she had the previous night, and this time, after a moment's careful consideration, deigned to take the offering.

"She says that a lot, too," Kleo observed. "I don't know what it means."

"Isn't it a saying, like caught between a rock and a hard place?" asked Jaide.

Jack nodded. Hector Shield liked to say that he was stuck between the Kettle and the Steeped Oolong Tea.

"So she was frightened at the estate and she's frightened here, too," Jack said. "But she's safe here, isn't she?"

"Perfectly, while Custer is keeping Ari distracted," Kleo said. "She might be the only witness who can tell us what really happened to Young Master Rourke on the night he died."

"Can you tell us, Cornelia?" asked Jack, offering her a big, shiny pumpkin seed this time. "We just want to stop it from happening again."

Cornelia raised her head and tilted it to one side, glancing at Jack first, then Jaide, then back again. She seemed to be trying to work something out.

"Out of the rain," she said.

"That's new," said Kleo, ears pricking up.

"Out of the rain," Cornelia said again, more firmly than before.

"What are you trying to tell us, Cornelia?" asked Jack.

"That's not rain."

"What isn't?"

"You daft old fool. Batten down the hatches! Rourke! Rourke!"

Cornelia spread her wings and flapped them up and down, sending tiny feathers and seed husks flying all around them. Jaide retreated, spluttering, while Jack tried to calm the bird down.

"Shhh! Cornelia, it's all right! We're here — you're safe!"

But the bird couldn't be consoled, and in the end they had to throw the cover back over the cage in the hope that she would settle down. Slowly, with the occasional raucous "Rourke," Cornelia did become quiet, although Jack could hear her moving about inside the cage.

Kleo went back to the dragon seat and sat like a sphinx, facing the twins.

"Well." She sighed. "That was all new. I don't think it means anything, but it's progress of sorts. She likes you, Jack."

"She still doesn't like the way I smell, though," he said, sniffing his fingertips. They didn't smell like anything more sinister than hamburger, and perhaps a small amount of dirt. Next time he would wash his hands to be sure.

"I'm just going to look in the *Compendium*," Jaide told Kleo, giving Jack a *keep her distracted* look as she went to the desk.

"Not gold cards again, I hope," said the cat, looking amused.

"No," Jaide said truthfully. "We're just worried about getting out of touch while Grandma's in the hospital and we're busy helping Rodeo Dave."

She opened the *Compendium* and began to focus her thoughts on the idea of skeleton keys in general, since she didn't know what this one looked like.

"Speaking of Rodeo Dave," said Jack, "has he seemed all right to you lately?"

"Not really," Kleo said. "He has been very tense since the old man died."

"Were you with him the night it happened?"

"I was. The phone call woke us both up."

"What phone call?"

"The one from the old man."

"Young Master Rourke called Rodeo Dave?" This was a twist Jack hadn't anticipated. "What did he want with him?"

The cat shook his head. "I don't know, but it was definitely him. Rodeo Dave said "Rourke" three times, then he went out to the estate in a hurry. That's why he was the first to find the old man."

Jack sat on his knees in front of Kleo, struggling to absorb all this new information. Rodeo Dave had spoken to Young Master Rourke while he was still alive. Then Rodeo Dave had rushed out to the estate and found the old man dead and the lodge thoroughly ransacked. Or *had* he? Had he taken the opportunity to look for the Card of Translocation while Young Master Rourke had been out of the picture? Or had he killed the old man himself because of something he had been told on the phone . . . ?

That was a picture of Rodeo Dave quite unlike the man Jack thought he knew. But as Jaide said, nothing in Portland was ever simple.

"Jack?" said Jaide. "Come look at this."

There was something odd about Jaide's tone, and with good reason. Her thoughts had been distracted by Jack and Kleo's conversation. Instead of focusing on skeleton keys, she had been thinking about Young Master Rourke, living alone on the giant estate, the son of a man who had made such an impact on Portland's prosperity but had not been terribly well liked.

Then she had turned the page and seen a familiar picture.

"This one again?" said Jack, leaning close over her shoulder. "Portland in 1872." It showed a whale carcass being winched ashore in front of a crowd of old-fashioned people. Everyone in the photo had wide white eyes, indicating that they belonged to The Evil.

"Look at him," said Jaide, pointing.

Standing with one arm upraised, facing the camera, was a man in a black suit.

"Do you recognize him?" Jaide asked.

Jack squinted, then gasped.

"That's Young Master Rourke's father!" he said. "The one in the portrait and the statue in the library . . . but it can't be, can it? I mean, it's too long ago."

"It looks like him," said Jaide. "And he was Evil."

Kleo made them both jump as she hopped up onto the desk and nosed the picture.

"That's the first Rourke," she said. "The grandfather. He started the whaling, but it was his son who built up everything else. They looked very alike. And the white eyes there might just be because it's an old photograph."

"Oh," said Jaide, disappointed. "There's too many Rourkes."

"Only three," Jack pointed out. "Grandfather Rourke, the whaler. Mister Rourke, the rich one who built everything. And Young Master Rourke."

"I still think Grandfather Rourke was part of The Evil," said Jaide, studying the photograph again. She shuddered and said, "Look at all those white eyes. . . ."

"Can you imagine what it would be like to have a dad who was part of The Evil?" Jack wondered aloud.

Jaide shuddered again, as though something slimy had slithered down her spine. She didn't want to imagine anything as horrible as that — not on top of Grandma X in the hospital and Rodeo Dave a possible sleeper agent.

"I don't think I want to look at this for a while," she said, shutting the *Compendium*. "I guess we should go to bed."

Jack looked at her in surprise.

"I don't want to go to bed. It's too early."

"I suppose we could stay here and keep Cornelia company for a while," said Jaide, with a wink that the cat couldn't see. "Do you want a break, Kleo?"

Kleo's ears twitched.

"I could do with a stroll," she acknowledged. "The night does beckon."

"Well, we'll stay here for, say, half an hour," said Jaide. "Would that be okay?"

"That is most considerate of you," said Kleo. "I'll be back shortly."

She jumped down from the table, shot up the steps to the tapestry-covered door, whisked behind one corner, and was gone.

Jaide waited for a few seconds, in case the cat came back, then shut her eyes and placed her hands on the *Compendium*. This time she thought ferociously about skeleton keys and, in particular, the one owned by her grandfather.

She felt the book shuffle under her hands, and though she didn't lift them, when she opened her eyes, the folder was open, this time displaying a handwritten note that said:

Sam didn't have the hooks. I've put all the keys in the top drawer of the snake bureau for now, will make the board when the hooks come in. And I picked up the cake, so you don't need to go.

Jack was reading over Jaide's shoulder.

"I guess that's Granddad's writing," he said. "Weird."

Jaide looked around the blue room. Over in one corner there was a teak bureau wound about with carved snakes.

"That must be it," she said, pointing. "Check it out. I'll ask about the witching rod."

Jack went over and pulled out the top drawer. It was full of numerous differently shaped and colored wooden boxes. He opened the lids of each of them in turn until in one of them he found a large ring of keys. The keys ranged in size from half the length of his little finger to one big key as long as his hand. They all had ivory handles, carved in the shape of a crescent moon, and the key parts were bright silver and surprisingly simple.

"We still don't know which one is the skeleton key," Jack said, holding them up. They made a sound like a wind chime. "I guess we take them all and try them one by one."

Jaide didn't answer. She was concentrating on the *Compendium* again. It fluttered open, but this time revealed only some hasty but well-executed sketches. One showed a close-up of a thick wire that had been bent in half and twisted in the middle. Underneath was an inscription in very small handwriting that said *Makeshift witching rod, made from fencing wire, works just as well as the one the blacksmith made. Comes in handy for toasting marshmallows.*

The second drawing showed a hand gripping the very end of the wire with just two fingers and thumb, and the note beneath that said *Of the two grips suggested, this one works best for me. Hard on the fingers, but the rod responds strongly, so strongly sometimes it jumps from my grip!*

Jaide stared at the drawing.

"This isn't much use," she complained. "It shows what a witching rod looks like, but not *where* one is."

Jack came and looked, too, bringing the keys. He tilted his head sideways, then laughed. "I know where it is," he said.

"Where?" asked Jaide.

"In the living room, next to the fireplace. In that box with the poker and stuff. I'll go get it."

"Don't wake up Mom by jangling those keys!" warned Jaide.

Jack closed his hand tight around the keys to stop their noise, and went up into the house. Jaide put her hands back on the *Compendium*, ready to ask it about one more thing that she thought needed investigation.

When Jack came back, he was holding a soot-blackened wire rod with a twist in the middle. He barely had time to show it to Jaide before the tapestry twitched and Kleo returned.

"What's that?" asked the cat.

"Um, a toasting stick," said Jack. "For marshmallows."

"Or sardines," mused Kleo. "I like a fire-toasted sardine."

"I guess I could toast you a sardine," said Jack, wrinkling his nose. "Not right now, though."

"Yeah, we'd better go to bed," said Jaide. "Night, Kleo!"

"Thank you for watching over Cornelia, troubletwisters." Kleo rubbed her head against both of them as they filed through the door. "Good night."

As Jack pulled the elephant tapestry back into place, he heard Cornelia call out quietly.

"The devil," she said, "or the deep blue sea?"

It was definitely a question, but Jack didn't feel as though it was directed at him. It might have been nothing more than random words from an old parrot. Still, it made him sad to think that she was still worried about something she couldn't communicate to anyone. If only she could talk properly like Kleo and Ari.

Back in their room, Jaide took the witching rod. It didn't look like anything magical, little more than a bent old coat hanger, but slightly thicker.

"Well," she said, "I guess this *is* it. It looks just like the picture."

Jack took the witching rod back from her and held it as the drawing had shown, with just two fingers and his thumb. It immediately quivered and the end arched back, toward Jack himself.

"It works!" exclaimed Jack. "I've got the skeleton key in my pocket."

"I looked up something else while I was in the *Compendium*," Jaide said.

"What?"

"The death mask you found — Professor Olafsson. He was a Warden, just as he said. He was very controversial, though, even among Wardens. He had a theory that in addition to the world where The Evil comes from, there are other parallel worlds around us that we can't see or access, but if we could work out how The Evil gets into our world we might be able to get into all the other worlds, too."

"Wow!" said Jack. "Interesting guy."

"Interesting extremely *old* guy," said Jaide. "He died in 1763. So I guess he won't be very in touch with anything going on more recently."

"He might still be able to help us find the card," said Jack. "We can ask him tomorrow."

Jaide pulled back her covers and crawled gratefully under them.

"*If* we can get away from Rodeo Dave . . ."

CHAPTER TEN

Every Castle Has Its Secrets

While they were getting ready for their trip to the castle the next morning, there came two loud knocks at the front door. Susan opened it and stared out at a high-cheeked man with long, blond hair. There was something about his eyes that unnerved her — they were so close set, and disturbingly intense. He seemed to be staring right through her, or into her.

"Susan Shield, I presume," he said.

"Yes, but I'm afraid —"

"I am a friend to your husband," he said, offering his hand. She took it. His grip was gentle, but his fingernails were surprisingly long. "And to your children."

"Oh," she said, backing away, feeling as though the wind had been knocked out of her. "Yes, I . . . think I understand."

Jaide had poked her head around the kitchen door. "It's Custer!" she cried, running out to meet him. Jack followed.

"What are you doing here?" he asked. "Is something wrong?"

"Nothing is wrong."

"Would you . . . would you like to come in?" asked Susan. "I've just made some coffee."

"Thank you, but all I require is a moment with Jack and Jaide, here."

He gestured at the twins. Susan nodded, turned as though in a fog, and walked three steps up the hall.

Custer squatted down in the doorway in front of the twins.

"We saw you yesterday," said Jaide. "Out on the estate."

"Indeed you did, and I will be patrolling again today while your grandmother remains in the hospital." His upper lip curled, revealing his opinion of modern medicine. His teeth were long and sharp-looking. "Ari tells me that you, too, are returning to the estate. You must be careful. The boundary of the wards stretches across the property. It would be dangerous for you to step beyond that boundary."

"Why?" asked Jack. "Is The Evil around?"

Custer glanced over their shoulders to where their mother stood just out of earshot, gnawing on a thumbnail.

"That is not what I am saying. I am asking merely for you to be careful." He reached into an inside pocket of his long, leather greatcoat. "Take these. They'll tell you when you reach the boundary."

He handed them a leather wristband each and helped tie them around their wrists. Colorful beads dotted the bands, apparently at random. One of Jack's beads looked like a tiny six-sided die.

Jaide opened her mouth to ask Custer the first of the many questions she had, but a horn tooted outside and the chance was lost.

The three of them went out onto the veranda to meet Rodeo Dave. He was driving an enormous red car — long, wide, and rectangular, with enormous fins at the rear and a top that was folded down behind the backseat, leaving the interior open to the sky. Two longhorns adorned the grille at the front, looking as though they came from a real steer. The car's engine sounded like the growl of a giant dog, slowed down to a rumbling throb. Rodeo Dave looked small and insignificant behind the wheel, even with his enormous mustache and an equally incongruous cowboy hat, which was also new to the twins.

"The old companion?" said Custer.

"It seemed fitting," said Rodeo Dave.

"Young Master Rourke would have hated it."

"This isn't about George."

The exchange revealed nothing to the twins, except that Custer and Rodeo Dave knew each other.

"Hop aboard!" Rodeo Dave called over the grumbling engine. Jack looked at Jaide, who shrugged. The chassis hardly shifted as they climbed in, Jack in the front, marveling at the chrome-finished dashboard and the depth of the seats, and Jaide in the seemingly infinite rear.

Susan hurried out of the house carrying packed lunches, as though they were going to school. She gave them to the twins with a kiss each good-bye, and waved as the giant automobile slid smoothly into motion. They watched her recede into the distance behind them. Custer disappeared as though he had never been there.

"This is Zebediah," said Rodeo Dave over the engine noise, patting the dashboard. "I only bring him out for special occasions."

"What's the occasion?" asked Jaide, wondering if this had something to do with Grandma's accident. Could he be hiding the van to get rid of evidence?

"Zebediah *creates* the occasion," he said. "Without Zebediah, this'd just be another ordinary Wednesday. And that's absolutely what it should not be."

Jack couldn't believe the car was going to fit down the lane, but it did, just.

"Where do you keep him?"

"Gabe Jolson lets me use the dealership's shed on Station Street. Zebediah doesn't take up much space when you park him carefully."

Gabe Jolson ran Portland's sole car yard, Gabriel's Auto Sales. Rather like the Book Herd, the twins had hardly ever seen anyone looking at the cars, let alone buying one.

Zebediah glided through the town like a cruise liner, barely bumping when they went over the bridge, and turning into corners as smoothly as cream. People stopped to look as the car swept by, and some of them even waved. It was as Rodeo Dave had said — Zebediah did create an occasion. Jack would have liked to drive around a little longer, but it seemed to take them no time at all to reach the castle gates.

Thomas Solomon waved Rodeo Dave into a parking space large enough for Zebediah. Dave put on the emergency brake and turned the key. With a smooth clearing of its mechanical throat, the car's engine shut down.

"I reckon you can leave the top open," Thomas Solomon said to Rodeo Dave. "No rain forecast today."

Jaide looked up. The sky was cloudy with patches of blue. It seemed the weird weather of the previous days had passed.

As she slid across the backseat to come out the far door, she saw a ginger tail poking out from under the front seat. She reached down and tugged on it gently.

The tail retracted and Ari's face appeared.

"Hey, watch it!" he hissed.

"What are *you* doing here?"

"Shhh. I'm supposed to be keeping an eye on you."

"Why?"

"Who knows? I think Custer wants me out of the way so Kleo can get up to . . . whatever it is she's getting up to."

That was a possibility, Jaide thought. If Ari suspected that there was a giant, vulnerable bird cooped up, who knew what he might get up to? But couldn't it also be that Custer didn't trust *them*? Or maybe it was Rodeo Dave he didn't trust. . . .

She wished they'd had time to talk to Custer properly that morning. It occurred to her only then to wonder if Rodeo Dave's arrival had been timed to cut them off.

"All right," she whispered. "You stay there and I won't say anything. Just try not to get in our way, okay? We've got something important to do."

"Don't worry," he said before she could explain. "I don't care a bit for old books. I'm mainly here for the mice."

"Coming, Jaide?" asked Rodeo Dave.

"Uh, yeah, just getting my bag."

Ari stayed under the seat as Jaide left the car, slammed the door behind her with an echoing boom, and ran to catch up with Jack and Rodeo Dave as they crossed the moat bridge to the castle. Rodeo Dave had a backpack of his own, filled with things that rattled and clanked. He didn't explain what they were, but it certainly didn't sound like lunch. He had left his cowboy hat behind, on the car's dashboard.

Nothing had changed inside the castle. Everything was frozen just as it had been for all the years after Young Master Rourke had moved out. Jack assumed that other assessors would be moving in at some point to look over the furniture, paintings, and other valuable items. Hopefully that wouldn't happen before they had found the Card of Translocation.

Rodeo Dave put his backpack on the floor of the library and took stock of the job ahead of them.

"Right," he said. "Here's how we start. I've made a rough list of the titles across these three shelves. I need you to take the books out, check them off against the list, dust the covers, and put them carefully in the boxes over there. If I've missed a book, write in the title, author, publisher, and year of publication on the right side of the list. If anything looks really fragile, leave it where it is. Don't even try to dust it. Okay?"

"Okay," said Jack.

"I'm going to check the collection in the lodge. It's mostly paperbacks, but even so, some of those old pulps can be very valuable. You'll be okay here while I'm gone?"

"We'll be fine," said Jaide.

He nodded, picked up his backpack, and left.

"That's great," whispered Jack. "Now we can start looking!"

"Not yet," Jaide said. "First we have to wait, in case he doubles back to get something and catches us gone. We also need to make it look like we did *some* work. We don't want to make him suspicious."

"What if the card is in the lodge?"

"He's already searched it — or someone has — and it wasn't there. I don't know why he's searching again. Let's get started, Jack. Otherwise he'll come back before we've even gone."

Together they went through about half the shelves Dave had indicated, marking off and cleaning the books, flicking through them as they went, before boxing them up as instructed. They were soon filthy, with blackened fingers, and dust and cobwebs in their hair. Jack had found an old notebook (blank) slipped between two volumes of a massive history of the steam engine, and Jaide had found the skeleton of a mouse or a small rat, squashed under a giant book about ship maintenance, but apart from that they found nothing out of the ordinary. No gold card, and no map showing them where it might be hidden, either. Just books, the bust of Mister Rourke, and the painting of the woman in yellow, smiling to herself as though she knew something they didn't.

Jack put his latest armful onto the ground, puffing up a cloud of dust that triggered a coughing fit.

"I think that's been long enough now, Jaide, don't you?" he said when he had recovered.

"All right." She climbed down from the low ladder she was using to check the top shelves. "Let's go."

They took the ring of keys and the witching rod from Jaide's pack and eased slowly through the library door, after first checking for anyone in the hallway outside. It was empty apart from several enormous tapestries, two suits of armor, and one wooden chest. The air was still and quiet. The only echoes came from the small sounds they made as they shuffled forward and stood for a moment, deciding where to go first. There was no sign of Ari.

"Let's try the keys on the chest," whispered Jack. "It looks locked."

There was no doubt of that. A huge iron padlock hung off the front, shaped like a lion and as big as two fists gripping each other.

Jack moved forward to try one of the keys in the lock, but Jaide held him back.

"Let's test the witching rod first, before we know what's in there," she said, raising the bent wire and gripping it in the way the *Compendium* had recommended. The wire was surprisingly difficult to keep still, once it was under tension. It flexed and shifted in her hand like a kitten ready to spring on a toy, and it took all her concentration to keep it steady.

She swept it across the wall in front of her, and felt nothing more than its usual jitteriness. They moved closer and she tried again. The wire felt taut in her hand, but it didn't bend down toward the chest.

"Nothing," she said. "Okay, open it."

Jack looked at the lock and then at the ring of keys in order to choose one at random. As he held the ring up, however, one of the keys swung out so it was pointing at the lock, as though magnetic. It looked like it would fit, so he slid it into the lock and tried to turn it. For a moment, it was stuck. He jiggled it a little and it went in far enough for him to turn it with ease.

The lock clicked open, but it took both of them to lift the mighty lid. When it fell back against the wall with an echoing boom, Jaide gasped with surprise. A hideous face was peering up at them with wide, staring eyes and long, sharp teeth.

Then she laughed.

"Another head!" she said.

This time it was a bear's head, stuffed and mounted, mouth open as though roaring. Its fur was matted and covered with dust.

Jack let out a sigh of relief. His heart was pounding, too, but at least this head wasn't likely to come alive and bite them, if the witching rod was to be believed. And now they knew that the skeleton key worked perfectly.

"Let's shut it again," he said. "Then go get Professor Olafsson."

"All right. Hey, look — more whales."

The underside of the lid was engraved with whales, whaling boats, and sailors with harpoons.

"The Rourkes were *obsessed*," said Jaide. "There are whales everywhere."

Together they lowered the lid, unable to avoid another loud boom as it closed. As Jack turned the key again to lock it, he thought he heard the soft chiming of a clock in the distance.

"Did you hear that?" he asked.

"What?"

"A clock, chiming. It was kind of faint. . . ."

"Nope," said Jaide. "Come on. I want to talk to the professor."

The death mask was exactly where they had left him, dozing patiently under the dust sheet. His eyes jerked open with a sneeze when they pulled it off.

"Ah, it's you again. The midgets from the future — no, wait, children, you said. You're looking for a golden card. You're starting your collection rather young, aren't you? Perhaps that's how you do things in this future of yours."

"What collection?" repeated Jack, confused.

"Of cards. Every Warden has one, but not usually in my time until they *were* Wardens."

Even though the death mask only had blank spaces for eyes, Jack and Jaide had the uncomfortable feeling that the professor was looking right into them. "Perhaps it is the same in this time, too. Why do you seek this card, exactly? And for whom do you seek it?"

"Our father asked us to find it," said Jaide. She figured she could trust a Warden with the truth, even if he had been dead for hundreds of years.

"What is this card called?"

"The Card of Translocation," Jack said. "Do you know what it's for?"

"There are thousands of gold cards. I don't recall that one in particular. They are, in general, *For the Divination of Potential Powers and Safekeeping Thereof*. Beyond that, however, I can only speculate. The name is somewhat curious."

The death mask raised its plaster eyebrows and dropped the left corner of its mouth in something that conveyed the feeling of a shrug.

"Can you tell us where it might be?" Jack asked.

"I can do better than that, if you put me in one of those satchels of yours. That would be a practical solution to my non-ambulatory state — my lack of legs, I mean."

"You want to come with us?" asked Jaide.

"Of course! I can't very well help you stuck here on this table, can I?"

She had hoped for directions rather than lugging the death mask around with her, but the professor's suggestion did make sense. And besides, he had been trapped under a sheet for more years than she could imagine. It seemed only fair that he should have a change of scenery.

She and Jack arranged his pack into a kind of harness around Jack's neck and shoulders, so it hung down his front. Then they tied the death mask of Professor Olafsson on the front, using the ends of the straps.

"No' 'oo 'ight — ah, yes, yes, that's perfect."

His grin widened as they approached the door and opened it.

"What a marvelous opportunity! I imagined I would be forgotten there forever, you know. A terrible fate for a brilliant mind like mine."

"Shhh," Jack said. "We're not the only people here."

"Is someone else looking for the Card of Translocation?"

"We don't know for sure," said Jaide. "Maybe."

"We should hear Rodeo Dave coming," said Jack. "His boots make a lot of noise on the stone."

"Well, I will endeavor to speak quietly," said the professor, only slightly more quietly than he had spoken before. "Tra-la-la! I see you have a witching rod. Yes, hold it like that — I believe it is the more efficacious of the two methods. Now, if we take the left corridor ahead, that would be our best course."

"Why?" asked Jaide. "What's there?"

"A very large window," said the professor with dignity. "I have not seen the sun for many decades. After a brief interval there, I will lead you on our search."

As quietly as they could, the twins moved off down the corridor, with the death mask of the professor humming something softly to himself, a tune the twins did not know, but long ago had been written in tribute to the glory of the sun.

CHAPTER ELEVEN

THE HIDDEN DOOR

The professor was completely silent as Jack stood in the shaft of sunlight that came through the tall window. After a few minutes, when Jack began to fidget, he sighed and said, "Enough. Let the hunt begin."

The twins took turns with the witching rod. It was difficult to hold, and they soon became quite sensitive to its every twitch and tremble — perhaps oversensitive. They spent a lot of time examining empty rooms and unmarked stretches of walls. They opened countless chests, drawers, and doors, the skeleton key working every time. Often Jack heard the distant chime of a clock when he turned one of the keys. Eventually, he realized it must be an echo of some old power, and wondered if the keys had been used by Wardens as well as by their grandfather. That would explain why the key apparently was physically drawn to the locks they presented it with, as though it had a mind of its own.

Unfortunately, when the twins got the chests, drawers, and doors open, they usually found nothing but dust. There were occasional surprises that under other circumstances would have piqued their curiosity: a brass bell hidden under a sagging bed, four pitted cannonballs in a pyramid in one corner of an otherwise empty attic, several coils of rope that rats had nibbled at, a shield leaning up against the side of an empty barrel, even a moth-eaten jester's hat in a glass case with a label that had faded into unintelligibility.

They *did* find lots more whales: in carved flourishes on the banisters, on dinner services and cutlery stacked neatly in the lifeless kitchen, even on a handkerchief someone had dropped long years past behind a sagging baseboard. Jaide supposed the whales made sense, given the family's fortune was made through whaling, but it was still a bit grotesque.

They also found the castle's medieval toilets.

"Is that what I think it is?" asked Jack, pointing at a piece of wood with a round hole in it, lying flat in a niche that stuck out of the wall in one corner of the castle's solar.

"It's a garderobe," said Professor Olafsson. "Has the future no need of such things anymore?"

"We call them toilets, and yes, we still need them," said Jaide, looking down the hole. It led to a pit outside the castle walls. A strong draft made her shiver. The air smelled of rain. "I wonder if the Rourkes used these? You know, being super realistic with the history and everything?"

"There were proper toilets in those bathrooms upstairs," said Jack. "And next to the library. Besides, wouldn't they stink?"

"Not if properly cleansed," said the professor. "A few buckets of water every time, mixed with a solution of hyssop and rosemary. Or you could lower a small child with a brush —"

"Okay, okay!" interrupted Jack. "That's enough about garderobes! Let's get on with finding the card. We're running out of time."

"I'm not getting any twitches," said Jaide, waving the witching rod slowly across the walls and furniture. The solar was one of the few places where the twins had found anything actually made of gold. Here, it was in the form of a candelabra and a cufflink case shaped like a fish. Downstairs they had found gold mugs in the dining room and a gold pen in the study, looking as though it had dropped on the desk decades ago and never been moved.

"Maybe that's a good sign," said Jack, kicking at the foot of a bed in frustration and provoking a rain of dust. "It never seems to point to anything interesting. Could it be faulty, Professor Olafsson?"

"That is a remote possibility," said the death mask. "The wire mechanism is simplicity itself. The fault might lie in the operator —"

"Are you saying I'm doing it wrong?" asked Jaide, looking under the bed and finding only an ornate chamber pot.

"— *or* in the nature of the card's hiding place. What if we can't find this card because it is not truly here?"

"Huh?" said Jack.

"There are more worlds than we can imagine brushing up against this one, realms separated from ours by the simplest thought, the merest breath. What if the card is in one of those? The witching rod might glimpse it, but we cannot because we lack the key to enter the realm the card occupies."

The twins glanced at each other. The *Compendium* had mentioned Professor Olafsson's ideas about parallel universes and how they were controversial among Wardens, with the majority not believing him. But the twins didn't want to show signs of skepticism in case he became offended and wouldn't talk to them anymore.

"We have the skeleton key," said Jack, hefting the ring in his hand. "Could that help us?"

"I don't mean that kind of key," Professor Olafsson said. "These locks aren't physical. They're mental. Only with the greatest effort of mind can we unpick them. I was working on such keys when I died, but my work was sadly incomplete."

"So the card could be here and at the same time . . . *not* here?" said Jack, trying to get his head around the idea.

"Exactly. We are surrounded by things we can't see that *are* there and things we *can* see that aren't. Like salt dissolved in water, or a reflection in a mirror. Have you never wondered where The Evil comes from, what its reality is like? It has its own world from which it attempts to break into ours, a world with its own rules . . . horrible ones, no doubt, quite inimical to our own.

"I'm not saying that the card is with The Evil," he added hastily, seeing the alarm blossoming on their faces, "but that it might be somewhere like that. Another world with its own rules, connected to our own by some means of passage that *someone* fathomed and which we, too, now must."

Professor Olafsson looked satisfied with that conclusion, but the twins were still frustrated.

"Like a secret passage?" said Jaide.

"Yes, exactly like that, between one world and the next."

"Do you know if the castle had any secret passages?" asked Jack.

"None that I saw, in the attics or the areas in which I was on display."

"You wouldn't put a secret passage where just anyone could bump into it," said Jaide. "You'd put it somewhere safe, somewhere private."

"Somewhere like the solar," said Jack excitedly.

"Exactly!"

Jaide leaped off the bed and began poking things at random — carved knobs on the mantelpiece, gas-lamp brackets and joins — looking for loose panels or hidden switches. Jack did the same, abandoning the mysteries of the witching rod for something more concrete.

"I didn't mean to be taken so literally," said Professor Olafsson, jostling from side to side as the twins competed over likely possibilities. "I hardly believe that a passage between worlds would be revealed in such a vulgar way as —"

He stopped talking when, with a solid click, a carved whale sank one inch into the wall under Jack's insistent thumb, and a panel slid aside next to it, revealing a dark, dank space beyond.

"Oh my," said Professor Olafsson. "You do appear to have found something."

Jaide peered inside the hidden panel and saw narrow stone steps leading downward. The walls of the secret passage were wood, once polished but now stained with age and damp. There were brackets for torches, all empty, and the light from the solar petered out after a few steps. Beyond that point, Jaide could see nothing at all.

Jack fared better, thanks to his Gift, but even he could see just ten feet forward, to the point where the stairs turned left. The ceiling was very low, and he was horribly reminded of the sewers under Portland, where The Evil had once chased him. He still had nightmares about those terrible experiences. Here at least there was no slime, and the air smelled stale, not foul. And the odds were that the realm of The Evil probably wasn't at the end of the tunnel . . . or so he hoped..

"After you," he told Jaide.

"*You* found it," she shot back. "Besides, you can see in the dark. I can't."

He swallowed his fear with a gulp and stepped inside.

As though sensing his reluctance, Jaide put one hand on his shoulder and followed closely behind him. He was glad for his sister's presence. In the sewers he had been entirely alone, and that had been the worst thing of all.

They descended four steps. Behind them, the panel closed with a soft click, plunging them into total blackness.

It was Jaide's turn to be frightened, and to be grateful for Jack's confident guidance. Fortunately the dark didn't last long. Four more steps took them to the corner, and as they turned it, she found that a notch in the wall farther down allowed a sliver of dim light into the tunnel. To her dark-adjusted eyes it was more than enough to see by. As they passed the notch, she saw that it opened onto a room they had visited before: a pantry on the first floor that had seemed utterly unremarkable.

"There might be holes like this all over the castle," she whispered.

"We should've checked the paintings," said Jack. "You know, like in old movies. There's always someone peeping through the eyeholes."

That prompted a creepy thought. What if someone had been watching them as they searched the castle? The stalker might be in the tunnels with them right now. . . .

Don't be silly, she told herself. *There's no one in the castle but us.*

But the creepiness remained as they followed the tunnel down through switchbacks and past several more peep-holes. At the bottom was a narrow storeroom, one of several, judging by the arched doorways leading from it, with curving ceilings above, like a vault. There were no chests or drawers, just stuff piled up or leaning against walls in apparently random fashion. Some of it was unidentifiable — implements or machines made from metal and wood, some of it rusted or rotten almost to nothing — but much was eerily familiar, after three visits to the Rourke Castle. It was the legacy of two generations of whaling.

There were harpoons corroded and stained by the blood of all the whales they had killed. There were carving knives as big as scimitars, with grips large enough for two hands. There were hooks and ladles and spades and tubs, along with compasses, cables, and oars that could have had innocent uses, but probably hadn't, considering the company they were keeping. There were sheets of whalebone in its raw form, which Professor Olafsson called *baleen*, plus numerous white objects that he assured them were whale's teeth, carved decoratively by the crew of the long-gone ships.

Jack and Jaide moved among them slowly and carefully, feeling a kind of revolted reverence normally reserved for graveyards and their father's old record collection. There was other stuff, too — a collection of artifacts from Asia and Polynesia, consisting of leering carved heads and wooden spears, and other artifacts difficult to identify — piled high in places like backyard junk, although once it had been precious to *someone*, Jaide thought. It might have been an exhibit, in a time when taking such things from the people who owned them was acceptable.

"What's it all doing down here?" Jaide asked. Echoes whispered back at her like a hundred voices.

"I guess he had to put it somewhere," said Jack. "Mister Rourke, I mean. With whaling being banned and so unpopular and everything."

"But why keep it at all?" She flicked open an old journal, the topmost of several stacked in a pile. The copperplate handwriting within was hard to decipher, but it seemed to be a captain's log from 1891. "He should've just thrown it all out."

"Whaling is banned?" said Professor Olafsson in amazement. "What oil lights your homes, then? What material strengthens your ladies' corsets?"

"Uh, we don't do stuff like that anymore," said Jaide. "Whales are almost extinct. It's wrong to kill them."

"Maybe he kept it for a reason," said Jack, getting out the witching rod. "To hide something else."

He gripped the wire tightly and swept the business end over a pile of rotting tarps. He tried the walls in case there was another secret passage. He scanned everything he could see, even if it didn't gleam or couldn't possibly contain anything.

Nothing — until the rod was pointing at the third entrance on the right. Then the wire twisted in his hand like an eel, so powerfully he almost lost his grip on it.

"Through there!" he said. His feet moved as though of their own accord. The rod was tugging him forward, pulling him toward the doorway.

Jaide fell in behind him, breath tightly held. They entered another narrow storeroom, lit by the faint light shining through two narrow peepholes. This storeroom held more of the same, with one important difference.

Next to a doorway on the other side of the room was a large suit of armor — but this wasn't the usual plate-and-mail variety. This was made of overlapping leather, gilded at the edges, with a wide skirt and sloping shoulders. The helmet was crested in red, sporting a nose guard and a gorget, a long, spreading collar that protected the neck. Ornate serpent patterns covered the chest and shoulders.

"Chinese," said Professor Olafsson. "Ceremonial, by the looks of it."

Jack shushed him. The witching rod was pointing at the suit of armor. He approached warily. The space inside the helmet was dark and empty. Could the Card of Translocation be hidden inside?

They had barely crossed halfway across the storeroom when the rod twitched again, tugging Jack to one side. At the same time, the light coming through the peepholes brightened, and they heard footsteps.

Jaide's breath stopped in her throat. They weren't alone!

The beams of light shifted as though someone holding a torch was moving on the other side of the wall. Someone coughed — a man. Jack put a hand over the death mask's mouth and inched closer to the peephole, Jaide close alongside him. They crowded together and peered through to see what lay beyond.

It was a cellar filled with wine barrels. A man moved among them with a light strapped to his head — like a miner's lamp but modern, with LED globes. It was hard to see his face for the shadows it cast. His hands held simple L-shaped pieces of wire that Jaide recognized from the *Compendium*: It was another sort of witching rod, different to theirs but designed to do the same thing. If they were pointed at something magical, the weighted ends would swing together.

"Where is the wretched thing?" the man asked himself.

Jack suppressed a gasp of realization. The face might be hidden, but the man's voice was immediately familiar.

"It *must* be here," muttered Rodeo Dave, pointing the witching rod methodically at each of the barrels in turn.

And Jack understood. It was Rodeo Dave's rod that their rod had detected — which meant . . .

Jaide realized before him, but pulled him away a second too late. Rodeo Dave's rod twitched at the same instant the one in Jack's hand did. They had detected each other!

Rodeo Dave's head came up. He stared for a long moment at the unbroken wall before him. The miner's light shone directly through the peephole. Jack and Jaide retreated from him. Rodeo Dave seemed to be staring *right at them*.

Jaide's foot kicked a fallen machete, which scraped along the cobbled floor with a terrible grating noise. Rodeo Dave froze.

"Who's there?"

The twins acted instinctively. Jack reached out with his Gift to snuff out the miner's light, while Jaide whipped up an obscuring whirlwind, thick with choking dust. Darkness and grit blinded Rodeo Dave's sight. He staggered back with a howl, tripped over his feet, and fell heavily onto his backside, blinking uselessly.

"Run!" Jaide hissed, pushing Jack ahead of her.

CHAPTER TWELVE

MEET THE MENAGERIE

Jack was already moving. Wiping grit from his eyes, Jack took his sister's hand and tugged her toward the nearest doorway. He couldn't remember which one they had come through, but that didn't matter. Getting away from Rodeo Dave was the important thing. The death mask bumped against his chest as they ran from storeroom to storeroom, past a seemingly endless exhibition of humanity's cruelty to whales, fleeing the sound of Rodeo Dave cursing and spluttering behind them. He seemed constantly close on their heels — a result, perhaps, of the acoustics of the cellars, but the effect was the same. The twins didn't let up their pace.

Jaide could see nothing at all as she ran, and Jack could barely breathe through the roaring dust. Only dimly did he perceive a door larger than any of the others looming ahead, double the width, made of sturdy aged oak with a beam lying crossways across the middle, sealing it shut. He fumbled at the beam and eased it as quietly as he could to one side. The door creaked open, letting in a rush of fresh air and natural light. Jaide lunged forward, not caring what lay on the other side. She could see again. Her Gift rose up and pushed them forward, lifting both of them to their feet for an instant, then setting them back down.

They stumbled up a flight of stairs, the light growing brighter with every step. At the top was a metal gate, easily unlocked with the skeleton key. Through its bars they could see the green mayhem of an overgrown kitchen garden. They passed through the gate, out of the secret storerooms and into daylight that seemed bright to them, even though the sky was overcast. They were outside.

Jack slammed the gate behind him and ran with Jaide through the garden. He didn't know if Rodeo Dave was behind them or not, but every instinct told him not to take any chances. They headed for a clutch of nearby outbuildings, over a low stone bridge that crossed the moat in a graceful arc. Dark water churned below, as though stirred by invisible beasts. Thick dark clouds gathered above. A natural, gusty wind tugged at them, made them hurry.

They reached the outbuildings and stopped, gasping.

"Did we lose him?" asked Jaide.

"Probably — that is, I'm sure we" — Jack was interrupted by a low growl coming from very nearby — "did?"

Only then did the twins notice the inhuman faces staring from all around them. They stepped closer to each other, and the growling doubled in volume.

"Is that a wolf?" asked Professor Olafsson, rolling his eyes around to look in every direction at once. "I'm not edible per se, but I'm undoubtedly chewable."

A gangly, humanoid figure leaped at them, shrieking like a banshee. The twins retreated until their shoulder blades crashed into iron bars. Another set of bars caught the attacking figure in mid leap, and that seemed only to enrage it more.

"It's a monkey!" said Jack in relief. "We're in the old menagerie!"

Jaide drew in a sobbing breath. "Of course. They must've reopened it when the animals escaped from their other pens."

A monstrous howl came from right behind them, and they leaped away from the bars. Turning, they saw a tremendous gray wolf standing alone in the cage with its legs braced wide apart, poised to spring. It growled again. If the bars hadn't been between them, thick and sturdy despite their age and the weeds sprouting from their base, the twins would have instantly bolted.

The wolf's and chimpanzee's cages were just two of at least two dozen cages of varying sizes to match their inhabitants. There were at least ten animals scattered across the cages. Quite a few of the animals were ones the twins had never seen before outside of a nature documentary, including a warthog, who looked asleep until they realized his eyes weren't completely closed and the very end of his tail was twitching slightly.

At least the animals' eyes were normal, Jaide reassured herself. There was no sign of The Evil here. But there was something strange about the animals nonetheless.

"Why are they all staring at us like that?" she asked. "They look like they want to eat us — even the ones that don't normally eat meat."

"That's because you're troubletwisters," said Professor Olafsson. "And you've recently used your Gifts. Surely this can't be the first time animals have acted strangely around you?"

Jack shook his head, remembering kamikaze insects that had been drawn toward him, only to die upon touching his skin.

"Could that be why Cornelia has been weird with me?" he asked.

"Who's Cornelia?"

"A macaw. She used to live on the estate, too. A couple of other animals escaped and —"

"Can we go somewhere else, please?" Jaide asked. The staring animals were putting her on edge. "I don't like it here."

"Back to the library?" Jack suggested, peering around the cages to the gate they had passed through. There was no sign of Rodeo Dave, who Jack was now convinced had to be a sleeper agent for The Evil. Why else had he lied to them about what he was doing in the estate?

And more than that. Rodeo Dave was looking for the Card of Translocation, too. It was now a race between them and The Evil to get to it first.

"We'd better get back there before Rodeo Dave does, anyway. Otherwise he might wonder if it was us he detected in the cellar."

"All right, but not the way we came," Jaide said. She didn't want to retrace her steps through the storerooms, with the stained harpoons and whalebones, and the brooding armor guarding the doors. "Let's go around the front."

They set off, leaving the staring, restless animals behind them. Jaide was glad to put them behind her. They had disturbed her far more than they had Jack.

"So how *are* we going to find the card?" asked Jack.

"We keep looking," said Jaide. "When we can."

"But where? We've gone all over the castle."

"Maybe it's on the grounds somewhere, not in the castle itself."

"That's not what Dad said."

Jack was firm on this point, even though he knew Hector Shield wasn't infallible. He was always losing his glasses, for one. And his phone, keys, wallet, and way. But Warden business was different. He would never make a mistake about something *important*.

“Maybe there are other secret passages we haven’t found yet,” said Jaide.

“Don’t forget my other-world theory,” said Professor Olafsson. “All we need is the right doorway and right key, and we will have that card found before you know it!”

Neither twin shared his optimism. As well as being worried that they might let their father down, they were nervous about facing Rodeo Dave again. What if he *did* know they’d been in the cellar, and it was their Gifts that had struck him down?

There was a slight rise on the south side of the moat, partly covered by a copse of ancient fruit trees. They trudged uphill, tired, dirty, and hungry. Jack stopped at the top to reach into his bag in search of the lunch Susan had packed. As he did so, a gleam of sunlight caught the corner of his eye.

He looked up. The gleam came again. It was reflecting off something in the woods bordering the estate, where his father was hiding. The light flashed like Morse code, fast and slow, fast and slow — an unmistakable signal.

Jack gripped Jaide’s arm and pointed.

“Look!”

She had seen it. “Is it him?”

“It must be.” He smacked his forehead with the palm of his hand. “Jaide, we forgot to check the phone. I bet he’s been trying to call!”

They pulled it out of Jack’s bag. They had kept it on vibrate so Rodeo Dave wouldn’t hear. There were several missed calls from an unlisted number but no messages. For the millionth time, Jack lamented the fact that they didn’t have their father’s number.

Jaide waved the phone above her head and jumped up and down, hoping he could see her through his binoculars, or whatever he was using to watch the castle. But the flashing continued and the phone didn't ring. Maybe he was looking at the drawbridge, not the back of the castle.

"We'd better go to him," said Jack, already moving down the hill away from the castle, Professor Olafsson bouncing once more against his chest. Jaide followed closely behind. They cut a straight line across the estate, not needing to cross the creek because that was the other side of the castle.

As they approached, the flashing grew brighter, then ceased.

"He's seen us!" said Jack, starting to run. Jaide ran, too, and Jack put on an extra burst of speed to keep ahead of her.

That was when he felt a sharp tug on his left wrist, as though someone had grabbed him. But Jaide was on the other side of him and there was no one else around. No one with a body, anyway.

"Ouch! Hey, Professor — what are you doing?"

"I have done nothing but attempt to hang on with my chin!"

"It's the wristband," Jaide said, holding up her right arm. "Custer gave them to us, remember?"

Jack had forgotten completely about the narrow coil of leather wrapped around his wrist. It tugged at him again, uncannily as though an invisible hand was holding him back, almost pinching his skin. He imagined the ghostly form of Custer reaching across the horizon to remind him of what he shouldn't have done.

They had left the wards.

Jack broke his pace for a second as reason undermined his original sense of urgency.

"We should go back," he said. "We can tell Dad about Rodeo Dave when he calls us later. He's bound to, isn't he?"

"Yes, but we can't go back *now*," said Jaide. "He's on his way — and I'm sure if we're quick and don't use our Gifts, nothing will go wrong."

Jack put his head down and pressed on, but even though the ground was perfectly flat, he felt as though he was running uphill. Worse, the slope was increasing, so every step took more energy. No matter how he huffed and grunted, he slowed down rather than sped up.

Beside him, Jaide was experiencing the same problem. To her it felt as though the invisible hand on her wrist was not only slowing her down, it was pulling her back to the safety of the wards. She gritted her teeth and fought as hard as she could, but there was no resisting the power of Custer's charms.

"This is useless," she gasped, as both of them were practically running on the spot. "We're never going to make it!"

The tree line was still some dozens of feet away.

"Where is he?" asked Jack. "I can't see him."

Jaide scanned the trees for any sign of their father.

"There!" She pointed.

A shape was moving through the undergrowth, low and hunched, like someone trying not to be seen. Jack waved his arms, and Jaide called out, "Dad! Over here!"

The bracken parted. Something stepped into view.

It wasn't their father. It was something totally unexpected.

A chimpanzee, riding on the back of a very large, savage-looking gray wolf. The chimp grinned, showing its huge yellow teeth.

But it wasn't the chimpanzee's teeth the twins were looking at. It was its eyes. Eyes that were completely white, without pupils of any kind. The wolf's eyes were just as white, horrible milky orbs set in the deep fur.

Jaide gasped. "The Evil!"

"Retreat!" shrilled Professor Olafsson, just as Jack shouted, "Let's get back!"

Jack was already moving as he spoke. Jaide was barely a pace behind him. This time, the bracelets worked in their favor, pulling them back toward the wards' influence.

Behind them, the chimpanzee pointed and the wolf broke into a trot. They looked like a miniature horse and jockey, heading right for the twins. The chimp lowered its arm as the trot became a run.

Jack looked over his shoulder, and was shocked by how fast the wolf was moving. The boundary of the wards was invisible, so there was no way of knowing how far they had to go. Could they outrun a wolf?

Ten scrambling, panicked steps later he glanced over his shoulder again and wished he hadn't. The grinning wolf was almost close enough to snap at his heels. The chimp was crouched low on its back, like a champion jockey, its arm whipping the flank of the wolf with a twig.

++Turn back, troubletwisters,++ said The Evil, directly into their minds. **++There is no escaping us!++**

Jack and Jaide unleashed their Gifts at the same moment, though not under control. A sudden darkness fell upon them, but vanished as quickly, even before Jaide could cry out in fear, closely followed by a wind that roared past ahead of them, flattening the grass but not doing anything else.

The chimpanzee chittered and the wolf howled, and though Jack didn't dare look, he knew that any moment he would feel the wolf upon him or — even worse — might see Jaide fall under its great weight.

++Your Gifts are strong, troubletwisters. We will use them well when they are ours!++

At that moment, a cloud formed above them and rain bucketed down, lashing the twins like whips, turning the already sodden grass into a playground slide. Jack lost his footing, and in reaching for Jaide, tripped her over, too. They fell onto the suddenly muddy soil, and slid to a stop.

++Ours at last! All ours!++

The wolf leaped toward them, the chimp jumping from its back to target Jaide as the wolf sprang at her brother.

But they did not land. They were met in midair by the rain, a solid *force* of rain, like a giant baseball bat made of compressed water. It met wolf and chimp with a liquid snapping sound, both animals disappearing right into it, before they were suddenly ejected out again and sent flying back up the slope in an explosion of mist and raindrops.

"What was *that*?" gasped Jack.

"Who cares!" said Jaide, slithering backward through the mud. Even the ordinary rain was torrential, getting in her eyes and making it hard to see which way she was going. The castle was a distant blur, far out of reach. "Let's get out of here!"

The wolf sprang up and headed back toward them, the mud-spattered chimpanzee struggling along at its side.

++One of you,++ growled The Evil inside their heads. **++Grant me one of you and we will let the other go free.++**

"No!" cried Jack, as he tried to get up and slipped all over again. He reached for Jaide's hand and gripped it. "Never!"

++Never is a long word for such a small boy.++

"You're just trying to drive us apart!"

++We merely hasten the inevitable.++ The wolf was prowling toward them, the chimp clambering onto its back. There was no sign of the mysterious watery force to protect the twins now. **++Spare yourself the agony, troubletwister, before she decides for you!++**

The raindrops suddenly got bigger, and fewer. They were so large, each made a sound like a small gunshot as it hit the ground. Then a really enormous raindrop fell, and there was a thunderclap, though neither twin saw lightning.

Wiping their half-drowned faces, the twins saw a sodden figure appear out of the rain.

"Dad!"

"Stay back!" said Hector Shield, splaying the fingers of his right hand wide to drive them away from him. "This is my fight."

++You dare? Do not come between us and our troubletwisters,++ said The Evil.

"Keep away from them." Hector's voice was faint but strong through the rain swirling around him. "Don't do this."

++You know we do what we must do. You cannot fight us!++

Hector Shield did not answer. Instead, he raised both arms, and with another thunderclap so loud the twins felt it in their chests, an absolute river of rain fell out of the clouds to smite The Evil where it stood. Stinging spray blinded the twins, and they recoiled from where their father had been standing, calling for him and hearing only the roar of water all around them.

Then two strong hands grabbed each of them by an elbow.

"Hurry," said their father, pulling them, twisting and sliding, back down the slope. "Get inside the wards!"

"Come with us, Dad," pleaded Jack. "I swear we can control our Gifts —"

But already the light was flickering and the rain was swirling around them with the beginnings of a hurricane.

"Listen to me, Jaidith and Jackaran." And they did. There was no arguing with their father's tone, and he only ever used the twins' full names when he was mad or in a hurry.

"The Evil is trying to distract us," he said. "It wants to stop us finding the card before it does."

"But we know who's looking for it," said Jack. "The sleeper agent is Rodeo Dave!"

"That explains a lot, but it doesn't change anything. You still have to go back. If he doesn't know you know, he won't act openly against you. The search for the card will keep him busy — he won't hurt anyone else now."

"Can't you just . . . I don't know . . . have him arrested?" said Jaide. "Or whatever it is Wardens do?"

She could feel Hector's hand shaking where he held her. Not only was he drenched, he looked and sounded as if he'd run a marathon. His glasses were askew on his nose. He pushed them back up as he hustled the children closer to the castle, bringing his eyes back into focus.

"It's not that simple, Jaide," he said. "The Evil already senses your grandmother's weakness. That's why it's here, now, acting so openly against the wards. If she finds out that Rodeo Dave is an enemy agent, it could weaken her even further, and not even Custer could keep The Evil out then. What have you told her Companions?"

"Nothing," said Jack. "We only just found out."

"Then we'd better keep it that way. Act as though nothing has happened, and let me and the other Wardens keep The Evil at bay. We'll do our job while you do yours. Okay?"

"Yes, Dad," said Jaide, even though it warred with her instincts. First Rodeo Dave was a traitor, then The Evil was actively looking for the card, too, and now they were keeping secrets from Grandma X and her Warden Companions. But it wasn't their fault, she supposed. It was The Evil's, for putting them in this situation.

"I'm sorry we came out to see you," said Jack. "We should've waited for you to call."

Hector shook his head.

"Never mind, what's done is done. It'll all be over soon, once the Card of Translocation is in our hands."

++Come back to us!++

Hector pushed the twins the last few feet, and they fell sprawling again. This time there was no tug from their wristbands. They were inside the boundary of the wards.

But their father did not follow.

++Come back to us now!++

"Go! Find the card, quickly!" Hector Shield shouted to them.

With that, he flung himself back into the rain. Back toward the wolf and the chimpanzee. Back toward The Evil.

"Dad!" cried Jack and Jaide together, but he was gone.

CHAPTER THIRTEEN

THE *LADY IN YELLOW*

Jack started to get up to run after his father. Jaide grabbed him around the waist and pulled him back into the mud.

"Don't, Jack!"

"This is not for troubletwisters," agreed the professor's muffled voice between them. "Live to fight another day — thus we keep The Evil at bay. But could you get my face out of the mud first?"

"What if he loses?" Jack said, but he did stop trying to get up and instead took his bag off and started carefully scraping mud from the death mask. "What if The Evil beats him?"

"It won't," said Jaide, although she was worried about that, too. "It can't."

"Jack! Jaide!"

The twins heard their names and looked around. It didn't sound like Rodeo Dave.

It was Ari, running across the lawn with dripping, rain-flattened fur.

Jack flipped the professor around so he could look the death mask in the eye.

"Don't say anything about what you just heard," he whispered. "We have to keep this a secret!"

"Why?"

"Because Dad says so!"

"But —"

"Maybe we'll just put you back in the backpack for now," said Jaide, taking him from Jack and zipping the pack up tightly so the sound of his muffled protests was inaudible over the rain.

"What are you doing out here?" asked Ari as he came within earshot. "Custer sent me to bring you inside while he braced the wards. The Evil is about. It hasn't breached the wards, so there's no reason to panic, but you're dangerously close to the boundary."

"Oh, really?" said Jaide innocently, glancing anxiously over her shoulder. Behind them, in the thick of the squall, there was no sign of either their father or The Evil. "I guess we got lost in the rain."

"How did you get past me?" asked Ari. "I've been watching the front door all day."

"We came out the back way," she said.

"Oh. But what are you doing out here in the first place? Why aren't you sensibly inside the castle, where it's dry and you're supposed to be anyway?"

Jack said the first thing that came into his head.

"We, uh, came to shut the car's roof to keep the rain off. And then we got lost."

"All you had to do was follow the castle wall around. Even a mouse couldn't get that wrong."

"All right," said Jaide, throwing up her hands in mock surrender. "We were exploring."

"In the rain? I will never understand humans." Ari lifted his nose to sniff the air. "Hey, that smells like wolf. Wasn't the vet looking for one of those earlier?"

That galvanized the twins into action.

"If it is a wolf," said Jack, heading toward the castle at a brisk pace, "we don't want to get any closer to it."

"Good thinking," said Ari, trotting close by his heels and looking nervously over his shoulder.

The three of them hurried back to the castle, the rain slowly petering out behind them. By the time they reached Rodeo Dave's car — whose roof was closed — there was little more than a drizzle. The damage had been done, though. The twins were soaked through, covered in mud, and felt exactly like Ari looked. Thomas Solomon waved from where he'd taken shelter in his golf cart, wrapped up in a raincoat, but didn't offer them a lift.

They stopped in the courtyard to try to clean and wring out their clothes. They managed to get most of the mud evenly distributed, if not actually off, and their clothes moved up from sodden to no longer dripping. They particularly didn't want to drip everywhere on the way to the library, or get any water on the books. Ari shook himself like a dog and sent a fine spray into the air around him.

When they were merely damp, they retraced their steps through the castle, past the chests, tapestries, and suits of armor — which now seemed perfectly ordinary to them after the discovery of the secret cellar, or *the dungeon*, as Jaide had begun to call it to herself — back to where they had started that morning.

Rodeo Dave was waiting for them there. The twins had been nervous all the way back to the castle, knowing that they would have to face him again, the sleeper agent who put Grandma X in the hospital. They braced themselves for what might come if he suspected they were seeking the card as well, but he seemed merely concerned, not angry. In fact, Jaide thought, she had never seen Rodeo Dave angry, or overly excited, or anything. It was almost as if he was never entirely in the moment, a watcher rather than a participant. He had obviously learned to keep his true self deeply concealed.

"I've been looking for you," he said. "Where did you get to?"

"We heard the rain," said Jaide. "We were worried about your car."

"You left the roof open," added Jack, reviving the excuse he had attempted with Ari earlier. "It could've been ruined."

Rodeo Dave put a hand on each of their shoulders. They held their breath. Did he know that they had in fact been out of the library for hours and that they had seen him in the dungeon?

"That's kind of you to think of Zebediah," he said. "I'm sorry you got wet doing it. At least it washed off the dust, eh?"

"I think it turned the dust to mud," said Jaide, thankful for one less thing they would have to explain away on their own. Her elbows and knees were brown from where she had fallen onto the ground outside.

"I'd better take you home. You must need a warm shower and a change of clothes."

"That's okay," said Jack, not yet ready to give up the chance to look for the Card of Translocation, impossible though that task seemed now. "We'd rather stay and help you."

Rodeo Dave frowned and looked at them, then back at the library. Clearly he was torn between what he wanted to do, what he thought he ought to do, and what The Evil had told him to do.

"I see you've made a dent in the work . . . I guess we could have lunch first and then see how you're both feeling?"

"An excellent idea," said Ari to Jack. "I've had a small appetizer of mice, but I am still hungry. I don't suppose you'd consider sharing what's in your lunch box?"

They sat on some upturned tea chests and opened the lunch boxes Susan had given them. Jack fished out the ham in his sandwich and gave it to Ari, who swallowed it in two gulps.

"So he followed us here, eh?" Rodeo Dave tossed Ari a pickle, which he sniffed warily, then ignored. "Curiosity and cats. Imagine what he could find, digging around in here."

The twins stared at Ari, struck by the same thought at exactly the same time. He could look for them, in all the places they couldn't get to, while they were stuck in the library.

"Excuse me," said Jaide, putting down her sandwich. "I need to go to the bathroom."

"You remember where it is?" asked Rodeo Dave. There were toilets just up the hall that must have seemed modern when the castle was renovated but now looked hulking and antiquated to the twins. Though at least they were better than the medieval garderobes.

"Yes. I won't get lost this time, I promise. Come on, Ari. Let's see if we can find some mice on the way."

"If wishes were fishes the sea would be full," he said, "and I would be down at the beach." But he trotted after her anyway.

"How many Wardens have you met, Ari?" asked Jaide when the library door was safely shut behind them.

"Quite a few."

"Do they all have collections of gold cards?"

"You mean like Custer and your grandmother? I don't

know. All of them collect something, though. They're like magpies."

"Jack and I want to collect gold cards, but we don't know where to start looking."

"You need somewhere the other Wardens haven't already picked over, somewhere full of old stuff and — hey, like this castle!"

Ari scampered ahead of her and jumped onto the nearest chest. He did a quick turn, as though chasing his tail, then looked down the back.

"Nothing behind here. Want to have a look inside?"

The twins had already checked that chest.

"I don't have time, Ari, or a key," she said. "I have to get back to the books. But why don't you have a look around for us, now you're inside the castle? You'll probably find more mice to eat as well."

"If I didn't know you better, I'd suspect you're up to something." Ari looked at her suspiciously. "In fact, because I *do* know you, I'm sure of it. Do you really think there are cards here or are you just trying to get me out of the way?"

"Grandma thought there were," she said. "She was on her way here when the accident happened."

"Was she? I don't know anything about that."

Jaide tried her best to look innocent.

"Well . . . I just thought . . . you know, collecting stuff, it's a Warden thing, and I want to be a Warden, so I should start now. . . ."

Her voice trailed off as Ari's eyes got narrower and narrower.

"All right," he said, "if it'll stop you from going exploring again. Custer's instructions were quite explicit."

"Done," said Jaide, kneeling down and hugging him. "Ari, you are a prince among cats."

"Of course," sniffed Ari, and expertly wound his way out of her embrace. "Don't go home without me. It's a long walk."

"We won't," called Jaide, as Ari disappeared around the corner.

Returning to the library, Jaide found Rodeo Dave high up a ladder, passing books down to Jack, who put them in piles up against one wall. They were mainly histories and biographies of people she had never heard of, some of them running to many volumes. Jaide helped, and between the three of them, they emptied one of the long bookcases that lined the enormous space. There were many more to go, and the twins stared around them with heavy hearts. While their father was out in the storm fighting The Evil with the other Wardens, they were stuck with Portland's traitor, helping him catalog books.

Jaide consoled herself by remembering what their father had said. While they were watching him, Rodeo Dave couldn't be getting up to any more mischief — and he wouldn't hurt them unless they revealed what they knew about him. The key was to act normal until the card was found and Grandma X was better. Then, they supposed, the Wardens would pounce.

The woman in the painting above the fireplace played on as they worked, eternally picking up the same card, over and over again. It was the two of hearts, something Jack wondered about as he worked. Had the number been significant to someone? Had the suit? Could she have been the painter's wife, perhaps? Or could she have been the wife of one of the Rourkes?

Sometimes she seemed to be looking at him out of the corner of her eye, not as creepily as the bust of Mister Rourke, but twice as enigmatically.

"You two are very quiet," said Rodeo Dave as he moved the ladder over to the next long bookcase.

"I was just, um, wondering about the painting," Jack said, saying the first thing that came to his mind. "Do you know who she was?"

"The *Lady in Yellow*?" Rodeo Dave's forehead wrinkled, as if he was trying to recall some distant memory. "I'm afraid I have no idea. She's been there as long as I can remember. It's my favorite painting in the whole place. And just look how dusty she is. . . ."

Rodeo Dave tut-tutted and turned his end of the ladder, guiding Jack across the room so they stood below the painting.

"Here, give me a hand getting her down."

Together they awkwardly lifted the painting off the wall and put it on the floor, where it stood almost as high as the top of Rodeo Dave's head. The rectangle of wallpaper exposed by its removal looked as good as new, not faded at all. Producing a huge spotted handkerchief from his pocket, Rodeo Dave lightly brushed dust off the paint and wiped down the gilded frame.

"There," he said, standing back to get a better look. "Considerably improved, don't you think?"

Jaide had been half expecting to see a secret door behind the painting. They hadn't thought to check there before.

"She looks a bit like Grandma," Jaide said.

"Do you think?" Rodeo Dave cupped his chin in one hand. "Yes, I suppose she does, as she was as a young woman. You must have seen her in photos."

"Er, yes, that's right," said Jack. He couldn't let on that they had seen Grandma X's younger self when she appeared in spectral form. "Did you know her then?"

"We met in our teens, a few years older than you are now." His eyes took on a slightly glazed look. "She was a firecracker back then, let me tell you —"

Jack cut him off in some alarm. "But it couldn't *be* her, could it?"

"What? Oh, no. I'm sure your grandmother would have had nothing to do with the Rourkes back then. They were bad seeds, through and through — but not George. It always amazed me that such a rotten old branch could still grow true at the end. It's a shame he never settled down. Besides, this painting is much older than your grandmother, or the Rourkes. It looks like early eighteenth century to me. . . ."

His eyes drifted back to the painting.

"There *is* something about the *Lady in Yellow*, though, isn't there? Just can't put my finger on it."

They left the painting where it was and moved on to a series of shelves that contained hundreds of novels all bound in the same stiff leather with gold letters pressed in the spines. Some of them looked as though they had never been opened. In the middle of a shelf at eye level, not placed with any particular prominence, were three narrow, gray books where the gold letters spelled out: *The Whale by Herman Melville.*

"Didn't Melville write *Moby-Dick*?" asked Jaide.

"That *is Moby-Dick*," said Rodeo Dave, delicately removing the three volumes and placing them in a special pile of their own. "The first British edition had the simpler title, and is extremely rare. Mister Rourke was an excellent collector, if not much of a reader. His son, George, was quite the opposite, and happier for it."

"So why did Mister Rourke have all these books?" asked Jack.

"To impress people. How does that line go? 'Of all tools used in the shadow of the moon, men are most apt to get out of order.' Never a truer word spoken, by Mr. Melville or anyone."

Rodeo Dave glanced at his watch.

"It's getting late in the day," he said. "You've worked long enough, and I thank you for your help, but now I'd better be getting you home. I promised your mother I'd have you back before dark."

"What about you?" asked Jaide. "Will you be coming back?"

"Not today." He sighed and rubbed his back. "I'm afraid this old boy needs some rest. And a bit of a read, too. Looking at all these books has definitely put me in the mood."

"Good idea," Jack said, thinking that if Rodeo Dave really was going to stay in and read there was nothing he could do to help The Evil. He wiped his hands on his pants but feared it would take a good wash to get the dusty smell off them. "We'll come back with you tomorrow."

"No need, no need." Rodeo Dave avoided their eyes as he cleaned up the remains of their lunches. "You've been a big help, but there's your schooling to consider. I've been lucky to have you this long."

They tried to change his mind all the way back to the moat, but he was adamant. It bothered Jack to the very core: Rodeo Dave seemed perfectly normal, his usual friendly self, but it was clear he didn't want them in the castle any longer. The only reason Jack could think of was so Rodeo Dave could keep searching for the Card of Translocation himself.

But how could Rodeo Dave possibly be a good enough

liar to fool both of them *and* Grandma X, whom he had known most of his life?

Jaide looked around outside for any sign of either The Evil or their father and the other Wardens, but the woods were empty and the rain had blown away. There was no movement along the fringe of trees. Maybe The Evil had been driven off, for now.

As Thomas Solomon drove up in his golf cart to see them off, Jaide remembered Ari. She called his name into the entrance of the castle, and seconds later he came loping out to join them.

"You've got him well trained," said Rodeo Dave. "Not like my Kleopatra. I think she's trained me."

"Any luck?" Jaide whispered as they climbed into Zebediah, whose roof seemed to have opened itself now the rain had passed.

Ari jumped onto her lap. "Just bones and old feathers." He stuck out his tongue. "All I can taste is dust."

Rodeo Dave put on his hat and started the car. Zebediah rumbled deep in its belly and the castle fell away behind them. If Jack concentrated, he could imagine that Zebediah was perfectly still and the world was moving around it. The gates of the estate, the outskirts of town, the town hall, the fish markets, Watchward Lane . . .

Susan was standing on the steps by the front door as though she had been expecting them. She waved as they drove up the drive and came down the steps to meet them, then she waved again as Rodeo Dave drove back down the lane, minus his passengers.

"How was your day?" she asked.

"What's wrong?" asked Jaide. There was an odd look in her mother's eyes that told her there was something up. "Is there something wrong with Grandma?"

"With Dad?" added Jack, feeling his heart thump hard suddenly in his chest.

"Why would you think that?" Susan asked them in return. "All I did was ask you how your day was."

"It was . . . fine," said Jack slowly. He looked down at his mud-streaked clothes, wondering if that was where the problem lay. "We got pretty dirty, though. All that dust and grime in the books."

"Nothing a bath and laundry won't fix."

The twins took a step forward to go inside, but Susan didn't move out of the way. She stood there, as if waiting for them to confess something.

Jack and Jaide just stared at her, completely at a loss. Which part had she guessed? That Grandma X's accident was the work of The Evil? That Rodeo Dave was a sleeper agent? That their father was not on the other side of the world at all, but in their very neighborhood, fighting to keep them all safe?

Susan did something entirely unexpected. She took her hand from behind her back and held up a small black box with an electric cord dangling from it.

A cell phone charger.

"Perhaps one of you could tell me what this is and *who* it belongs to?"

CHAPTER FOURTEEN

MULTIPLICATION AND DIVISION

The twins stared at the charger with their mouths open. Jaide felt a wild urge to laugh hysterically. This was about nothing more than the secret of the cell phone?

"It's the charger for our phone," blurted out Jack in relief. "Dad gave it to us — ow!"

Jaide kicked him in the shin. One secret led to another. If they started down the path to the truth by telling where the phone had come from, it would all come out and they would never be allowed to keep looking for the card, no matter how much they wanted to help.

Luckily, Susan didn't believe them.

"Your father and I agree that you're much too young to have a phone. And besides, how could he give you a phone when he's in Italy? Tell me the truth this time, or you'll be in real trouble."

They had to say something.

Jaide opened her mouth, but nothing came out. Fortunately, this time Jack was quicker off the mark.

"We know you told us you weren't going to give us a phone," he said, "but we really need one to text Tara about homework and stuff, and everyone else our age has one, so we got it for ourselves from one of the kids at school. It's an old one that doesn't do very much. See? They would've thrown it out if we didn't take it. We're not wasting time or money on it. We pay for the minutes out of our allowance."

Susan looked at the phone in Jaide's hand, clearly weighing up the veracity of their explanation. She had no reason to suspect that the phone came from their father, though it was clear she was still not entirely satisfied.

"Please, Mom, can we keep it?" asked Jaide.

Jack's heart sank as Susan shook her head.

"I don't like you going behind our backs like this," she said. "It sets a bad precedent. If you're good, maybe you'll get it back one day, but not today."

The twins argued, but they had no choice but to hand over the phone. It joined the charger in Susan's back pocket, firmly switched off, and eventually she raised her hands to bring their pleas for clemency to an end.

"All right, enough! Go inside, both of you. I've got some homework for you to do, after you've had a shower. I'm just going to the store to get ingredients for dinner. There's a recipe I saw on the Internet at work — it sounds delicious."

"That's my cue to go elsewhere," said Ari, who had watched the confrontation from the sidelines. "If it's anything like last week's chili con carne with white chocolate, I'd rather be patrolling with Custer in the rain."

He sprang off into the dusk, leaving them to their fate.

Jack and Jaide slouched up to their room as their mother scooped up her keys and bag and headed out to the car.

"I can't believe it," said Jaide. "This is a disaster!"

"I know," said Jack. "But what else could we have said to Mom to make her change her mind?"

"You could have told her the truth," said a muffled voice from inside Jack's backpack.

The twins had completely forgotten about the death mask. When they peered in the bag, Professor Olafsson was indignantly tangled up in old plastic wrap and a damp sock.

"She'd never believe us!" said Jaide.

"Not about the devices you people employ to avoid talking face-to-face," he said. "About everything. You should tell your grandmother, too."

"We can't," Jack told him. "Mom wouldn't want to know about it and Dad told us not to worry Grandma."

"Do you trust him?"

"Of course," said Jaide. "He's our father!"

"*And* he's a Warden, too," Jack added.

"What kind of father knowingly puts his children into danger?" Professor Olafsson asked them. "What kind of Warden keeps the near presence of The Evil secret from the Warden in charge of the wards?"

"He hasn't really put us in danger . . . has he?" said Jack.

"I guess he has, kind of — if Rodeo Dave ever finds out what we know. But he won't do that," Jaide told Professor Olafsson. "We're good at keeping secrets."

"Secrets, like lies, multiply in the keeping," said the professor. "Have you never thought to ask *why* this card is so important?"

"Of course!" said Jack again. "There hasn't been time, and we keep getting interrupted."

"And we're just troubletwisters," said Jaide miserably. "No one tells us *anything*."

Professor Olafsson's expression softened.

"I, too, was once excluded from Warden activities," he said after a moment, "because I argued too strongly for my theories to be tested. You know your father best. Perhaps you are right to do as he says, and I am wrong to question him. As a fellow Warden, I will keep the secrets he has asked to keep, and I will help you find this Card of Translocation for him."

"But how *are* we going to find it?" asked Jack. "If we can't go back to the castle tomorrow, Rodeo Dave will beat us to it."

"Was that Rodeo Dave you were talking to earlier, when we left the castle?" asked Professor Olafsson. "Talking about someone called Kleopatra?"

"That's his cat," said Jaide, "although she's not anyone's cat, really. She's Grandma's other Warden Companion."

"Odd. I recognize his voice from somewhere, but I can't recall where."

Jaide zipped up the backpack and headed to their room.

"I want to check on Cornelia," said Jack, continuing on up the stairs. He needed to do something other than stew over the lost phone.

"Okay," she called after him, "but don't think I'm doing your homework for you!"

Jack found Cornelia and Kleo sitting in the blue room exactly as they had been last time. The macaw's royal blue head came up as soon as she saw Jack and she began walking rapidly from side to side as though pleased to see him. He crossed to the cage and fed a nut through the bars.

"Hello, Cornelia. How are you doing today?"

"Shipshape and Bristol fashion," she declared, taking the nut.

"Is that good?" he asked Kleo.

"I think so," said the cat, extending her chin so Jaide could skritch under it. "But she still hasn't said anything sensible. Maybe she will now that you're here."

"You can trust us," said Jack. "Whatever you have to tell us, we'll believe you."

Cornelia bobbed up and down, sending bits of nut flying in every direction.

"Rourke!"

With short but confident strides, she walked along the perch and climbed down the inside of the cage to the door. Gripping the wire in her powerful beak, she pulled the door upward and, with a deft and obviously well-practiced maneuver, flipped herself through it. Then she climbed to the top of the cage and fluffed up her feathers.

Jack took a step backward, unsure where this was going, while Kleo watched from the dragon chair.

"Is this the first time she's left the cage?" he asked.

"Hasn't so much as put her head through the door," said Kleo, "until now."

Cornelia looked at Jack, and then Kleo. The presence of the cat didn't seem to worry her.

"Rourke!"

The macaw's wings unfolded, flapped, and suddenly she was airborne. She didn't fly far, just to the other side of the room, where her beak tugged the elephant tapestry aside. Two swift hops took her through the door.

Jack heard her wings flap again. He ran to lift aside the tapestry to see what she was doing. He had a fleeting glimpse of blue flying down the stairwell, then she was gone.

"Why did she do that? Is she coming back?"

Kleo shrugged. "If she won't tell us, we can't know."

"But she *can't* tell us. She's not like you, a Warden Companion." Frustration boiled in him. Had they failed Cornelia somehow by failing to understand?

"What if we made her a Companion?" Jack asked. "Is there a way to do that?"

"There is, and it's very difficult. Far too difficult for troubletwisters," said Kleo firmly. "Speaking of which . . .

Custer left exercises for you. You'll find them on the desk. I'm to make certain you do them before you go to bed."

Jack groaned. *More* homework? It wasn't fair.

"I advise getting it over with," said the cat. "Let me fetch your sister for you. I'll keep guard for your mother's return, and check on Cornelia, too, in case she's thinking of getting up to any mischief."

"All right," Jack said, rubbing his stomach. He was still looking at the tapestry, worried about Cornelia, but at the same time, their late lunch felt like days ago, *and* he had shared it with Ari.

He slouched up the short flight of stairs with his sister when she joined him. There he found the homework as promised, a series of fiddly optical illusions for Jack (involving mirrors and lenses and beams of light in a wild variety of colors) and twelve triangular flags for Jaide that she had to make flap in a particular order using carefully targeted jets of air. Jaide joined him, and they set to their tasks with their minds on other things, so half the time their efforts were to no avail. Flags whipped back and forth, lights flashed on and off, and inevitably their Gifts began to interfere with each other. One particularly uproarious mishap had both of them running for cover under a bureau as objects swept around the room in the grip of an invisible tornado.

The twins each felt five tiny pinpricks of pain in the small of their backs. Startled, they turned around.

"I'll take this as a sign," Kleo said, as the wind ebbed, normal visibility was restored, and a hundred tiny knick-knacks fell with a clatter to the floor, "that you are tired and in need of dinner. I suggest you call it a night and head down, once we've tidied up here."

Jaide brushed her hair out of her eyes. "Can I take the *Compendium* with me to read later?"

"You may — although your grandmother says it's terrible bedtime reading. It gives her bad dreams."

"Did Custer say anything when he came by today?" asked Jack as they picked themselves up off the floor.

"Only that he has observed several unusual meteorological phenomena near the estate." Kleo followed them and began batting hidden trinkets into view. "He mentioned a storm and all three of you getting wet. But there was no lightning, at least none that he saw. Did you see any?"

The twins shook their heads, wondering why that might be important. Their father traveled by lightning, using his Gift. They didn't know what the absence of lightning might mean.

"But the wards are strong, aren't they?" This was as close as Jack dared to asking outright if the fight against The Evil that afternoon had gone well.

"If The Evil was to seriously test the wards," said Kleo, rounding up a series of chess pieces that were trying to run away from her, "I would know. Wardens aren't infallible, and as you now know, sometimes they fall ill. They can be distracted by human concerns and affections. That's why they have Companions: We can see things they do not. We are their eyes and ears when they are blind and deaf."

With a gentle nip, as if she was picking up a kitten, Kleo scooped up the last wriggling pawn and tossed him into the box with the other chess pieces.

"Thank you, Kleo," said Jaide, rubbing the fur under Kleo's ears. "We'd better go back upstairs before Mom gets back."

At that moment, the crash of breaking glass sounded from the living room.

Kleo led the charge to find out what was going on, Jaide almost treading on the cat's tail as she ran after her.

Cornelia was crouched on the mantelpiece, clinging to the edge with her powerful claws and peering downward. On the ground below her was a picture frame lying in a field of glass shards. She glanced up at them, then back at the wreckage. Instead of exhibiting remorse at the accident, Cornelia flapped down and landed gingerly among the splinters and began pulling at the frame with her powerful beak.

"That's no way for a guest to behave," said Kleo, running toward her.

Cornelia looked up and stretched her wings, flapping them violently.

"Rourke! Rourke!"

Kleo retreated, and Cornelia returned to the frame, tossing it back and forth with wild jerks of her feathered head until it broke and the picture within fell facedown onto the carpet.

She tossed the frame away, nipped the corner of the picture in her beak, and flipped it over. The picture was a black-and-white portrait of the twins' family taken when they were nine, showing them all dressed in Wild West outfits. Hector looked out of place in a cowboy hat, sheriff's badge, and chaps, but Susan looked totally convincing with a six-shooter in her hand, despite her frilly dress. The twins were dressed in old-fashioned "Sunday best." Jack remembered the way his stripy suit had smelled, of mothballs and faintly of sick, as though the last person to wear it had thrown up in it.

"'ourke!" said Cornelia, hopping across the floor to him, holding up the photo in her beak.

"What's that, Cornelia?" he asked, crouching down to her level. "Are you trying to tell me something?"

" 'ourke!" She dropped the photo in front of him and nodded her head up and down. "Rourke!"

"Something about the photo?"

She stretched out and tapped it with her beak. "Rourke! Killer!"

"Yes, that's me in the photo, and Susan, and Mom and —"

She tapped more insistently, putting a hole in Hector's face. "Rourke! Killer! Rourke!"

"I don't understand, Cornelia. That's my dad, yes, but —"

The tapping became more insistent, and the hole bigger still.

Jaide squatted down next to Jack.

"Cornelia, are you saying that Dad was the one who frightened Young Master Rourke the night he died?"

Cornelia stopped tapping, hopped backward, and waddled around in a circle. The message was clear: *Finally!*

"But that's impossible," said Jack. "Dad wasn't there. He couldn't have been."

"Was he the one who frightened you?" asked Jaide.

Cornelia nodded. "Visitor! Killer!"

"And is that why you were frightened of *us*, because you could tell we were related to him?"

Cornelia's blue head bobbed rapidly up and down. "Visitor! Killer!"

"Stop saying that!" shouted Jack. The parrot stopped squawking, but gave Jack a very beady-eyed look.

Jack backed away until he bumped into Jaide's shoulder.

"Cornelia can't be right," he said, shaking his head. "Dad wasn't there, and even if he had been, he wouldn't have hurt Young Master Rourke. He wouldn't have!"

Jaide was just as bewildered, but she was trying to think it through. "There must be some explanation. Perhaps he *was* there, and Master Rourke died of fright for reasons we don't know anything about, or —"

"There's very little we can be certain of right now," said Kleo. "Let's just be glad that Cornelia is starting to talk about what happened, and worry about making sense of it later."

"You don't believe her, do you?" asked Jack.

"I believe your mother will be home soon, and we have some cleaning up to do. It would be best to hide Cornelia, too, to avoid making a scene."

"Good thinking," said Jaide. "Come on, Jack."

"But if Dad didn't frighten Master Rourke, who did?" he said in a dazed voice. "I bet he wasn't there at all! You're just making stuff up!" he yelled down at the parrot. "And I thought you were my friend!"

The parrot lunged for the photo but Jack yanked it out of the reach of her sharp beak. He ignored her when she flapped and squawked in protest, thinking only of his father hiding in the forest in the rain, mistrusted by everyone. He couldn't have killed Master Rourke, he wouldn't kill anyone.

Jack wanted to run back to the estate and find his father, to be told the truth of the matter and comforted. Instead, he settled for fleeing upstairs and flinging himself onto his bed, clutching in one hand the ruined photo that, for a reason he could never admit to himself, he was unable to look at.

CHAPTER FIFTEEN

THE CORNELIA CONUNDRUM

Downstairs, Jaide felt similarly stunned. Cornelia quieted when Jack left the room and eyed Jaide warily, as though sizing her up.

"You're a weird old bird," she said. "Maybe your eyes are going."

"Walk the plank! Keelhaul the landlubber!"

"All right, I'm sorry. But I just don't see how you could be right. I mean, it can't be Dad."

But for the life of her, Jaide couldn't think why Cornelia would pick out her father and screech "Rourke! Killer!" like that, and she couldn't talk about it with the parrot.

"I'll keep guard," said Kleo, heading for the front door. "You do what you can to make it look like nothing happened here."

Jaide sighed in frustration and confusion. There was nothing else to do until Jack came out of his funk, so she took the dustpan and broom from the laundry closet. Watched by Cornelia every second, she tipped the remains of the picture frame into the garbage can and brushed up every last splinter of glass as best she could.

Kleo came running back in. "She's here!"

Jaide met Cornelia's beady eye.

"You've got to go back in the blue room," she said. "After the business with the phone, I have no idea how to explain where *you* came from. Either you go now, or I'll throw a rug over you and carry you there. That way you won't be able to bite me."

The parrot bobbed her head and made a low clicking noise, as though considering her options.

"I'm serious," Jaide said, doing her best Grandma X impersonation.

"Rourke!" Cornelia came up to her full height and flapped her wings. Two mighty sweeps saw her in the air, and a third sent her swooping for the door. The front door opened as Cornelia vanished up the stairs to the top floor and through the door leading to the blue room.

"Finished your homework already and doing your chores?" asked Susan, seeing Jaide with the dustpan and broom. "That's a step in the right direction."

"Thanks, Mom," said Jaide. "Do you think we could have —"

"Your phone back?"

"Yeees," replied Jaide slowly, thinking she might be pushing her luck too far.

Susan frowned.

"I'll think about it. Now, I couldn't find all the ingredients I needed so I got us stuff for sandwiches instead. How's that?"

Sandwiches at dinnertime might have been a bit weird, but it was better than the alternative. "Great, Mom."

"Don't look so pleased. I know that when it comes to cooking, I make a great paramedic." She gave Jaide a quick hug. "Where's Jack?"

"Upstairs finishing his homework."

"Okay. I'll make him something and you can take it up to him later."

Jaide put the utensils away and helped her mother

unpack. The thought of eating dinner led to the unexpected discovery that she was actually hungry. Susan had bought fresh bread with sliced meat, cheese, and vegetables, creating a spread almost identical to the first meal they had ever had in Portland. Jaide made herself a lettuce, ham, and tomato sandwich, and contemplated all the things that had happened since that first day. They had learned about their Gifts and The Evil. They had made several new friends, two of them cats. They had been in danger many times, and would certainly be in danger again. Maybe they were in great danger at that moment and didn't know it. She thought of her father and wondered how he was doing, but there was no way to find out unless Hector called or Custer dropped by.

"Can we go back to the castle tomorrow?" Jaide asked, figuring she might have better luck on that front.

"That wasn't the deal," said Susan. "You've missed enough school for one week."

"But Mom —"

"No buts. David Smeaton's been very good to put up with you two, but I think it's time you let him get on with his work."

Jaide wanted to protest that this was exactly what they didn't want him to do, but she couldn't say anything like that. If Grandma X had been there, maybe they could have talked her around.

"Is Grandma any better?"

Susan sighed and looked down at her plate. "Doctor Witworth has her under heavy sedation in the hope of reducing the pressure on her brain. Maybe we can go see her tomorrow, if she improves."

Jaide put down the rest of her meal, her appetite gone.

Susan made Jack a sandwich and Jaide took it upstairs to him, but not before detouring through the blue room to pick up the *Compendium* on the way. The chances of finding anything in it were slim, but she had to try.

Jack was lying facedown on his bed and didn't look up when she entered.

"Are you hungry, Jack?"

"No." He rolled over onto his side, his back to her.

"Well, here you are anyway." She put the plate next to him and sat on her own bed, setting the *Compendium* down in front of her. Concentrating briefly on the notion of Warden Companions, she opened the folder and began to read.

After a minute or two, Jack stirred.

"Where's Cornelia?" he asked, still without looking up.

"Back in the blue room. Do you want me to get her? I could probably sneak her in here without Mom noticing."

"No. I never want to see her again."

One hand reached out and snared half the sandwich. The smell of it had reminded him that there were more immediate concerns than what a mad old parrot thought of his father. The first mouthful went some way toward filling the aching void inside him. The second mouthful did more.

"Listen to this," said Jaide. "One of the earliest steps toward inviting an animal to be your Companion is to spend three days in their mind, experiencing everything they do. That means Grandma X has been inside Kleo's and Ari's minds. I wonder if they got to be in hers in return."

"It doesn't work that way," said a muffled voice from Jack's bag.

"Professor Olafsson!" Jaide jumped off the bed to rescue him. "We forgot you again. I'm sorry."

"No apology necessary," he said when released from captivity and placed on the chest beside Jaide's bed. "But it is nice to be part of the conversation again."

"So what *does* happen when a Warden makes a Companion?" Jaide asked him, putting the *Compendium* aside.

"May I ask why you're asking?"

"Well, I thought that if we made Cornelia Jack's Companion, she'd be able to talk to us properly about what she saw that night."

Jack rolled over.

"No way!" he exclaimed. "I don't want anything more to do with that treacherous old bird."

"Calm down, Jack. It's possible we're still misunderstanding her, isn't it?"

"I don't think this could be a misunderstanding." Jack held up the photo, where Cornelia had bitten a hole right through Hector Shield's head. "She kept saying *killer.*"

"That does seem most definite," said Professor Olafsson. "But in any case, I assure you that enlisting the services of a Companion takes a great deal of time, energy, and trust — three things I fear you entirely lack at the moment."

It was Jaide's turn to flop hopelessly on the bed.

"We can't just lie here and do nothing," she groaned.

"I want to talk to Dad," Jack said. "I'm sure he could tell us what really happened to Master Rourke. I mean, we know Rodeo Dave went over there that night. It's more likely that he was the one who did the frightening, if The Evil told him to."

"I don't want to think about that," said Jaide. "It's too horrible, and besides, there's no way to talk to him without the phone. We just have to find the gold card first. Then everything will be all right."

"How?"

"I don't know, but it will be!"

"I mean, how are we going to find it? We tried a witching rod. We used a skeleton key. We got Ari to look around for us. We've found nothing, and now I'm out of ideas."

"The solution might be right in front of you," said the death mask, "or behind you, or above you, or all around you. If it's in the universe next door, it could be anywhere, and nowhere."

"But how does that help us?" asked Jack. "If it's in another universe, we can't get to it because it's . . . in another universe, right?"

"Not so. All we need is a cross-continuum conduit constructor."

"Is that something Grandma might have?"

"Not likely. It was never considered . . . uh . . . mainstream Warden equipment. Very few were made — though now I come to think about it, I suppose more must have been built since I've been . . . ah . . . resting. . . ."

"If Grandma hasn't got one of these construct things, then I don't think there's much hope —" Jack started to say, but he was interrupted by the gleeful professor.

"That's where you're wrong! There's one in the castle. I saw it while we were searching the second floor."

Jaide and Jack sat up at the same moment.

"What?!"

"The castle contains a cross-continuum conduit constructor that I suspect now was used to hide the card you seek in the first place. If we go back, I can show you where it is. I can even show you how to use it!"

"Wait." Jaide rubbed at her tired eyes. Her brain was beginning to shut down from exhaustion. "You're telling us that with this thing you can open a tunnel to another world, where the Card of Translocation is hidden?"

"Yes. A world among many possible worlds."

"What kind of world?"

"It could be like ours, or it could infinitely stranger, built from an entirely different number of dimensions and physical laws. I glimpsed some of these places during my own research — endless flat plains with no height or depth at all, giddying vistas boasting an extra version of left and right —"

Jack cut him off. "Could someone use one of these conduits to connect to somewhere else in this world?"

"Yes, of course."

"So *that's* how the back door to the blue room works!"

He felt pleased to have worked that much out, even though he was no closer to a solution to their current problem.

"Okay, so it could be done," Jaide said. "But we can't search every possible universe. That would take us forever."

"That's true. Fortunately, in this case you would simply look for an existing doorway into the world where the card is hidden, not create a new one. Then we would use the cross-continuum conduit constructor as a key to open it."

"Would the witching rod help us find the doorway?"

"Yes. Just deduce where such a doorway would likely be, point the rod at it, and see what happens."

"And how exactly do we do the deducing?" asked Jaide.

"Well, in my day people tended to make otherworldly doorways in things that already looked like doors. You know, they tend to the rectangular. A window, for example.

Or even an actual door, since it would only open to the other world if it was activated by the device."

"That's all great, but we still have to go back to the castle," said Jack.

"Somehow." Jaide felt gloomy again.

"I find," said Professor Olafsson with persistent cheer, "that the best ideas come when the concerns of the mundane world are set aside and the conscious mind submits to the ruminations of the unconscious."

"When *what*?" asked Jack.

"When you get a good night's sleep, in other words, and that's what I advise for both of you right now. By the time you wake up, I'm sure you will have the answer."

"I hope so." Jack was too tired to argue, even with a full belly. He got up and slipped into his pajamas.

Jaide went to the bathroom to brush her teeth. There was no sign of Cornelia or Kleo, and by the time she went back, Jack was already out cold, the damaged picture sitting on his chest, resting under his limp hand. The bracelet charm Custer had given him gleamed in the low light. Jaide browsed through the *Compendium* until Susan came and told her it was time for sleep.

"Do *you* sleep?" Jaide asked Professor Olafsson as she got into bed.

"No, but there are times when I fade out. When nothing is happening and there is no one to talk to." He smiled at Jaide. "I would not want to sleep now. This puzzle has given me much to think about!"

"Well, that's good," she said. "Happy thinking. Maybe one of us will have the answer by morning."

"I believe that is entirely likely, Jaide."

Jaide closed her eyes and, within moments, started to snore.

"Cards, parrots, and cats," said Professor Olafsson softly to himself. "Now, where *did* I hear that voice before . . . ?"

Jack woke the next morning from a nightmare about giant parrots picking up members of his family one by one and biting their heads off, while Jaide had dreamt about flying in the rain and dodging lightning bolts. Neither dream brought any kind of revelation or solution to any of their problems. Professor Olafsson had nothing, either, and he didn't look happy about it. The night's fruitless thinking had put him in a sullen mood.

"The entrance could be anywhere in the castle," said Professor Olafsson. "It could be disguised as anything. We need another clue to guide us."

"Will you be okay if we leave you here?" asked Jaide. "I don't think we should take you to school."

Jack agreed, fearing what Miralda King would make of the death mask if she got her hands on it. Professor Olafsson assented. He was getting bored of sitting around, thinking, but it wasn't as if they had many choices.

Susan was distracted and irritable over breakfast, as though she hadn't slept well. Jack assumed she was worried about Grandma X and their father, as they were. She didn't know anything about The Evil, but distance and car crashes were enough to make anyone unhappy.

"I don't want to hear any more talk about going to the castle," Susan said, although they hadn't said anything about it at all. "I checked the homework I gave you. You didn't do any of it. You're going to school and that's where the matter ends. And don't even think about asking for the phone."

They knew better than to argue with that tone, just as they understood when to obey their father. Feeling trapped between two parents who weren't talking to each other about what really mattered, they had no choice but to grit their teeth, make their own lunches, and get themselves to school.

"What are we going to do?" Jaide asked as she untangled their bikes and pushed hers out of the laundry room.

"Beats me." Jack followed her, almost running over two feline shapes sitting by the back door, one a scruffy ginger and the other a glossy blue-gray.

"So *this* was the big secret from the other night?" Ari was looking up at the rail of the widow's walk high above, where Cornelia was visible as a blue smudge against the tiles of the roof. His eyes were narrowed and suspicious. "What's so special about a bird? They're just dinner on legs."

"Exactly what we thought you'd think," said Kleo. "I asked Custer to keep you busy so you wouldn't scare her off."

"So he didn't really need my help?"

Ari looked hurt, and Jaide hastened to distract him.

"Not all birds are stupid," said Jaide. "This one can talk."

"About what, how she really wants a cracker? Pffft." Ari rolled his eyes. "No respectable animal would eat *crackers*."

"I'm on your side, Ari," said Jack. "Why doesn't she just fly away?"

"Because she's still trying to tell us something," said Kleo. "She stirred when you woke, troubletwisters, and came out through one of the upper-floor windows. I don't know what she's doing, but she definitely has a purpose."

Jaide climbed on her bike. "Come on, Jack, or we'll be late."

Ari returned his attention to the bird.

"Just come down here," he called, "and we'll see whose claws are sharpest. . . ."

They pedaled down the lane, leaving Ari to his fantasies of a parrot breakfast. Neither of them saw Cornelia stretch one wing and then the other, as though waking herself up, then launch herself into the air. She flapped twice, banked to avoid a tree, and disappeared from Ari's frustrated sight.

CHAPTER SIXTEEN

A TWIN THING

Zebediah was just pulling away from the curb with Rodeo Dave behind the wheel as the twins approached the Book Herd. *On his way to the castle,* Jaide thought glumly, *to continue his search for the Card of Translocation.* He waved, but their return waves were halfhearted at best.

"Good morning, troubletwisters," Rennie called from the doorway with her rough voice. She waved, too, and it took both twins a full second to realize that she did so with a complete left hand. They screeched to a halt, not believing their eyes. Grandma X had told them that there was no way even the Wardens could heal so great a wound.

"Come inside," Rennie said, crooking one impossible finger. "I want to talk to you."

They propped their bikes against the window and followed her into the shop, where she led them through the door at the back and up a narrow flight of stairs, to the room she slept in. It contained very little in terms of furniture, just a single bed and a cupboard with one door, but was plastered floor to ceiling with hand-drawn pictures.

They were the pictures of Rennie their class had drawn when they'd thought she was dead, Jaide realized, looking around in wonder. Tara must have given them to her in the end.

Rennie sat on the bed, surrounded by pictures of herself, and brought the twins to her for a quick hug. She was like that sometimes. The Evil had used her when she was grieving over the deaths of her own children. Now that she was a ward of Portland, that protectiveness had been transferred to them.

Jack felt hard, mechanical digits digging into his shoulder and realized that the hand wasn't real flesh at all.

"Rodeo Dave gave it to me," Rennie said, holding up the hand for closer inspection. It was strapped to her wrist, a device of fiendish complexity made of thin slivers of wood and metal, with thousands of tiny gears connecting them to a complex of nested springs within. They could hear the mechanism ticking when it was still, then whirring into busy life when Rennie moved it. "He said your grandmother had ordered it from her 'special connections' before her accident, but it only just arrived."

Jack stared at it more closely, looking for evidence that it had come from The Evil. What if the hand went crazy and attacked them? But it showed no immediate sign of going on a rampage.

"Does being touched by The Evil change you permanently?" Jaide asked, emboldened by desperation. Everyone else who understood The Evil was busy fighting it, or forbidden by their father from talking about it. "I mean, would there be some way to tell if it had happened to someone we know, even if it was a long time ago?"

"Maybe," Rennie said. "Why do you ask? Have you been threatened by someone?"

"Not exactly . . . but he has been acting pretty weird lately."

"Who? Tell me at once, Jaide."

Rennie took her by the shoulders. There was no refusing that anxious stare.

"Rodeo Dave," Jaide said in a weak voice. "I mean, he was friends with Young Master Rourke, whose grandfather was definitely Evil, and he's doing some pretty strange stuff out at the castle, and we thought Grandma might have sent you here to keep an eye on him, and —"

Jaide stopped as the mechanical hand closed firmly over her mouth.

"I still have much to learn about The Evil, the Wardens, and the wards," said Rennie. "But I do know that people who have been taken over by The Evil have been released without permanent damage. In rare cases, people have even managed to free themselves, without the intervention of Wardens. But if you are part of The Evil for too long, it changes you. It steals away your humanity, your love. You become hollow, twisted, lost. . . ."

She hesitated, and looked at her artificial hand.

"I was a part of The Evil for long enough to feel that I was lost, but I wasn't. And now I am a Living Ward. Such a thing has never happened before, and it is hard to deal with. Rodeo Dave . . . David has had some similarity of experience, so he can help me —"

"You mean Rodeo Dave was once part of The Evil!" Jaide couldn't believe her ears.

Rennie hesitated again, biting her lip.

"Don't jump to conclusions," she said firmly. "David's history is his story to tell. Ask him and perhaps he will share it with you. Let me just say that he, too, has known sorrow and loss, and he has helped me."

Jack and Jaide looked at each other. That explained why Rodeo Dave was somehow connected with Warden business, and wasn't freaked out by weird stuff happening. But if he had once been part of The Evil or working for it . . . maybe he wanted to go back to it, and finding the card was how he would make up for leaving The Evil before.

"I didn't bring you here to show off my new hand," Rennie said, snapping its fingers to bring their attention back to her. "I want to tell you something important. I have felt The Evil nearby, through the wards. It has come very close in the last few days, to the west and north, but not once has it directly tested the strength of the wards. I sense that it is waiting for something."

"Like what?" asked Jack.

"That I do not know," she said. "But I feel it . . . where I felt it before."

"In your hand?" asked Jaide.

Rennie shook her head. "The Evil burns like a fire, but it is not fire. It is nothing, and it leaves nothing behind. I feel it in the *absence* of my hand."

She raised the clockwork hand and flexed it again, marveling at its complexity.

"In losing much, I have gained much," she said. "But I would not lose any more. Be careful, my troubletwisters. If you leave the boundary of the wards again, as I sensed you doing yesterday, I will have to tell your grandmother."

Jaide and Jack nodded very seriously, struck by the thought that Rennie could barge into the hospital and wake up Grandma X if they didn't obey the rules, even if it was for a good purpose.

"Listen, Rennie —" Jaide started to say, wanting to explain.

Rennie cut her off. "You are late for school. You'd better get going before I land you in more trouble."

"But we just want to tell you —" tried Jack.

"Enjoy your ordinary life while you can," Rennie insisted, ushering them down the stairs. "It won't stay ordinary for long."

Outside, they found Cornelia sitting on Jack's handlebars.

"What are you doing here?" asked Jack angrily. "Are you following us?"

"Rourke!"

"Well, don't. Go away and leave us alone."

Jack tried to shoo her from his bike, but one sharp lunge reminded him of the vicious hole in the photo where his father's face used to be.

"Here, Jack, let me."

Rennie held out her clockwork hand. Cornelia nipped at it, but soon realized it was immune to her formidable beak. Leaving barely a scratch, she gave up and hopped onto the hand and was lifted away.

"Off you go now," said Rennie. "I'll find something to keep her occupied."

The twins pedaled furiously down the street, leaving Rennie and Cornelia behind to take each other's measure.

School had never seemed more pointless. After the usual welcome and group discussion about dreams (which the twins joined halfway through, making stuff up) the first lesson was Artistic Expression, which involved drawing or writing while Mr. Carver improvised on a variety of musical instruments. Students were encouraged to join in, or even to dance, but no one ever did that. While the others sketched horses or spaceships, Jack concentrated hard on drawing a map of the castle from memory, looking for any secret spaces they hadn't visited yet. Maybe one of them had been where the entrance to Professor Olafsson's other universe was hidden.

Tara, who normally sat with them, had greeted them warmly enough that morning, but soon picked up on their mood and went to join Kyle, who had been sitting alone at the table in front of them. Ever since he had argued with Miralda, no one else would talk to him.

Now the two of them were whispering excitedly with their heads close together, and Jaide was unable to avoid hearing what they were saying.

". . . Peregrinators pick a mystery every month, and they explore it until they figure it out or get bored," Kyle was saying. "I followed Dad once and listened in. They were talking about giant rats living in the sewers. Some of them wanted to go down there and check it out."

"Eww."

Jaide agreed with Tara. She had seen what Jack had looked like after he had been down there.

But it wasn't that that made her want to join in the conversation.

"Did the Peregrinators ever hear anything weird about the Rourke Estate?" Jaide asked, switching tables while Mr. Carver wasn't looking.

"Sure," said Kyle. "I was just getting to that bit."

But with a sniff, Tara leaned back with her arms folded. "So *now* you want to talk to us — when we have our own thing going?"

Jaide stared at her in surprise. "What?"

"It's really difficult being friends with you and Jack. You know that? You're always whispering and skulking around, keeping things secret from me. Sometimes I wonder if you want to be friends at all."

"I do," said Jaide. "That is, we both do. It's just really hard to explain."

"Is it?"

"It's a twin thing," said Kyle. "I've got identical sisters, Esther and Fi. They can be real pains, too, but it's not their fault. It's the way they're made. You just have to get used to it." He smiled calmingly at Tara. "Don't let it get to you. That's my advice."

"All right . . . I guess. But why do I have to do all the work?"

"I'm sorry," said Jaide. "We'll try harder, I promise."

Tara relented a little. Her arms unfolded. "Okay. Good. Because I want to hear about what you did yesterday."

"You first," said Jaide to Kyle. "What were you about to say?"

"What? Oh, yeah. The Rourke Estate." Excited to have doubled his audience, Kyle recommenced his story. "A few months ago, Dad had this thing in his head that there was buried treasure there."

"What kind of treasure?" Tara asked.

"Gold."

Jaide leaned even more closely, excitement rising in her.

"Did they find anything?" she asked.

"No," said Kyle.

"So why did your dad think there was a treasure there in the first place?" asked Tara.

"There's always been rumors, and then a few months ago Dad found this weird thin strip of cloth with some words stitched on it. Not stitched very well, like maybe a kid did it for a craft project, but you know what?"

"What?" asked Tara and Jaide together.

"The thread was pure gold wire. And the cloth was velvet. So Dad went out a few nights in a row to search — I guess it was easy for him, since he's the groundskeeper there and no one would've thought it weird if he was poking around with a shovel. But he never found anything. I assume he didn't, anyway, because we didn't suddenly become rich or anything."

"Maybe it never existed," said Tara.

"Or it's still there, waiting for someone to find it," said Kyle. "Wouldn't that be cool?"

"What were the words embroidered on the cloth?" Jaide asked him.

Kyle nodded. "Dad used to walk around the house saying it under his breath. We all knew it, eventually."

He leaned in closer and in a low, breathless voice intoned:

"The path between fields,
the season grows old,
the deuce is revealed —
there lies the gold."

"What does that mean?" asked Jaide.

"If only we knew! There are fields on the estate, and lots of paths, too. The rest, though, is a bit of a mystery."

"How big was this cloth again?"

Kyle held up his ruler. "About the same width as this, only half as long."

"Sounds like a bookmark," said Tara. "A bookmark of velvet with gold embroidery."

"Where did your dad find it?" asked Jack, who had overheard and come over.

"Just on the ground near the new menagerie cages, outside the lodge.

"Did he ask Young Master Rourke about it?"

Kyle put his ruler back under his desk and mumbled something that sounded like "Finders keepers."

Jaide leaned back, frowning. The bookmark must have fallen out of one of Master Rourke's old paperbacks, and it certainly sounded like a clue to something. But if the groundskeeper of the estate hadn't worked out the landmarks, how would she and Jack possibly do it?

"What's a *deuce*?" asked Tara.

None of them knew.

The school's ancient dictionary proved to be of some use, unlike the last time Jaide had used it. There were two definitions for the word *deuce*. The first was "an expression of annoyance or frustration." She could see how that could come in handy at that moment, but it didn't help. The second was all about sports and games. Deuce was when two tennis players were tied at the end of a game. It was when someone rolled two in a game of dice. A deuce was also "a playing card with two pips."

Jaide blinked. Suddenly, she knew. She knew what the path between fields was, and what it meant when the rhyme talked about the season growing old. That and interworld doorways being rectangular! It had been staring at them in the face all along.

Before she could whisper what she'd figured out to Jack, a commotion on the other side of the class distracted her. Fingers pointed and a cluster formed around the windows, oohing and aahing.

"Isn't he just adorable?" exclaimed Miralda King. "I think he wants to come in."

"Don't open the window," said Mr. Carver hastily. "He

could be dangerous. They carry parasites, you know. And just look at that beak!"

Kyle and Tara hurried to see. So did the twins. There was a large blue bird pacing up and down outside the window, craning to see past the faces peering out at it.

"Oh, no, not again," said Jack. "What's she doing *here*?"

CHAPTER SEVENTEEN

HIDDEN IN PLAIN SIGHT

On seeing Jack, Cornelia began to pace more quickly, rolling her head from side to side.

"Rourke! Rourke!"

"She's a she, not a he," said Jack, feeling defensive of Cornelia despite everything, "and she doesn't have parasites."

"You know this bird?" asked Mr. Carver.

"You could say that. But I don't know what she's doing here."

He pushed through to the front of the throng.

"Go home, Cornelia," he said, waving his hands at her through the glass. "Go on! Get out of here!"

The bird just watched him with a quizzical expression, as though he had gone mad.

"Rourke?"

"Is that all she says?" asked Miralda. "I thought parrots were supposed to be intelligent."

"She *is* intelligent," said Jaide. "We just can't understand her."

"Rourke!" Cornelia tilted her head and bit at the window frame, pulling free a chunk of wood. Spitting it aside, she began digging again, widening the hole with her sharp beak.

"Shoo!" said Mr. Carver, flapping at the window with an open book. "That's town property!"

"Rourke!"

She kept on digging.

With a sinking feeling, Jack realized that Cornelia was his responsibility. She thought he was her friend, even if he didn't feel the same way in return anymore. If he didn't do something about her, she would only get into more trouble.

"I'll take her away," he said. "If I can be excused . . . ?"

"Yes, yes, do what you need to get rid of that feathered vandal." Mr. Carver was normally a fervent advocate of animal rights, but not for anything that disrupted his school, it seemed. He gathered up Jack and practically pushed him out the door. "Don't come back until it's safely locked up!"

Jack came around the side of the school, acutely conscious of everyone watching him. Cornelia stopped digging at the wood the moment he appeared and waddled over to him.

"All aboard," she said. "All aboard."

"What? Cornelia, I can't understand what you're saying."

She opened her wings, flapped mightily, and launched herself onto Jack's shoulder.

He almost fell over backward in surprise. Cornelia rocked from side to side, her powerful claws digging into his shirt and not letting go.

"What are you doing?" Jack asked her.

"Shake a leg," she said, folding her wings and doing an odd and slightly painful dance on his shoulder.

"You want me to take you somewhere?"

"Rourke!"

"I'm not allowed to take you to the estate. I'm at school."

But her dance got only weirder, shuffling from foot to foot and pushing one knobbly leg into his face.

"Everyone is watching, Cornelia. Wait . . . is *that* what you're talking about?"

Jack had forgotten the tiny metal ring attached to Cornelia's left ankle. She was waving it under his nose, trying to get him to look at it.

Jack gingerly took her leg in his hands. She didn't protest, and she kept her claws carefully away from the palm of his hand so she wouldn't scratch him.

There was a piece of very thin paper tucked into the ring. He pulled it out and delicately unfolded it, expecting a note or even — his heart pounded — another clue, perhaps more of the treasure poem Kyle had recited.

Instead, it was a page from a dictionary, with a hole in one corner where Cornelia's beak had gripped it.

"Did you take this from Rodeo Dave's shop?" he asked her.

"Rourke!" She tapped the page with her beak.

"Rennie must have folded it for you. Which means you're trying to tell us something again."

He scanned the page. It came from the *T* section of the dictionary. The word *twister* leaped out at him.

"Hey," he said, "that's a secret. You're not supposed to tell people."

"Rourke!" She tapped the page again. "Rourke!"

"I know, but what does that have to do with anything?"

She tapped so hard, her beak slashed the page and almost cut Jack's thumb, making him drop the paper onto the ground. She threw up her wings and squawked in frustration.

Jack sympathized. It *was* frustrating, constantly banging up against this block in communication. Cornelia mainly talked in nautical phrases, probably picked up from the captain of a whaling ship long ago. It was lucky, he supposed, that she wasn't singing rude sea shanties. Maybe it was some kind of trauma, a throwback to an earlier phase of life brought on by what she had seen the night Young Master Rourke died — understandable but not terribly helpful.

"I don't know what you're trying to tell me," he said, "but I know my dad had nothing to do with what happened to your old master. He just couldn't have. Still, I don't think you're lying or trying to trick us — and you're definitely not Evil. Just a bit destructive sometimes."

He picked up the torn piece of paper and put it in his pocket.

"One of us is wrong."

Cornelia head-butted him on the nose. The message this time was unmistakable.

You are.

"We have to figure this out, Cornelia," Jack said, "but I'm supposed to be at school. If I don't go back in, I'll get in trouble. Why don't you go home and we'll try again later?"

Cornelia looked uncertain.

"Oh, right — Ari. That was why you didn't come down earlier, wasn't it? Okay. I'll come with you and see if we can find a way past him."

She nodded, then said, "Anchors aweigh! Push the boat out!"

"Just let me get my bike."

Jack glanced at Jaide, who was peering out at him with the others. Jaide was practically bouncing up and down on the balls of her feet, as though there was something she desperately wanted to tell him, but there was nothing he could do about that now.

Cornelia stayed put as he pedaled up to speed, and as they swept over the bridge at the center of town, she opened her wings and held on so the wind of their passage could ruffle her feathers.

"Full steam ahead!"

If only, thought Jack.

There was no sign of Ari back at the house, or anyone else. Jack and Cornelia sneaked inside without incident. The house was empty and silent, apart from the usual creaks and ticks that made it sound sometimes like a giant clock. Cornelia didn't want to go back into the blue room, so Jack put her in the bedroom he shared with Jaide, where she seemed happy enough.

"I'll be back later," he said. "Please don't bite any more books or photos. Or Olafsson. He'll be here if you need to talk to someone."

"Indeed, I appear to be going nowhere," said the death mask grumpily.

Cornelia nuzzled her downy head into Jack's hand and softly clucked her tongue. He grudgingly tickled her under the ridge where her ears would have been and said goodbye to both of them.

Satisfied that they would keep each other company, Jack returned to school the way he had come, conscious of the curious stares of his classmates and enduring Miralda King's sharp remark that she hoped he had the proper license for such a wild and dangerous animal.

"I mean, it's bad enough that some of Young Master Rourke's menagerie animals are still prowling around town," she said. "But when they could swoop down on you from above, at any moment . . . ?"

She shuddered in theatrical horror.

"Captivity is just as cruel for animals as it is for people," said Mr. Carver, eyeing the damaged woodwork. "Perhaps your feathered friend deserves a home somewhere else, Jack, somewhere far away from here. In a forest."

Jack slipped into his seat, hating the blush he felt boiling up over the collar of his T-shirt and turning his face pink. Mr. Carver had written a series of mathematical equations on the board, and Jack tried to concentrate on what they said in order to blot out his embarrassment.

But Jaide was still bouncing.

"I know where it is!" she whispered to him when everyone's attention returned to the front.

"What?"

"The card!"

She nodded furiously, and pointed to her exercise book, where she had written out the words Kyle had told them.

The path between fields,
the season grows old,
the deuce is revealed —
there lies the gold.

"It's the painting," she whispered.

"What painting?"

Jack had spoken more loudly than he intended, loud enough for Mr. Carver to come over. Jaide hastily shut her exercise book as Jack looked up at their teacher and gave him an innocent smile.

"Do you need help with the questions?" asked Mr. Carver. "If so, that is what I am here for, and I expect I will be able to answer your questions more effectively than your sister, smart as she is."

"No, no, I'm okay now," said Jack. "I just got a bit distracted, with the parrot and all."

He looked at the math questions and realized that he did need help. But it was too late to ask now. Sighing, he bent his head and tried to concentrate.

It wasn't until just before lunch that the twins got the opportunity to talk again, because Mr. Carver had to go to the office five minutes early to play his welcome to the midday meal song over the PA system.

As soon as he went out the door, Jaide leaned in close.

"The painting in the library — the woman playing Solitaire — remember? The leaves on the tree are brown, so it's autumn. *The season grows old*. There are fields behind her with a road between them. And she's holding the two of hearts. The *deuce* of hearts! Jack, it has to be her. It has to be — and it was right under our noses all the time!"

Jaide's excitement was infectious. Jack felt himself getting caught up in it even as he got stuck on the obvious question.

"But there's nothing behind the painting, remember? We took it down. The wallpaper is unbroken."

"That's because it's not behind the painting. It's *in* it."

"How can the gold card be in a painting?"

"Think, Jack!" Jaide sighed. "It's just like Professor Olafsson said. It's a door to another dimension. All we have to do is open it and we can go through!"

"Yeah, right," said Jack. "How are we going to get back to the castle in the first place? Mom won't let us go."

"I don't know." Jaide deflated a little at that. "We'll just have to think of *something*."

They sank back into their seats, minds whirling with possibilities, most of them discarded instantly.

"I wish we could call Dad," said Jack. What if he hadn't escaped The Evil after all? What if he was out there, needing their help? What if, this time, being troubletwisters wasn't enough to help anyone?

"Oh, hey, that reminds me. . . ." He pulled the scrap of paper from his pocket and laid it out flat on the table. "Cornelia gave me this."

Jaide scanned it, but the mystery was as opaque to her as it was to Jack. It seemed relatively unimportant, too. So what if Cornelia knew they were troubletwisters? The main thing was that they had figured out where the card was. All they had to do was get their hands on it before Rodeo Dave did, and then get it to their father.

Tonight, thought Jack, as the now-familiar notes from the nose flute came drifting through the speakers in the corridor outside. *Tonight could be our last chance.*

Tara and Kyle had also been whispering all through class, and they took their conversation out onto the playground, where the twins interrupted them.

"Can we tell Mom that we're going to stay at your place tonight?" Jaide asked Tara.

"All right," she said, "but only if I can tell my parents that I'm going to be staying at yours. Kyle and I are going to the estate to look for the treasure!"

For a second, Jaide just blinked at her in surprise.

"But . . . aren't you afraid of rats?"

"They're only inside the castle, Jaide," Tara said. "We're going to look outside. I think *season* refers to seasoning, which is like spices, and Kyle says there's an old herb garden on the estate. He's going to sneak out and show me where."

"Sometimes there are advantages to being the youngest in a big family." Kyle grinned.

Jaide's instincts were to try to talk them out of it. The Evil was still sniffing after the wards, after all.

"Do you really think the treasure's still there?" Jaide asked. "What if it never existed at all?"

"What if you're planning to go treasure hunting, too?" said Kyle. "I saw the way you two have been twin-thinging all day. You don't want us to go because you want to find it first!"

There was no denying that, because it was utterly true. But if Jack and Jaide were inside the castle, where Tara wouldn't go, there was no possibility of being in direct competition.

"It'll be like a race," said Jack. "The first to the gold wins."

Kyle's green eyes twinkled with the challenge. "It's *so* on."

The afternoon seemed to drag and race by at the same time. Jack's stomach was full of butterflies as the farewell song sounded and the class dissolved into chatter and scuffling feet. Kyle and Tara hurried off in one direction, waving and promising to see them later, while Jack and Jaide got on their bikes and rode up the street, keeping their fingers crossed that Susan would let them go. That was the first hurdle to overcome.

They skidded their bikes to a crashing halt by the back door and ran inside.

"Mom?" Their voices echoed up the stairs and through the house's many rooms. "Mom, where are you?"

There was no answer.

"The car isn't there," said Jack. "Maybe she went to work."

"Or maybe she's at the hospital. . . ."

Both twins jumped at the sound of a crash from upstairs, followed by a distant squawking.

"That was Cornelia," said Jack, already running for the stairwell.

Jaide overtook him, her Gift lifting her up so she could take four steps at a time. What if something was attacking Cornelia so she couldn't tell them what she knew? *Inside the house!*

"Rourke!"

There was another crash. It came from the bedroom. The door swept open ahead of Jaide and the twins crashed through it.

Within, they found a scene of utter chaos. Curtains were torn, books had been knocked over, the sheets were pulled off their beds, and their clothes were scattered into every corner. It looked like they had been burgled by a thorough but incompetent burglar.

The source of the mess, a rather harried-looking Ari, was currently running in circles in the middle of the room being dive-bombed by Cornelia.

"Rourke! Rourke!"

Ari took a running leap for the macaw but only succeeded in knocking over Jack's bedside lamp.

"What are you doing?" Jack asked, skidding to a halt with his sister at his side. "Ari, what's going on?"

With one last squawk, Cornelia landed on the top of Jaide's four-poster bed frame.

"She started it," said Ari, looking up at Jack with slightly addled eyes. He looked that way sometimes on a full moon, but this time he didn't have that excuse. The old moon was barely a sliver in the evening sky.

"Started what, exactly?" asked Jaide. "Have you been trying to kill each other?"

"I've been trying to make them stop," said the death mask from where it had been tipped into a half-empty garbage can.

"Professor Olafsson!" Jack fished him out and put him upright next to where his lamp normally went.

"I'm so sorry," said Jaide, before turning on Ari and Cornelia. "You two should be ashamed of yourselves. What were you thinking?"

She sounded very angry. Even Jack was scared of her when she was like this. Ari stood behind him with only his tail and his face showing.

"Were you trying to eat Cornelia?" Jaide asked him.

"A fat old bird like that? No, thanks."

Jaide ignored Cornelia's squawk of indignation. "So what were you doing?"

"She was calling me names," Ari said, scuffing at the ground with one of his front paws.

"Sound the bell, Mr. Dingles!"

"See? Why, you —"

Ari ran for the bed, but Jack caught him. Cornelia danced from foot to foot, cackling, "High and dry, high and dry."

"Cornelia, stop it," said Jack. "That's not very nice."

"I tried to explain to your furry friend here," said Professor Olafsson, "that Mr. Dingles was probably a ship's cat Cornelia once served with, but he won't listen."

"I don't even know who you are!"

"He's a former Warden," said Jaide. "We found him in the castle. You should do as he says."

"Why, when *she* won't?"

"Is that it, Cornelia?" asked Jack. "Do you think Ari is Mr. Dingles?"

Cornelia looked down at him with one yellow-ringed eye, and slowly nodded her head. Jack didn't know if Cornelia genuinely understood or not, but that was something.

"Ari, if I let you go, will you leave her alone?"

"Oh, all right," said the cat, going limp in his arms. "But why does she get to call *me* anything at all? What's she even doing here? I'm the Warden Companion, not *her*."

Jack and Jaide exchanged a glance. It hadn't occurred to either of them that he might be more jealous than hungry when it came to the new animal in their midst.

"You *are* one of Grandma's Warden Companions," Jack said, "and you're still our friend. Having Cornelia here doesn't change that one bit."

"Jack's right, honest," said Jaide, bending down to give him a hug.

"You promise?" he said into her neck.

"We promise," said the twins together.

"Okay, then. You can let me go now."

Jaide stood back, and Ari put his rear down and began licking his fur flat again.

Only then did it occur to Jack that they couldn't talk to Professor Olafsson with Ari in the room. Grandma X may have given them permission to go back to the estate when they visited her in the hospital, but if she knew the full story about Rodeo Dave and The Evil, it would only make her upset, which their father had told them not to do.

"Erm, Ari, we need to talk in private," he said.

"About what?"

"I can't tell you. . . . It's private."

Ari narrowed his eyes and looked from one twin to the other.

"But the bird gets to stay?"

Jaide glanced at Cornelia, who looked back at her innocently.

"I guess not," Jaide said, holding up her arm for Cornelia to climb down.

One swift jab with the beak made her reconsider the wisdom of doing that.

"Jack, could you . . . ?"

He coaxed Cornelia down from her perch and took her out of the room, putting her on a banister. Once she was outside, Ari followed, taking a seat a foot or two away from Cornelia. They did nothing but glare at each other as Jack closed the door behind him. He hoped it would stay that way.

Jaide was crouched down at eye level with the death mask in the wreckage of their room.

"We've done it, Professor Olafsson," she said. "We've found out where the card is, and we think it's in one of your weird universes."

"Really? How absolutely marvelous!" Professor Olafsson grinned from ear to ear. "Well, the first thing we must do is get back there and apply the cross-continuum conduit constructor to the portal."

"I know," said Jack, "but —"

He stopped at a shrill noise coming from the chest next to Jaide's bed.

"That's the phone!" she cried.

Jack couldn't believe it. The phone was sitting on a piece of paper covered in Susan's neat writing, charger plugged into the wall, as though it had been there all day.

They both lunged for it at the same time, but Jaide got there an instant before her brother's grasping hands. Susan's note fluttered to the floor, unread.

"Dad? Dad? Where have you been? We've got good news!"

"How can you have good news?" Hector Shield said, voice harsh through some kind of heavy interference, perhaps even rain again. "I've been calling you all day and you didn't come to the castle even once. I'm beginning to wonder if I made a mistake entrusting this mission to you. Perhaps it's not too late to give it to someone I can truly rely on."

CHAPTER EIGHTEEN

THE FIELDS OF GOLD

The twins rocked back on their heels, feeling as though they had been punched in the guts. The lights flickered and the air swirled around them as their Gifts reacted. They had never heard their father speak so cruelly before, not even when he was mad at them. He was never mean to anyone, really, and only ever raised his voice when certain household appliances didn't behave as they were supposed to. Which was pretty much everything with an on/off button, all the time, for him.

"But we couldn't come today," said Jack, feeling sick to his stomach. "Mom wouldn't let us. And she took the —"

"Your mother has nothing to do with this. The Card of Translocation is what's important, not the petty rules and regulations of the ordinary world."

"We tried, Dad," said Jaide, fighting hard not to stammer. "And we know where the card is, now. All we have to do is get it."

"Why should I believe you?" The static was so thick they could hardly hear him.

"Because it's true!" Jaide stamped her foot, something she hadn't done since she was five years old. It wasn't fair that he should treat them like this, not when they were so close to getting the card. "It's in a painting in the library. And we know how to get it out. We can do it — I know we can!"

"I gave you a simple task," Hector Shield said through the background noise. ". . . I'm really disappointed. . . ."

"We just need a little more time," said Jaide.

". . . no time left . . . can't hold it back much longer without the card . . . taking all our energies just to protect the wards . . ."

Behind their father's distant voice they heard the sound of a wolf howling. Jaide shuddered, and Jack reached out to take her hand.

"We can do it," Jack told him. "Mom's not here but we can leave her a note —"

"But what if she calls Tara's parents?" Jaide asked, seeing the flaw in that plan immediately. "She'll know we're not where we're supposed to be."

"Yes, but she won't know where we are, right? As long as we find the card, we can deal with her afterward."

Jaide groaned. Success was dangling just out of their reach, but to attain it they would have to play one parent off against the other. It would be so much easier if they could just talk to Susan about what was really going on!

There was a moment's roaring silence over the phone.

"Dad? Are you there, Dad?" she said. "We can do it. I know we can."

"All right," he finally said. "But you mustn't fail me! This is your final chance."

"You can trust us," said Jaide. "You really, really can."

"We honestly won't let you down, Dad," said Jack.

"Be sure you . . . I mean, we're counting on you. . . ."

The static rose up, cutting the call off. The twins sagged, feeling emotionally drained. Their father must have been under incredible pressure to speak to them like that. Whatever was going on out there in the fight against The Evil, it was their job to help their father, as well as Custer, and whoever else was involved.

"You write the note," said Jack, leaping to his feet, grabbing the phone and the death mask, and putting both in his pack. "I'll get flashlights and — is there anything we'll need, Professor Olafsson?"

"Perhaps some rope," he said. "The way through the portal may not be in the same horizontal plane."

"What do you mean?" asked Jack.

"It might be the top of a hole, for example. Or you might come out the side of a wall, a hundred feet up a tower."

"Okay. Rope."

Jack opened the door to find Ari and Cornelia exactly where he had left them. Ignoring them, he ran downstairs to the ground-floor closet, a dark and cobwebby space full of all sorts of domestic odds and ends. Coiled up at the back was a length of slender, green nylon rope, which he scooped up and stuffed into his bag.

Jaide looked for a piece of paper on which to write the note telling Susan that they would be going to Tara's house for dinner, and found the note the phone had been sitting on. She started to read the message from Susan explaining that, on further thought, maybe Jack and Jaide were old enough to be entrusted with a phone, provided they understood that it was a responsibility. . . .

Jaide's eyes crossed. There wasn't *time*. Turning it over, she wrote *Going to Tara's for dinner. Thanks Mom. Love J & J.*

Running downstairs, she left the note on the kitchen table where Susan was sure to find it. When that was done, she turned and found Ari watching her.

"What's going on?" he asked.

She didn't have the heart to lie to him. He was their grandmother's Warden Companion. He was one of the protectors of Portland. He deserved to know at least part of the truth, didn't he? The only thing stopping her was the promise she had made to her father.

"Find Custer," she said. "He'll tell you."

"Mmm-hmm," he said. "Like how he told me he how useful I was yesterday?"

"Forget about that," she said. "This is a whole different thing. This is *important*."

"My feelings aren't important?"

She threw her hands in the air in frustration. "I don't have time for this!"

Jack was already outside, untangling their bikes. "All okay?" he asked when she appeared.

"I hope so," she said.

They put their heads down and rode furiously up the lane.

As they turned into Parkhill Street, a blue blur whizzed overhead in a flurry of feathers and wings.

"Rourke!" cried Cornelia, settling onto Jack's shoulders.

"Yes," he said with a grin. "This time we're going to the estate. Are you sure you want to come with us?"

The macaw bobbed her head up and down. "All parrots on deck."

"Okay. Let's go!"

Behind them, the weather vane turned against the wind to point northeast, directly at the Rourke Estate.

Clouds gathered overhead as they neared the castle. Sunset was still some way off, but the light failed steadily, until it seemed more like twilight than late afternoon. There was no rain yet, but Jaide had no doubt that it was coming. There was a thick, heavy feeling to the air, as though a storm was brewing. Somewhere nearby, Jack was sure, The Evil and the Wardens were doing battle.

They rode cautiously up the long drive past the lake, watchful for Rodeo Dave or Kyle and Tara, but the only person visible was Thomas Solomon. He held up a hand as they approached and drove the golf cart out to meet them.

"You've missed him," he said as they came alongside. "Rodeo Dave just left."

"I know," said Jack, thinking fast. "We saw him, and he said he'd left something behind."

"We volunteered to get it for him," said Jaide. "It might take us a while to find it, though."

"Okay, I guess. But I'll be closing the gates at six, so don't take too long."

"We won't," said Jaide. She hoped that this was true.

Barely a minute later, they reached the moat and trundled their bikes over. A rising wind whipped around them and made Cornelia grip Jack's shoulder tighter. Apart from that, she was quiet and still, and looked all around her, as though nervous. The shadowy courtyard appeared to be empty, but that was little consolation.

Jaide put the skeleton key into the lock, despite the serious mismatch in size, and turned it as hard as she could. She needed both hands but eventually the door groaned open, and Jack and Cornelia slipped inside.

As Jaide stepped over the threshold, a ginger shape darted out of the shadows and leaped onto her shoulders, clinging tight to her with what felt like hundreds of pinprick claws.

She fell forward with a scream that made Cornelia lift off in a flurry of wing beats and squawks. Jack spun around to drive off the thing that had attacked her, his Gift turning the dim light inside the castle even darker than before.

Ari rolled free of Jaide's flailing limbs and stood upright with his legs apart and hair raised along his back.

"I knew you were up to something," he said. "The note said you were going to Tara's. What are you doing here?"

"Doing something important," Jaide said, getting up and dusting herself off. "For Dad. You have to believe us, Ari. We wouldn't sneak around like this without a reason."

"What counts for a reason among troubletwisters is notoriously unreliable."

"But this is different! We're looking for a golden card — the Card of Translocation. Remember? You helped us look for it."

"Not intentionally! If it's so important, why don't I know about it already?"

"Maybe Grandma just hadn't got around to telling you about it yet," said Jack. "Young Master Rourke had only just died. And then she had the accident. And then Kleo was busy keeping you away from Cornelia — it's been a mess, but I swear this is all we know!"

"We can't stand here arguing, Ari," said Jaide, feeling desperate. "The Evil is just outside the wards, trying to get in. We have to do this now."

"How are you going to do it if no one else has been able to?"

"Everyone's been looking in the wrong place." Jaide grinned triumphantly. "Come with us and we'll show you."

"Oh . . . all right," he said, cat curiosity winning in the end, as it always did. "I'm all eyes. And nose and whiskers and tail."

Jack called Cornelia back to him and together they walked up the corridor to the library for the third time that week. A wide line of footsteps marked the way through the dust. Jack took out the flashlights and gave one to Jaide, but they didn't turn them on just yet. There was still enough light coming through the high windows to show the way.

The library was empty. Most of the books had been cleared. A stack of boxes rested behind the door, tagged with labels in Rodeo Dave's handwriting. Whatever else he was up to, he had been genuinely busy.

"So," said Ari, walking around the base of the boxes and emerging with his tail high, "where is it?"

"There," said Jaide, pointing at the painting. It was still leaning against the wall where Rodeo Dave had cleaned it. The resemblance of the *Lady in Yellow* to a young Grandma X was more striking than ever, despite the old-fashioned clothes.

"Behind the painting?"

"*Inside* the painting," said Jack, putting down his backpack and taking out Professor Olafsson and the rope. "Tell us where you saw that constructor thing and I'll go get it."

"On the second floor, two doors along on the left from the main flight of stairs," he said. "It's a long, brass tube that looks a bit like a telescope. You'll need both of you to carry it."

"Okay," said Jaide. "We'll be right back."

The twins hurried through the castle, past all the chests they had uselessly searched before, stiff-limbed suits of armor that contained nothing but wooden frames and cobwebs, and door after door of abandoned rooms full of dusty antiques. The room Professor Olafsson had identified was little different than the others, except for a tubular shape lying on a desk, six feet long and not tapering, as a telescope would. The sheet covering both tube and desk had pulled away, revealing one brassy end capped with a smoky glass lens.

The twins uncovered it completely and took one end each. It was too heavy to be hollow, but not so heavy that they couldn't lift it. Treading carefully, taking turns going backward, they retraced their steps to the library, where Cornelia, Ari, and Professor Olafsson were waiting.

"Now what?" asked Jack, mopping his brow.

"Make two stacks of books three feet high," Professor Olafsson said. "Put the constructor on top of them so it's lined up with the center of the painting."

Jaide hurried off to get some books from a pile that didn't look particularly valuable.

"How do we switch it on?" she asked.

"Switch what?"

"You know, make it work, like a machine."

"This isn't a machine in the usual sense of the word," he said. "It doesn't require activation. In the right environment, with the right operator, it simply does what it's supposed to. Now, let's make certain we do, in fact, have the portal before us, first of all. Jack, did you bring the witching rod?"

After a flicker of panic during which Jack thought he had left it behind, he discovered that it was indeed still inside his backpack.

"Yes, Professor."

"Please direct it at the painting and tell me what you feel."

Jack did so, and was rewarded by an immediate tremor

through the wire. When he lifted his hand, the wire bent noticeably down, striving to reach the painting.

"It's pulling me," he said. "Pulling me closer!"

"As expected. Good. Jaide, can you make absolutely certain that the constructor is aligned with the center of the frame?"

"Yes, Professor." She bent over the tube and sighted along it, shifting it an inch to the right. That was better, but it still needed a book or two under the end closer to her to make it perfectly level. Once she had done that, she nodded.

"Now, Jack, tie the rope around your sister's waist. I trust you can tie a good bowline?"

"A what?"

The professor explained how to tie the knot, and Jack quickly caught on, making a loop secure around Jaide.

"Now wind the rope around that column a few times and hold the end."

Jack wound the rope around one of the columns that supported the balcony above them and busied himself with another knot. Two of them, to be completely sure. Perhaps three.

"Are you sure this is safe?" asked Ari, peering out from behind the stack of boxes as Jack did as he was told, keeping a tight hold on the other end as he did so.

"Is a door safe?" asked Professor Olafsson.

"Of course it is," said Ari, "unless it slams shut on your tail. It's what might be on the other side that worries me."

"There's no reason to be fretful. This is a hiding place, nothing more. Were we attempting a journey to the Dimension of Evil, on the other hand . . ."

"What?" asked Ari nervously.

"The Dimension of Evil," said the professor calmly. "Where The Evil comes from."

"So this doorway could go *there*?"

"Oh, no, very little chance of that!" chuckled the death mask. "No Warden would hide a gold card there. You might as well just hand it over to The Evil."

"Little chance — that's still a chance," said the cat. "Maybe we should think about this. Jaide?"

Jaide wasn't listening to him. She had got the tube almost perfectly in alignment. It just needed a nudge back to the left. She checked again. Perhaps a touch more . . .

The moment her fingers touched the brass, she was wrenched off her feet and fired along its length like a cannonball down a cannon. The shelves of the library blurred around her. Jack's face, his mouth open in an O of shock and the rope whipping through his hands, flashed past in an instant. The canvas ballooned ahead of her, and the frame swept by, flashing gold all around.

She jerked to a halt, wobbling in space as though she'd landed on an invisible trampoline. Gasping, she looked around her.

Jaide was inside the painting. There was the woman playing cards just a step or two away, as three-dimensional as life, albeit frozen into immobility under the spreading branches of the tree. There were the fields, rising and falling in golden waves to the distant hills, and there was the brick path that snaked between them.

Funny, she thought. They had never noticed that the path was made of yellow bricks.

Follow the yellow brick road, she thought, and raised her right foot to walk farther into the world of the painting, where the sky was smudged and the hills were blurry, as though painted in a hurry.

"Jaide!"

The voice came from behind her, wobbly and distant, as though it had traveled through miles of water.

"Jaide, come back!"

It was Jack. She turned to look behind her, and saw his face in the frame, as though he was now a painting. A moving painting, hanging against an endless sunset-hued sky. He was banging against the invisible boundary separating them, calling her name. The rope around her waist pulled insistently at her, vanishing into thin air like the brass tube, where it entered the real world.

"Jack, what's wrong?"

"You have to come back!"

"But I'm perfectly safe here. See?"

She indicated the calm world around her with a sweep of one hand. What could be safer than a painting of a woman playing cards? All she had to do was find the gold card, and she could go.

"Jaide, quickly! We're under attack!"

There was an edge of panic to his voice that couldn't be denied. She took one step toward him, and was instantly snatched up by the cross-continuum conduit constructor and whisked back to her world in a breathtaking rush.

She staggered. Jack grabbed her arm and stopped her from falling. Before she could ask what was going on, there came a booming crash at the library door. Cornelia took off from the head of the Mister Rourke statue and flew squawking up to the landing. Ari stood between the twins and the door, staring up at the shivering wood with his fangs bared.

"What is it?" asked Jaide.

"I don't know," Jack said. "But I don't think the door's going to hold."

Another crash shook the door, then another. The wood splintered inward, making a gaping hole. A metal-clad hand reached through the hole and twisted around to grab the handle.

CHAPTER NINETEEN

BOOBY TRAP!

Quick!" said Jack, who had let go of the rope and was lifting a box of books. "We've got to barricade the door!"

Jaide was frozen for a second by a glimpse through the hole of a domed, metallic head. She thought it was a monster of some kind, but then she realized it was actually a suit of armor — the suit of armor that normally stood right outside the library, now moving on its own!

She ran to help Jack pile boxes against the door and was pulled up short by the rope catching on something. Quickly stepping out of the loop, she pushed a box up against the door. The armored gauntlet couldn't quite reach the doorknob, so it was making the hole larger, pulling off splinters of solid mahogany the size of Jack's hands as easily as he might snap a matchstick.

"What's making the armor move?" shouted Jaide. "Is it The Evil?"

"It can't be. We're inside the wards!" exclaimed the professor. "I don't . . . ah . . . It must have been you!"

"Me?" exclaimed Jaide. "I didn't do anything."

"You went into the painting. That's what woke them up. They're guards!"

"We triggered a booby trap?" said Jack, thinking of his father's old adventure novels. That was what criminals used when they really wanted to keep something hidden. "How do we switch it off?"

"I don't know, dear boy."

"There must be a way," cried Jack. He threw another box on the makeshift wall in front of the door, just as another hand punched through the wood, emerging just above his head. The jointed metal fingers lunged at him, snapping open and shut like the jaws of a metal mouth. Jack staggered back, the hand missing the collar of his T-shirt by a fraction of an inch.

With a deafening crash, the doors burst open, sending the twins and boxes of books flying everywhere. One metal figure thrust through the jagged splinters with arms outstretched, closely followed by a second. The visors on the second one flipped open, revealing that the space within contained nothing but a startled spider.

"Back!" shouted Jack.

Jack retreated, snatching up Ari, who looked as if he was prepared to stand up to an army of magical armor but was more likely to get squashed before they even noticed him, and ran to join Jaide, who had fallen back near the painting.

A breeze was beginning to whip up around Jaide, as she raised her hands and called upon her Gift. Jack's Gift was also stirring, reaching out to the shadows cast by the setting sun, which was painting dark lines down the walls and bookcases. Jack could hide in them, but that wouldn't do the others any good. Although maybe, he thought, if he held on very tight, he could take Ari with him. . . .

The leading suit of armor bulled through the hanging remnants of the door and the fallen boxes and clanked toward them. As it reached the first line of shadow, Jack had another idea. He reached out with his Gift toward the shadow, and it responded by twitching like a snake, the clear line from the window now rippling under his invisible hand.

Jack focused upon it, dragging it up the suit of armor, and then wrapping it around the helmet like a scarf of darkness. Even though the armor was nothing but metal and there were no eyes within the helmet to be confused or blinded, it still stopped and clutched at the veil of darkness that grew thicker and thicker around its head. Its strong metal fingers found purchase on nothing more substantial than air.

Jaide launched a very different attack. The helmet of the second suit of armor was still partly open, thanks to a splinter that had wedged in the hinge of the visor. Moving her fists as though wringing out a tea towel, she built a rapidly spinning rope of air that quickly took on solidity and form, like a spear. As the second suit of armor pushed past the first, which was still held back by shadows, she raised her right arm and threw the spear as hard as she could.

It flew straight into its face. The air rushed through the open visor down into the armor and ricocheted loudly off the hollow metal. Jaide's Gift made the wind steadily stronger and faster until, with a thunderous clatter, the staggering armor exploded. Its head went flying up and its arms went in opposite directions. The torso fell into halves like an exploded iron turtle. The legs stayed standing for a split second, then shivered into their component plates.

Jack cheered, perhaps prematurely, for the collapse of the armor also freed the force that had destroyed it. Both twins staggered back as a whirlwind erupted in the middle of the library, sending books flying in a mad spiral up to the ceiling. Cornelia was swept up into it, and she flashed in and out of sight, screeching madly. When the wind hit

Jack's web of shadows, the two Gifts became entangled. Long black streaks spread up through the funnel of air, threatening to snuff out all light with it.

"Control yourselves, troubletwisters!" The voice of Professor Olafsson was barely audible over the wind. He had been swept into the fireplace and wedged there. "Don't let your Gifts control you!"

"What he said!" added Ari from where he clung to Jack's chest with all twenty claws digging in.

"Stop it . . . please," said Jaide through gritted teeth. She clutched at the whistling air, trying to slow it down, but it slipped through her fingers with playful ease. "Stop it now!"

The remaining suit of armor stumbled into the maelstrom and was lifted off its feet. It turned around in accelerating pirouettes with both arms extended, creating a propeller effect that threatened to chop the twins' heads off when it came close to them. They clutched the fireplace to stop themselves from being swept up as well. Between the two of them, they kept the painting safe.

The spinning armor's left glove hit a bookcase, sending slivers of wood and iron fingers flying like bullets. The armor ricocheted into a wall, which hastened its disintegration even further. Jaide ducked her head as bits of curved metal whizzed around her, screaming for the wind to be still before it killed them all.

Finally, it listened. With a series of crashes and clatters, the whirlwind dropped its load of metal and books and shrank into a self-contained spiral. Cornelia flew out of the top and clung to the upper level's balustrade, feathers in brilliant disarray. The cross-continuum conduit constructor dropped onto the ground at the twins' feet. With a sigh of regret, the wind shrank down into a breeze and vanished.

There was no time to relax. From the hallway outside came the clanking of more metal feet.

"What are we going to do?" asked Jack. "We can't give up now."

"Why not?" said Ari. "That's what your father would want. If whatever's in the painting is so important, he should be the one looking for it."

Jaide was pale, but she shook her head.

"No," she said. "Our Gifts are too dangerous when he's around, and besides, he's needed outside the wards. We have to finish it ourselves."

Ari stared up at her with wide eyes. "Your *Gifts* are dangerous? What about those suits of armor?"

More clanking metal shapes filled the doorway, pushing among themselves to get through first.

"I urge a strategic retreat," said the death mask from the fireplace.

"All right," said Jack. "We can go upstairs and watch from there."

Jaide nodded, even though it felt like running away from the problem rather than solving it. She picked up Professor Olafsson, and together with Jack and Ari, they hurried to the spiral staircase that led to the second tier of books in the library. Rodeo Dave hadn't cleared out up there yet. The shelves were still full, thickly coated with dust and cobwebs that not even Jaide's hurricane had disturbed.

Cornelia greeted them with a weak croak from the balustrade. Some of her feathers had come loose and stuck out at weird angles, but apart from that she seemed unharmed.

"Three sheets to the wind," she said, which didn't make much sense to Jaide, but it made Professor Olafsson chuckle.

"Look," said Jack, still holding Ari close to his chest with one arm. His free hand pointed into the room below.

Three suits of armor burst through the doorway, knocking off chunks of wood and stone with their broad shoulders. None of them was carrying a sword, for which Jack was extremely grateful — particularly as one of them headed for the stairs while the other two stayed behind to protect the painting.

"We'd better get out of here," said Jaide.

There were no doors from the upper level, but there was a window that was just wide enough for the twins to fit through, which hopefully meant their armored pursuer couldn't pass. It was latched but not locked, and when Jaide tugged it open, cool, fresh air rushed inside. The light was fading fast, but she could see out to the tiled roof beyond.

"We could stay and fight," said Jaide, emboldened and energized by the breeze.

"There are dozens of those suits of armor all over the castle," said Ari. "And what's going to stop your Gifts blowing you up, too?"

"There must be a way to switch the booby trap off," said Jack. "Maybe . . . maybe we can look in the *Compendium*."

"We can't go back home!" said Jaide. "If Mom's there, she'll never let us leave."

"Let's worry about that later," said Jack nervously. "I think getting out of here is top priority."

He raised Ari so the cat could wriggle through the gap. Then he put his hands on the frame and hoisted himself up through it. Jaide pushed him from below, trying not to think of the heavy tread coming up the stairs behind her.

Cornelia flapped through next, calling "Rourke" softly until Jack put out his hand for her to climb onto. They were just behind one of the crenulated walls that ran around the outside of the castle. The sky above was as black as pitch and the air smelled of rain. His dark-sensitive eyes made out a way across the roof to another set of windows on the far side.

"Come on, Jaide," he said, hearing the crunch of heavy footsteps on the stairs.

Jaide started to climb out, then suddenly dropped back.

"Jaide!"

"There's someone down there," she said. "What if it's Kyle and Tara?"

She ran to the railing. As one of the suits of armor was laboriously clanking up the circular stair, down below, in the ruins of the doorway, stood Thomas Solomon. He was holding a flashlight limply in one hand and looking around in horror at the scattered books and wooden splinters that now filled the room.

"Get out of there!" Jaide shouted. "Run!"

"What the blazes —"

"Run!" shrieked Jaide. The suit of armor that was after her had almost reached the top of the stairs, and there were two downstairs that were turning toward Solomon.

"Why? What is going —"

He stopped talking suddenly, his eyes widening. Jaide sensed movement behind her and ducked just in time. A heavy iron first whizzed over her, missing her head by inches. Her Gift came to life as she rolled away, whipping books off the shelves and flinging them at the armor. It batted them away like flies, following her with thunderous footsteps. She tried to stand, but the books slipped underfoot, and her crablike backward crawl was taking her away from the window, into a corner. . . .

Finally, she got to her feet and looked around for some kind of weapon. The suit of armor lumbered closer, drawing back its fist for another all-iron punch. She froze, unable for an instant to think or do anything but stare at the gauntlet that was raised to deliver a killing blow.

"Jaide! Move!"

Jaide moved, ducking under the blow and diving past the suit of armor. The wind gathered around her like a cloak, lifting her feet off the ground so it didn't matter that they were slipping on books every time she tried to run. She wasn't really running anymore. It was more like flying, except this was nothing like having wings. This felt like being caught up in a hurricane, moving with the wind wherever it wanted to take her.

Luckily, it was taking her right for the window. Jack held out his arms, and then fell back as it became clear she was coming like a rocket, right for him. For an instant it felt as if she was shooting down the cross-continuum conduit constructor again, except this time it was a window frame, not a picture frame, and what lay on the other side was freedom, not the golden card.

Something cold and hard grabbed her ankle and yanked her back into the library.

"Jaide!" Jack gasped as his sister disappeared just as quickly as she'd emerged into the night. "Jaide!"

He scrambled to the window and peered in. Horrified, he stared at the suit of armor looming over his sister.

Neither of them believed their eyes when the armor let go of her, drew itself upright, and raised its right fist in salute.

CHAPTER TWENTY

TO TRANSLOCATE OR NOT TO TRANSLOCATE

Not very far away, in Portland, the man best known to the twins as Rodeo Dave sat upright at his desk.

"Oh my," he said, as a series of very strange and unlikely memories suddenly rushed back into his head at the instigation of a signal — a signal that had been prepared long ago in case certain events ever came to pass.

He stayed still for a long moment, absorbing everything: the what, the where, and most especially the why. He had chosen to forget so much — his memories had been hidden for good reason. Now that the reason had come back to him, he wished he didn't know again.

Another signal came to him, hot on the heels of the first.

"Oh my, oh my, oh *my*," he said, leaping to his feet and reaching for Zebediah's keys.

Jaide gaped up at the suit of armor that had gone from trying to kill her to saluting her, all in one second.

"Jaide, get away from it!" called Jack. "Now!"

She slithered back a few feet. The armor didn't move. It hadn't reacted to Jack, and didn't react now as she stood up and faced it again.

"Jack?"

She dashed forward and waved a hand in front of the armor's face, jumping straight back in case it was a trap.

But why would it *need* a trap? It had caught her just seconds ago.

"Jack . . . I think they've been turned off."

He climbed through the window and hesitantly approached the armor. When it didn't move, he tapped it on its cuirassed chest. The only thing this provoked was a deep, resonant *bong*.

"I guess they have," he said. "But why? And by who?"

"Let me see," said a muffled voice from his backpack. "Perhaps I can tell you."

Jack pulled out Professor Olafsson. He examined the armor with interest, squinting and pursing his lips until at last he nodded with satisfaction.

"Yes," he said. "Quiescent. Very clever use of the Gift for animating inanimate objects, very tricky, too . . ."

"So why are they suddenly *quiescent*?" asked Jaide.

"Again, I can only imagine that it was your doing."

"Mine? But I didn't do anything."

"You must have. Did you make any unusual signs or gestures —?"

"No."

"Call it by any particular names —?"

"No."

"Touch it, by any chance?"

Jaide opened her mouth to say no to that, too, but then she remembered otherwise.

"It grabbed my ankle," she said. "It touched me then."

"There you have it," said Professor Olafsson. "I expect it was designed to recognize a Warden . . . even a junior troubletwister Warden. The moment you touched one of its agents, the booby trap realized you weren't hostile and stood down."

"I'm glad it did," said Jaide. "But what about Thomas —"

She peered over the balustrade. Two suits of armor were frozen in mid-motion, with the unconscious form of Thomas Solomon hanging between them, his shirt bunched up in their gauntlets.

"Is he dead?" whispered Jack.

"I . . . I think I can see him breathing," said Jaide.

"We'd better go and check," said Jack. He looked around to make sure there were no other moving suits of armor lurking anywhere and suddenly added, "Where's Ari?"

"I don't know," said Jaide. There was no sign of him on either level of the library or on the roof when Jack stuck his head out the window to have a look.

"Perhaps he ran away," said Professor Olafsson.

"He would never do that," said Jaide.

"Unless it was to get help." Jack groaned. "I hope he hasn't gone to wake up Grandma."

They ran down the stairs, Cornelia zooming ahead of them and taking a perch on the picture frame.

Together, the twins gently lowered Thomas Solomon to the ground, though they ripped his shirt in the process.

"He *is* breathing," said Jaide. "But . . . I guess we'd better call an ambulance."

"What if Mom comes?" asked Jack, gesturing at the destruction all around. "How do we explain all this? Shouldn't we go and get the card first?"

"The man is not hurt," pronounced the professor. "He has merely fainted. He will come around in his own time, probably an hour or two."

"Are you sure?" asked Jaide.

"I am sure," said the death mask.

"Okay, let's go get that card," said Jack, "before something else gets in the way."

"Indeed," said Professor Olafsson. "I am curious to see

the cross-continuum conduit constructor in action again. It was a little quick that last time."

The cross-continuum conduit constructor was undamaged, apart from a small dent near one end that Professor Olafsson assured them would not affect its working.

As they lined it up again, Jack asked, "What's it like in there? Did you see the card?"

Jaide explained what she had experienced, then confessed that, no, she hadn't actually found the Card of Translocation yet.

"I'm going to come with you this time," Jack said. "Two sets of eyes are better than one."

"Who's going to watch out for more booby traps and hold the rope?"

"Cornelia and Professor Olafsson will yell if something happens. We can tie the rope to the column and pull ourselves back."

"Actually, I guess we don't need the rope," said Jaide. "I've been through, and we know it isn't straight down or anything. Come on. Let's line it up and we'll touch it together on three."

When the controller was aligned, Jaide counted.

"One . . . two . . . three!"

The twins pressed their hands to the cool, brassy surface. Once again, Jaide felt herself being whisked along from the normal universe of the castle to the one inside the painting. She blinked, momentarily dazzled. There was no visible sun, but everything was lit by a warm, yellow light. She hadn't noticed how dark it was getting back in the real world.

There was a rushing, tearing noise, and suddenly Jack was standing next to her, rocking faintly on his heels and blinking around him as she had done a moment earlier.

"Wow," he said. "That was amazing!"

There wasn't time to gawp at the scenery.

"I'm going that way," Jaide said, pointing along the yellow brick road to the horizon. "You look around here."

"Don't go far," warned Jack. "There could be other guards or traps."

"I'll be careful. I won't go out of sight."

Jack stared up at the strange yellow sky, devoid of a sun, and across at the blurred horizon. Then he put aside his amazement at being inside a painting to concentrate on the task at hand. Where would he hide a gold card if he was the one doing so? There weren't many places, or at least not many he could see close by.

First he tried the tree, peering around its roots and branches and into every knothole. Then he tried the ground around it, looking for signs that it had been dug up, but the ground was undisturbed. It didn't even look like real soil. When he poked at it, it dimpled like rubber instead of crumbling.

Next he tried the table on which the young woman who looked a bit like Grandma X was playing cards. There was nothing taped underneath and there were no visible drawers. The cards themselves were all ordinary cards, much too small to hide something made of solid gold. The young woman was wearing a voluminous yellow dress that Jack was afraid he might have to look under, but it, too, was rubbery like the ground and seemed solid all the way through. Her hair also had the same texture, close up. There was no way to hide anything there.

A gleam of light caught his eye as he was examining her hair. There was something around her neck, something real: a silver locket suspended from a crimson ribbon, studded with tiny jewels. He peered closer, irrationally afraid that she might come to life if he tried to touch it. But she remained exactly as she was, a facsimile of someone, not alive in her own right.

His fingers lifted the locket. It *was* real, not part of the painting. Thinking there might be a clue inside it, he untied the ribbon and pulled the locket free. It rested lightly in his hand, and opened easily when he flicked the clasp with a thumbnail.

Inside was a lock of hair and a photo. The photo had once been black and white, but was now mostly brown. It showed the woman in the painting standing on a jetty, looking out to sea. Next to her was a young man with a broad, infectious grin below a mustache so thin it might have been drawn with a pencil. Both wore old-fashioned clothes, but not as old as the woman in the painting, maybe early twentieth century. Behind them and to one side was the Portland lighthouse.

On the inside of the locket was written: *To Lottie, With Love.*

"Found anything?" asked Jaide from behind him.

He jumped. "No, nothing important." He put the locket in his pocket for thinking about later. "What about you?"

"Not a thing." She looked as frustrated as she felt. The yellow brick road had taken her over the rubbery hills, past fields of rubbery plants, and nowhere had she seen anything that looked like a gold card. And then, just as Jack and the tree had vanished from behind her, they had reappeared again in front of her. The road had looped back on itself, taking her to where she had started with nothing to show for it.

"This can't be a dead end," she said. "The card has to be here somewhere."

Jack agreed, but he couldn't see any way around it. They had searched everywhere and found nothing. There was just the tree, the table, the girl, and the yellow brick road.

Suddenly, he wanted to laugh. "Of course!"

"What?"

"It's like the painting itself, hidden right out in the open. What's the one thing you didn't look at?"

"Just tell me, Jack. This isn't a game."

"I know, but it's really very clever. . . ." He stopped at the look on Jaide's face. "Come on, I'll show you."

He tugged her by the hand.

"It's the road itself, see?"

And she *did* see, all of a sudden, as though a veil had been pulled from her sight. The yellow bricks were the exact size and shape as the golden cards. Any one of them could be the Card of Translocation. All they had to do was find it.

They ran back and forth at random at first, and then more methodically, scanning back and forth across the road surface, looking for telltale gleams of gold. Jaide didn't know how quickly time passed inside the painting, but it soon felt like hours. She tried not to think about how the fight with The Evil was proceeding. They could only go as fast as they could go.

And then, off to her right, she saw a brick that gleamed differently from the others. It had a distinctly flatter surface, and as she ran up to it she saw herself reflected back at her.

"Got it!" she cried, and Jack came running to join her.

"Are you sure?"

"Positive." She slipped the tips of her fingers under the card and lifted. It came free with a click. The Card of

Translocation was released from its long hiding place and into their hands.

"Finally," Jack breathed. "Can I hold it?"

For such a small thing, it was amazingly heavy. About the size of a book but much thinner, it was featureless on both sides and rounded on the edges. Jack turned it over in his hands, marveling at the reflections sweeping across it. As he stared, a faint black X formed on one side, and he felt an odd sensation, as though the gold was becoming icy cold under his fingertips.

For the Divination of Potential Powers, the *Compendium* had said. He wondered if this particular card was divining something in him at that very moment.

Jaide took the card back from him and put it in her back pocket.

"Now," she said, standing up and wiping her hands on her jeans, "let's go find Dad so he can translocate The Evil."

They hurried back to where the end of the constructor stuck out of thin air and they put their hands on it at the same time, returning to the real world in a wild, breathtaking rush. Nothing had changed in their absence: The suits of armor remained immobile, and the mess of books lay under a pall of settling dust.

"Pieces of eight," said Cornelia, dancing admiringly across the frame. "Pieces of eight!"

"We've been watching through the picture frame," said Professor Olafsson. "Congratulations, troubletwisters. You have accomplished something wholly singular and remarkable!"

"It's not over yet," said Jaide, gathering her things together and telling herself not to get too excited too soon.

"We've still got to get this to Dad so he can use it to fight The Evil."

Jack checked the phone. Three missed calls, but they were from earlier, when their father had been trying to get through. No texts.

"We'll have to go out to him," he said. "You saw those clouds before. He's got to be nearby."

"What about The Evil?" Jaide asked.

"We'll be careful. Anyway, we've got the card. We can, uh . . . translocate it, right?"

"You do know what *translocate* means, don't you?" asked Professor Olafsson.

"Sure, we looked it up. It means to move something somewhere else. So it must like getting rid of things."

"Getting rid of things?" asked the professor. "But to where? And what kind of things are translocated *exactly*?"

"I don't know," said Jack.

"It doesn't matter," said Jaide. "We've got it, and we need to get it to Dad."

Jack picked up the death mask and tucked it into his backpack.

"What do we do about Thomas?" he said. "We can't leave him here like this."

"Let's put him in a ground-floor room," Jaide suggested. "There's a bed in one of them, I'm sure. When he wakes up, maybe he'll think he sneaked off for a nap and dreamed it all."

That seemed a remote possibility to Jack, but together he and his sister managed to hoist the unconscious man's arms over their shoulders and drag him along the corridor, to the accompaniment of encouragement from the professor and comments about drunken sailors from Cornelia. At the door to the room Jaide had in mind, Jack took the skeleton key from Jaide's pocket while she held Thomas unsteadily aloft with her Gift. Jack unlocked the door, and Thomas rushed inside on the back of a tiny tornado and crashed onto a sheet-draped bed. The wind howled once around the ceiling and escaped up a chimney, leaving the room considerably less dusty than it had been before. Somehow Thomas slept through it all.

Jaide nodded in satisfaction. "Okay, that's done. Let's go."

Cornelia flew down onto Jack's shoulder as they hurried through the silent castle, Jaide lighting her way with a flashlight, Jack seeing by his Gift alone. They felt buoyed by their success in finding the card, but nervous all the same of what was to come.

There was no one outside, just Thomas Solomon's abandoned golf cart sitting slightly askew on the cobbled driveway. The air was thick with the threat of a storm. Jack could practically taste rain, and he braced himself for another soaking. They hadn't thought to bring raincoats.

Distantly, they heard a wolf howl, and Jaide shivered.

"Which way, Jack?"

Before he could answer, headlights flashed in the distance as a car pulled through the gates. A car engine growled low and deep, getting louder as it accelerated up the driveway. Even from far away, they recognized the light gleaming off the tips of long steer horns.

"Jaide, that's Rodeo Dave's car," Jack said.

"Quick," she cried, "into the cart!"

They leaped aboard, even though neither of them knew how to drive. Luckily, it was as simple as could be: There was a button that started the engine, and from there all Jack had to do was push down the accelerator and turn the wheel.

The cart accelerated down the hill, bouncing across the lawn and around the back of the castle. Jack left the headlights off so the person coming up the drive might not see them. He didn't need the lights — he could see the ground ahead perfectly well. For Jaide it was a far more terrifying experience, clinging to the dashboard in front of her as the cart hurtled off into the darkness, swerving around obstacles she couldn't see. Cornelia jumped ship immediately and followed above, shouting such well-meaning but unhelpful advice as "Trim the mainsail" and "Hard to starboard!"

As they passed the menagerie, they heard the animals calling in alarm. Something had riled them up, Jaide thought. Perhaps they could sense The Evil gathering outside the wards.

Two shadowy figures appeared from the nearest animal enclosure, waving their arms and running in front of the cart.

Jaide gasped and ducked. Jack wrenched the wheel to one side, narrowly avoiding a collision.

"Hey, that's cheating!" called a familiar voice.

"Come back here and give us a ride!" shouted another.

Jaide twisted to look behind her. It was Tara and Kyle. They jumped up and down, hollering for them to come back.

"I forgot all about them," she said. "I hope they're going to stay out of it."

Jack just grunted. The field ahead was rough and bouncy, and he was having trouble maintaining a straight course. He could see the copse where his father had been hiding that week. Getting there was all he could concentrate on at that moment. A heavy rain had started to fall, making it hard to see, and if the ground became too boggy they might get stuck and have to run on foot.

When a glowing blue figure appeared in front of them, the figure of a young man with outstretched arms, Jack gasped and slammed on the brakes.

++Stop, troubletwisters,++ the figure said. **++You don't know what you're doing!++**

"What is that?" asked Jaide, who had only just managed to stop herself from falling out of her seat, such was the violence of their abrupt halting skid. "Who is that?"

"I don't know," Jack said, spinning the wheel with the intention of going around the phantom.

++Jack, Jaide, turn back!++

"Is that The Evil?" asked Jaide, plugging her ears, but the voice in her mind was impossible to keep out.

Jack didn't know. When Wardens talked to them through their minds, they sounded just as echoey and strange. Besides, he was busy trying to get around the phantom. Everywhere he went, it stayed steadfastly in front of them. Stranger still, he could almost believe that he had seen the phantom's imploring face somewhere before.

++Listen to me, troubletwisters — you're making a terrible mistake!++

Another voice struggled to make itself heard over the whine of the cart's motor. It was coming from Jack's backpack.

"That's him!" Professor Olafsson was shouting. "That's the voice I've been trying to remember!"

Jaide pulled the death mask out and pointed him forward.

"Him?"

"Yes! I knew I recognized him from somewhere. He was in the castle, a long time ago. He — eeeeargh!"

Jack braked again as a long red car roared to a halt in front of them, driving right through the phantom and dissolving it into mist. Professor Olafsson flew out of Jaide's hands and went spinning out the window, striking the side of the car with a resounding crack and splitting in two, right down the length of his face.

"Professor Olafsson!" Jaide stood up in her seat but couldn't see if either piece was still moving. "Jack — he's hurt."

Jack was too busy trying to reverse, but the wheels were spinning in the wet grass.

In the rearview mirror, Zebediah's driver-side door opened with a creak and a grim-looking Rodeo Dave stepped out.

"Jack, get us out of here!" cried Jaide.

"I'm trying!"

The cart's engine whined uselessly.

"Don't run, troubletwisters," called Rodeo Dave over Zebediah's long front hood. "I know what you've done, but it's not your fault. You've been tricked!"

"Hurry up, Jack!"

"Don't listen to him!"

Rodeo Dave was coming around the front of the car now. Zebediah's blinding headlights cast his face into deep shadow. The cart was going nowhere. They would have to get out and run for it and hope youth would win out over his longer stride, or —

"The card, Jaide," Jack gasped. "Use it — quickly!"

"What?" Jaide fumbled at her back pocket. "Use it to do what?"

"Translocate him!"

"Translocate Rodeo Dave? But we don't know where he'll go —"

"We have to! He'll stop us from getting to Dad if you don't!"

Jaide pulled the card out into the light. It gleamed wildly in the reflected headlights. A wave of cold made her fingertips numb as she held it up in front of her. A series of black symbols swept across its face, settling on a bold, black X.

She called up her Gift and felt it swirl around her in the night air. Lacking any idea at all how the card was supposed to work, she simply raised it in front of her and said the first things that came to mind.

"Go, card — do your stuff!"

"Jaide, no!" said Rodeo Dave, holding up his hands in alarm. "Don't do that!"

But it was too late. The Card of Translocation had been activated.

CHAPTER TWENTY-ONE
REMEMBERING RODEO DAVE

Jaide's Gift vanished like the air leaving a burst balloon. She felt it going, bleeding out of her in a few seconds, leaving a terrible emptiness in its wake.

"What?" She shook the gold card as though it was a malfunctioning gadget. "My Gift's gone! That wasn't supposed to happen."

"Give it here," said Jack. "You probably didn't concentrate hard enough!"

He took the card and tried exactly what she did.

"No, Jack, wait!" cried Rodeo Dave, stepping out of the light and coming closer.

"Translocate!" said Jack.

Suddenly he could no longer see in the dark. His Gift was sliced away, leaving him blind apart from the dazzling headlights.

"It's not too late, troubletwisters," said Rodeo Dave urgently. "I can make everything right. Just don't run. I'm nearly there."

Jack almost gave in. The card was useless in his hands. They had no Gifts and no means of defending themselves. Perhaps if they gave him the card, they would live to fight another day, as poor Professor Olafsson had put it. Perhaps he would let them go.

Then a voice called out of the darkness to their right.

"Jack and Jaide! Over here!"

Hope returned. It was Hector Shield, and he sounded close.

"We're coming, Dad!" cried Jack, grabbing his sister's hand and tumbling out of the cart.

Rodeo Dave lunged for them, yelling, *"No, wait!"*

They dodged him, and then they were running across the muddy grounds of the estate, following their father's voice.

"That's it! A little farther!"

Jaide had her flashlight on. Hector Shield was just feet away. He waved them closer. He looked disheveled and his glasses were askew, but his face was eager, excited, and relieved all at once.

"The card has taken our Gifts," Jaide called to him. "Translocated them somewhere!"

"That's what it's supposed to do," he called back. "But don't worry — it translocates them into the card itself, with all the other Gifts he stole."

"I didn't steal them," puffed Rodeo Dave from behind them, "and you know it!"

"Shut up, old man. In a moment the card will be mine, and then I'll deal with you once and for all." Hector Shield hurried the twins onward, into his waiting arms. "That's it, children. Almost there. *Almost mine. . . .*"

Jaide hesitated. There was something so gloating and horrible about the way her father was speaking that she hardly recognized him. She had never heard him sound that way before, and she remembered Professor Olafsson asking, *What kind of father . . .* ? Her father would never talk like that. Her father would never threaten anyone.

"Wait, Jack," she said, slowing him by tugging on his backpack. "Something's not right."

"Don't listen to her, Jack," said Hector Shield, reaching toward him. His feet stayed just outside the invisible line marking the boundary of the wards. "Just come . . . a little bit . . . closer. Oh, curse you — I'll come in there and get you myself!"

With that, he lunged over the line, caught the card in one hand, and pulled it from Jack with a cry of triumph.

"No!" shouted Rodeo Dave. He grabbed the twins and pulled them farther back inside the boundary of the wards, away from their father. "This is the worst possible thing! Behind me, both of you."

"Nothing you can do will save them now." Hector Shield capered on the spot, holding the Card of Translocation over his head. Black symbols danced over its surface like numbers on a digital clock that was running too fast. "You were foolish to allow them near the card. Now I have their Gifts, and soon The Evil will have them, too."

"The Evil?" Jaide asked. "What are you talking about, Dad?"

"Just get back," said Rodeo Dave, putting himself in front of them.

"Dad . . . but you can't be Evil. You can't be," Jack said.

"Can't I, Jackaran Shield?" Hector Shield stared at him. "Just you watch."

He tapped the gold card with his right index finger and the symbols stopped moving. It showed a square with a straight line through it. What happened next, Jack and Jaide didn't understand at first, but the air changed around them. The ground beneath their feet also changed, and the rain hitting their faces, and the clouds high above. Hector Shield changed, too. He stood straighter. His face grew longer, more haggard. He didn't look like their father now. He looked like a different man hiding behind the same face.

"Dad . . ." said Jaide, but the word sounded uncertain in her mouth.

++Will you tell them or will we, David Smeaton?++ Hector Shield said in the voice of The Evil.

Not very far away, in Portland, Renita Daniels jumped at a searing pain between her ribs. It felt as though a dagger had stabbed deep inside her, so keenly and smoothly that she hadn't even felt it, until it reached her heart.

"No," she gasped, pressing her wooden hand to her side. "Not again."

And not very far from her, a much older woman, who no longer had a name at all, opened her eyes and took in the dim gloom of the hospital room around her. Her mind felt fogbound and sluggish, the exact opposite of how she prided herself on being, and for a long second she struggled to remember how she had come to be that way. There was a car . . . the river coming up to meet her . . . a series of doctors and nurses in white coats . . . a dark figure creeping in at night, fiddling with her drip . . .

. . . the worried faces of Jack and Jaide . . .

She sat bolt upright, startling the regal cat sleeping at her side, tucked under the sheet so a passing nurse wouldn't see her. The feeling that had woken her from her artificial slumber was strikingly clear. It was also unexpected and urgent. She was needed, and needed badly.

There was no phone by the bed, but she didn't require one. She was awake now. Fully awake. Soon, her powers would return, and until then she was sure there was an ambulance she could borrow.

"A mother," Grandma X whispered to Kleo as she swung her legs out of bed and began looking for her clothes, "never abandons her son."

"Run, kids!" yelled Rodeo Dave. "Run!"

"No!" Jack protested. "His eyes are normal. He can't be Evil. This can't be happening!"

Hector Shield bent forward and pulled down his bottom eyelid. Around what looked like perfectly normal brown eyes was a ring of white.

"Contact lenses!" gasped Jaide.

"But you can't be in here," said Jack, clinging to one last piece of hope. "The wards will drive you out."

++You would like to believe so, troubletwister, wouldn't you?++

To Jack's horror, the hideous parody of his father did another gleeful jig inside the wards' invisible boundary. And only then did the twins realize what had changed when Hector Shield had used the card. The wards had failed.

As though from very far away, they heard Rennie cry out in pain.

++Come to us now,++ said The Evil, raising the card and studying the symbols flashing once again across its face. **++This family reunion is long overdue.++**

++Indeed it is,++ said a voice to their right. **++Put the card down and step away from the troubletwisters.++**

"Grandma!" cried the twins. For it *was* her, as young and beautiful as she always looked in her spectral form, standing just yards away.

++You can't tell us what to do,++ snarled The Evil. **++We are beyond your authority.++**

It thrust the card at Grandma X's image, and a psychic whip lashed out at her, sending her reeling.

++Stop, H —!++

With a cry of pain, she vanished.

Aghast, the twins stared at The Evil as it turned, gloating, to face them again. It raised the card to attack them in turn.

"Rourke!" cried a voice from above. A blue-winged shape flashed in front of Hector Shield and snatched the gold card out of his grasp. "Repel boarders!"

++No!++

"Cornelia!" Jack cried in amazement. "Good bird!"

"Everybody run!" shouted Rodeo Dave. "Get back to the castle!"

He turned to face Hector Shield, who was advancing upon the older man with his teeth bared in a furious expression the twins had never before seen on their father's face. There were lines of white around his eyes, where he had dislodged the camouflage lenses.

++The wards are gone, and you are old and feeble, Warden. The castle will offer no protection to the children. Come to us! We don't need the card to deal with you.++

"Go!" ordered Rodeo Dave before either twin could ask him about what The Evil meant about him being a Warden. "It can't be very strong or it would have taken us already. Take Zebediah! Go!"

Powerless and terrified by the defeat of their father and grandmother, the twins had no choice but to obey. Zebediah's doors were open, and Jack ran to the passenger side, nearly treading on the two halves of Professor Olafsson where they lay in the mud. He scooped them up and jumped into Zebediah's expansive front seat. The doors slammed shut behind them, the engine roared, and Jaide took the wheel as the mighty car leaped forward.

The pieces of Professor Olafsson stared up at Jack from where they lay in his lap, frozen in shock, mirroring the exact way he felt.

"I don't believe it," said Jack.

"Dad being Evil or Rodeo Dave being a Warden?" Jaide couldn't believe either shocking revelation herself.

"Everything!" he exclaimed. "The wards are down, and it's all our fault!"

"If only the card had done what it was supposed to do . . ." Jaide suppressed a sudden feeling of panic that her Gifts might be gone for good.

Jack remembered Professor Olafsson asking them if they knew what *translocate* meant. He raised the two halves of the plaster mask and, figuring he had nothing to lose, pressed them firmly together.

Professor Olafsson sprang back to life with a start.

"Good grief," he said. "Where am I? What caused this terrible headache?" His rolling eyes caught sight of Jack. "Oh, yes. I remember now. The Warden who found me in the castle and asked for my advice. He's an old man now but I still recognized him . . . eventually. It must've been he who hid the card in the first place, set the booby traps and everything!"

"What?" asked Jack. "Rodeo Dave can't be a Warden! And why would he hide the card? What does it do?"

"To *translocate* something is indeed to move it somewhere else. Judging by the way the card affected you two, I'd say it moves not things, but *Gifts*."

"But The Evil said that it has our Gifts now, or will soon," said Jaide. "That they're in the card!"

"That sounds like a reasonable hypothesis. *For the Divination of Potential Powers and Safekeeping Thereof* . . . although it's not usual for cards to hold more than one Gift at a time. Perhaps this one is special because it holds the Gift of Translocation, which gives the Warden who possesses it the power to take other Wardens' Gifts."

"Who would want a gift like that?" asked Jaide.

"The Gift chooses the Warden, not the other way around." Professor Olafsson stared at her out of the corners of his eyes. "This card must *not* fall into The Evil's hands again or it will have all the Gifts it contains, as well as the ability to steal more. That's what makes it so valuable as a weapon."

Jaide brought the car around the estate. She had lost sight of Cornelia momentarily behind the castle. As they passed the menagerie, there was no sign of Tara or Kyle.

"How can we get our Gifts back out of the card?" asked Jaide.

"I suppose you would do the same thing you did before, only backward."

"Yes, but how exactly?"

Professor Olafsson shrugged with his eyebrows.

Zebediah bounced in and out of a deep rut. As they came up the other side, Jaide saw the golf cart accelerating toward them, headlights burning with a cold, Evil light. There was no driver behind the steering wheel.

"Look out!" cried Jack.

Jaide wrenched the wheel as hard as she could. The cart turned in the same direction, and the vehicles collided head-on. Jack and Jaide were flung forward onto the floor. The two halves of the death mask flew apart. Zebediah's engine coughed and died with a hiss, its radiator pierced by one half of the steer horns on its grille.

The twins picked themselves up and tried the doors. Jaide's was stuck, but Jack opened his fine. The Evil cart was a twisted mess of metal and plastic. As they stepped out of the car, it twitched as though still trying to get at them.

++Come to us, troubletwisters. Be one with us!++

They ran for the castle.

"Cornelia?" called Jack, scanning the skies. The torrential rain made it hard to see anything. "Cornelia, where are you?"

They heard a faint "Rourke" from up ahead.

"Jack? Is that you?"

"Over here!" That didn't sound like Cornelia, but it didn't sound Evil, either.

Tara and Kyle came running toward them out of the rain.

"What are you doing?" asked Jaide.

"Trying to round up the menagerie animals," said Kyle. "Their eyes went really weird, and then Chippy opened his cage somehow and they all ran away —"

"Chippy?" asked Jack.

"One of the monkeys. They all have names. I visit them sometimes, when Dad lets me."

"Which way did they run?" Jaide asked.

"That way," said Tara. "We were following when we heard you."

"Let's go," said Jaide, leading the charge.

They ran around the curving moat, and the drawbridge came into view. Next to it was the strangest thing Jack had ever seen: a giant creature made up of all the menagerie animals combined into one. The warthog and the zebra were at the bottom, holding up the lemurs and jackal, which in turn held up the wolves, on whose backs rode both chimpanzees, with all the forest creatures mixed in for good measure. It looked a bit like a gymnastic pyramid, but for the fact that it moved as one. Even through the rain, Jack could see how the fur mixed and mingled, creating a terrible hybrid of all of them at once.

The chimps were at the tip of two reaching limbs that swayed and clutched at something in the sky, gibbering excitedly.

"Cornelia!" shouted Jack.

"Rourke!" The macaw was a blue speck staying just out of reach of the monster.

Jaide was amazed. "Why is *she* still herself? Why hasn't The Evil taken her over?"

"The card must be protecting her," said Jack. "We have to help her!"

Cornelia was struggling to stay out of reach of The Evil. With the gold card heavy in her claws and her feathers full of water, it was amazing she was flying at all. But without their Gifts, what could the twins do?

"What's happening?" asked Kyle, his eyes wide with horror.

"I remember," said Tara in an amazed voice. "How could I forget? These guys are like superheroes. Kyle, wait until you see what they can do!"

"We're not anything at the moment," said Jack, thinking furiously. They couldn't attack The Evil directly, but there might be another way, if they could lure it to the cross-continuum conduit constructor. If they could get The Evil to touch it, it would be sucked into the painting and there might be a way to trap it.

"Cornelia," he called, "go to the library! We'll meet you there!"

"Aye-aye," she squawked back, banking sharply toward the window they had left open on the second floor. The motley creature lunged for her, lost its balance, and toppled with a roar into the moat.

"That's our chance," said Jaide. "Let's go!"

They ran across the drawbridge, dodging mutated limbs that reached up for them from below. They passed under the portcullis, which Jaide briefly considered trying to close. It looked merely decorative, though, so she kept running. When they were through the front door, Jack slammed it behind him and locked it with the skeleton key.

"What . . . what was that thing?" asked Kyle, his face pale.

"It doesn't matter," said Jack. "Don't worry about it."

"Don't *worry* about it? If my dad were here, he'd go mental. So would the Peregrinators. They'd never stop talking about it! That's if it didn't kill everyone first."

"You can't tell them," said Jaide. "It's a secret."

"There's this guy," said Tara. "Big beard . . . deep voice . . ."

She was getting vague and sluggish again. Jaide tugged her down the corridor after Jack, with Kyle bringing up the rear.

"Is this something to do with the treasure?" he called after them. "Did you find it?"

"We'll tell you later," Jaide lied.

As they ran for the library, they heard the distinctive *tramp tramp* of marching metal feet.

"Don't worry," said Jack. "That's just a booby trap to stop people stealing the, uh, treasure. Rodeo Dave must've switched it back on again."

But as they rounded the last corner, it wasn't the usual sort of armor they saw at the far end of the corridor. It was one of the leather suits from the hidden basement, covered with golden serpents. A ghostly white light shone from its eyepieces.

++Your father is ours,++ said The Evil. **++He has been all along. Join him now and give us the Card of Translocation, and we will spare your friends. If not, they will all die.++**

CHAPTER TWENTY-TWO

THE WRONG GIFTS

It's lying," said Jaide.

"I know," said Jack.

"That voice," said Tara with a shudder. "I dream about it sometimes. . . ."

Jack judged the distance to the library door. If they were quick they might just make it, and if they got there first they could retrieve the golden card from Cornelia and start fighting back. "Let's go!"

They sprinted for the door. Jack, normally the fastest runner, took the lead, but he was soon overtaken by Tara, thanks to her slightly longer legs. Once again Kyle fell behind, and Jaide slowed to help him along even though she could see the armor lumbering rapidly toward them, picking up speed with every step. Jack looked as though he was running right for the waiting armor, its arms opening wide to catch them, but when it was still some yards away Jack and Kyle took the turn through the doorway, feet skidding on the dusty floor, barely staying upright.

Jack looked wildly around for Cornelia.

The library was exactly as they had left it, with the two ordinary suits of armor standing on either side of the painting, the cross-continuum conduit constructor directly in front of it, and books scattered everywhere.

"Cornelia!" Jack shouted, struck by the sudden fear that someone — or something — had gotten her.

His flashlight picked out a flash of blue wings fluttering toward him.

"Mind the yardarm," she squawked, letting the gold card drop heavily into his hands, then flew to her usual perch on top of the statue of Mister Rourke.

Jack caught the card with both hands and turned it over to examine it from all angles. Now what? He'd gotten this far, but what could he do next? He didn't have a Gift anymore. Would the card even listen to him?

There was more skidding behind him as the others followed in his footsteps. Tara and Kyle turned to look at the armor as it reached the doorway and came to a complete halt.

Only Jaide didn't stop. She kept running, following a wild guess, right up to the nearest of the booby-trapped suits of armor. Without hesitation, she rapped twice on its chest.

"That thing's Evil and it's after us," she said, pointing, "and we're troubletwisters so you have to help us!"

The armor grindingly came to life. It looked at its neighbor and seemed to confer with it.

"Don't take too long. It's right behind us!"

The armor inclined its head, and the other nodded, too. Clenching their fists, they moved forward to tackle The Evil head-on.

Armor clashed with a sound of metal meeting leather. Jaide stepped hurriedly away from them, leading the others to the base of the spiral staircase.

"What did I tell you?" said Tara to Kyle. "They can do anything!"

Kyle was staring at the card. "Is that *real gold*?"

Tara's confidence washed away Jack's uncertainty. Gift or no Gift, they were still troubletwisters. And now that they had the Card of Translocation, he could get his Gifts back.

He raised the card. Symbols were flicking across its surface, almost too quickly to see.

"Give me my Gift back," he told it.

Something crackled through the skin of his fingers and rushed up his arms, making his hair stand on end and his legs go weak. He felt instantly complete, but weirdly, his eyesight didn't change. The shadows were still impenetrable. Maybe it took time to settle back in, he told himself.

"Did it work, Jack?" asked Jaide.

"I don't know," he said. Things did look a little different, but not in the way he had expected. Everything around him seemed to be growing taller, including Jaide, Tara, and Kyle.

"I think I'm shrinking," he said.

"No, you're not," said Tara. "You're *sinking*!"

He looked down at his shoes, which were already up to the laces in the library's stone floor, as if he was being sucked into quicksand. He lifted one foot, and then put it down and lifted the other. All that happened was that he sank even farther, up to his shins.

"You've got the wrong Gift," said Jaide.

"What use is this?" Jack gasped out in frustration. The floor was up to his knees now. If it continued, he would soon be in the basement — and what happened if he *kept* falling? Would he go right down to the center of the Earth?

With a weird, slippery sensation, the gold card fell through his fingers and clattered to the floor. Jaide snatched it before Kyle could.

"Here," said Tara, offering Jack a hand. "I'll pull you up."

But her hand went right through his without even slowing down.

Panic was rising as fast as the floor. Jack told himself to keep calm and breathe slowly. This was a Gift like any other. He could presumably learn to control it. *Someone* must have, after all, before it had ended up in the card.

He concentrated on making himself solid again, but a sudden pain warned him off that route. What would happen if flesh and stone tried to occupy the same place at the same time? Instead he thought about just his hands, and bent down and pushed against the floor. That worked. He could feel the stone distinctly against his skin. With an awkward push-up move, he brought his legs up out of the stone, concentrated on his feet, and managed to stand without slipping down again. It took constant focus, but he could do it.

Jaide studied the symbols flashing by on the card.

"You obviously have to pick the right one," she said.

"Can I have a Gift, too?" asked Tara. "I'd love to be able to walk through walls."

"I'd like to be invisible," said Kyle.

"Hang on," said Jaide, concentrating on a symbol she recognized: two connected curves like a kid's drawing of a bird, with squiggly lines underneath that might represent air. She had seen something like that the first time Grandma X had shown them the cards.

That was the best lead she had to go on, so the next time she saw it, she tapped the card like The Evil had and cried "Give me that one!" in a loud voice before it could flash away.

The Gift came in a rush that felt like going down an elevator really fast, and for a moment she wondered if she might actually take off.

But she didn't, and when she performed a quick, exploratory jump, she found that she weighed just as much as before. She wasn't falling through the floor, but she hadn't gained a new Gift, either.

"Jack, I don't think it worked."

He didn't answer, except with a long, drawn-out yawn.

She looked at him. He was sagging where he stood, eyes falling shut and arms dangling limp at his sides. Tara and Kyle were the same. As Jaide watched, Kyle drooped to the floor and started snoring.

"What's going on?" she asked. "Am I doing this?"

"So . . . sleepy," said Jack, beginning to sink into the floor again. Tara slumped down next to Kyle, fighting but steadily losing the fight to stay awake. Jaide knew she had to do something before she was the only one left standing.

Like Jack, it was a matter of finding enough control over her new Gift to make it stop working. Concentrating on Jack, she willed him to stop falling asleep. To wake up, in fact.

"Wake up now!"

Jack's eyes flew wide open, and he shot up out of the floor so fast she thought he might keep on going, right up to the ceiling.

"Are you all right?" she said.

"Wow, Jaide. What happened?"

"The gold card happened," she said. "It's not fair! You got a really useful Gift but all I can do is put people asleep, like I'm really boring."

A sudden crash returned their attention to the dueling suits of armor. One of the friendly ones had just been knocked to pieces. The other was still putting up a fight, but it was looking severely dented and its helmet had been wrenched off and was being used as a metal boxing glove by its attacker. A series of thudding footsteps announced the arrival of the third suit of armor from the library's upper floor, but at the same time, a second suit of Evil armor appeared in the doorway, and up above, a window shattered. Something big and angry growled.

"What are we going to do, Jack?" Jaide asked. They were hemmed in on all sides, with Tara and Kyle slumped at their feet.

"We'll just have to get some more Gifts," Jack said, bouncing up and down on his toes and sinking a little bit into the stone each time. He felt a bit too wide-eyed and alert now, but that was better than the alternative. The wave of sleepiness that Jaide had hit him with had felt like being buried in a landslide of cotton wool. "One of them is bound to be useful."

Jaide raised the card and randomly selected another Gift.

Nothing happened.

She tried another.

Still nothing.

"Jack, it's not working!"

"Maybe we can only have one at a time."

"Fiddly thing! Translocate!"

She felt something, presumably the sleeping Gift, leave her and quickly shook the card and watched the symbols flash by. How to choose? At random, she supposed.

Meanwhile, Jack considered his original plan of luring The Evil into the painting. That might fix one suit of armor, but not both, and not anything else The Evil might throw at them.

"Perhaps we could hide in the painting while we find a better Gift —"

The second suit of armor staggered backward into the cross-continuum conduit constructor and tripped over it. The copper tube ended up in an L-shape, and the armor into numerous pieces.

"Or not."

"Lucky we didn't," said Jaide, "or we'd be trapped now."

"Like we aren't already — what the . . . ?"

Jaide was shootings sparks out of her hair. Her skin prickled and tingled with swirling electricity. She pointed her finger at one of the suits of armor, but instead of a lightning bolt, all she got was more sparks.

"Try again!" Jack cried, curling into a ball so he wouldn't get scorched.

"Translocate!"

There were two Evil armors versus one, duking it out in the doorway, and when Jack peered out from his ball, he saw two gray snouts nosing through the balustrade, sniffing for them.

With a flap of wings, Cornelia circled Jack's head.

++Join us,++ she crowed.

Jack ducked back down as the hideous white gaze of The Evil swooped him at very close range.

"No!" he cried.

++Join us,++ growled the wolves, from the floor above.

"Never!" cried Jaide, blinking in alarm at a world that had suddenly gone inside out, thanks to the new and useless Gift of X-ray vision.

++Join us,++ said the two suits of armor. Tara and Kyle stirred, murmuring the same words weakly in their sleep.

"Stop saying that!" shouted the twins at the same time.

The suits of armor went still. So did the wolves. Cornelia turned a circle over Jack, and then flew back to the bust of

Mister Rourke, where she twisted her head from side to side and ruffled her feathers. Her eyes were black again.

"Out of the rain," she said, twisting around to face the doorway, where, with a clatter of metal on stone, the last surviving good suit of armor staggered and fell over, revealing someone new standing there.

++Join us,++ said Hector Shield. **++Don't you want to be reunited with your family?++**

Jack and Jaide drew together. Their father's eyes were hypnotically bright, growing brighter and brighter the closer he came. The natural brown color faded from them until two shriveled contact lenses fell down his cheeks, revealing in full the terrible whiteness beneath. The light made his face look cold and cruel.

He held Rodeo Dave with an arm twisted behind his back, and with one painful wrench, walked him into the room.

"You're not Dad," said Jaide. "You're The Evil."

"We're never going to do what you say," shouted Jack.

++But you did, didn't? And so well, too. You found the Card of Translocation for us — you even rid yourselves of your own pesky Gifts. We are proud of you, troubletwisters. You are practically one with us already.++

Jack and Jaide shook their heads.

"We'll never give you back the card," Jack said. "We know what it does now."

"We know you lied to us."

++Too late, troubletwisters. The wards are defeated. How long can you withstand us on your own?++

"Don't listen to him," gasped Rodeo Dave. "He's not — ah!"

He gasped as The Evil viciously wrenched his arm higher up his back.

"Leave him alone!" shouted Jaide.

++Would you trade his life for one of yours?++ The Evil asked.

The twins glanced at each other, wondering if it was being serious. It had made a similar offer earlier, but they had had no doubt then that it was just messing with their heads. And they came to the same conclusion now. Besides, neither of them was going to let the other go. There *had* to be a way to fight The Evil, even now. Perhaps with their new Gifts . . .

++We didn't think so,++ said The Evil with a sneer.

And with that, Hector Shield's eyes began to clear as The Evil left him and all its other hosts, withdrawing from them so it could gather all its strength to move into the troubletwisters.

The weight of The Evil bore down on the twins. They had felt this before, the terrible, soul-sapping emptiness that wanted to get inside them and make them hollow and lifeless. It was the blackness at the bottom of the ocean, the coldness of winter at the South Pole, and the emptiness of deep space all rolled up in one. They fought it with all their willpower, but The Evil at its full strength was too powerful. The colors in Jack's vision faded to white. Jaide felt her fear peak and then begin to dissipate — and that was the most terrifying thing of all. When she stopped feeling afraid, she would know that The Evil had her completely.

Hector Shield watched it happen with sad, brown eyes.

"Help us!" gasped Jack.

"Dad . . . do something!" Jaide said. *"Please!"*

They were shuffling forward like zombies, their limbs operating without their conscious control.

Hector Shield opened his arms to welcome them in.

CHAPTER TWENTY-THREE

NO ESCAPE

With a deafening crash, a bookcase collapsed in front of the twins, directly on top of their father. The falling bookcase dislodged the one next to it, which dislodged the one next to *it*, and soon the library was full of tumbling books and the shelves that had once held them. The twins reeled backward, released from The Evil the moment its attention was diverted. They blinked and shook their heads, feeling the horrible soul-sapping influence ebb.

"Got him!" cried Kyle, hopping in victory among the tumbled books and high-fiving Tara.

"Is that really your dad?" she asked the twins, poking his limp, outstretched hand with her toe. "And I thought *mine* was a loser."

"He's not a loser," said Jack, hoping Hector was just unconscious under the mountain of books. "He's just . . . it's not . . ."

"He's not your father," said Rodeo Dave, clambering out of a pile of books. "This is what I've been trying to tell you. He's not who he seems."

"Then who is he really?" asked Jaide. "Dad's identical twin?"

She had meant it as a joke, but even as she spoke the words, she was struck by the force of them. So was Jack. It couldn't be true, could it? If it was, that changed everything. . . .

"There's no time to explain," Rodeo Dave said urgently. "Make for the gates and get the card to safety."

"What about you?" asked Kyle.

"I'll follow. Don't worry about The Evil attacking me. The card is what it wants. Go!"

They didn't need to be told twice. Jaide and Jack led the charge through the castle and back out onto the grounds, with Tara and Kyle hot on their heels and Cornelia above, matching their pace.

Outside, the night was storm-racked and furious. Wind buffeted them from all sides. Rain lashed their faces. It was difficult to talk, and nearly impossible to see where they were going. They could only find the road leading to the gates and remain on it by bending low, holding one another to stay together as they ran around the lake.

Jack glanced behind him and saw several dark shapes running after them. It was hard to tell from the water in his eyes, but it looked like chimps on wolf-back again. Their eyes shone like cold stars, fixed permanently on the children's retreating backs.

"And The Evil is . . . ?" shouted Kyle over the sound of the storm.

"Evil!" said Jack.

"Why?"

"I don't know."

"Like you didn't know your dad had an identical twin?"

"We don't . . . that is, he doesn't . . . I mean . . ."

The unreality of the situation struck him hard. He couldn't decide what was stranger — that The Evil had somehow created a mirror image of their father to lure them into a trap, or that Hector Shield really did have a twin brother he had never told them about.

Despite the storm and The Evil and everything else that

was going on, the weirdest thing in Jack's life was suddenly the realization that he might have an uncle he hadn't heard of before.

"Where are the reinforcements?" shouted Tara as the gates loomed ahead.

"I can't see anyone," said Jaide, scanning the road outside. She had been randomly trying Gifts while they ran and had stumbled across Jack's Gift by accident. Using the Gift, she could see the white-eyed animals trailing them with chilling clarity. The chimps weren't riding the wolves — they were now part of them, like miniature, wild centaurs. And they were catching up fast.

Any hope of escape through the gates was snatched from them when the gates themselves came alive and slammed shut in their path.

++Halt!++

The metal whale woven into the gates flapped its tail and snapped its jaws at them. The four kids retreated.

"That way!" shouted Jaide, pointing. Through the wind and rain, the stone walls of a building were visible near the gates. The porter's lodge, Tara's father had called it. It wasn't much, but if they could barricade the doors behind them, that would at least slow The Evil down.

Jack used his grandfather's skeleton key to unlock the front door, and they tumbled inside, one after the other.

"This is where he died, isn't it?" said Tara, flicking on a light switch and looking around. "Young Master Rourke, I mean."

"I think you're right," said Kyle.

Cornelia swooped with practiced ease around light fittings, coatracks, and high-backed chairs, and occupied a familiar perch on a curtain rod in the main room.

"Rourke," she said, dipping her head. "Daft old fool."

A chill wind whipped around the room, riffling book covers, swaying the sheets that covered the furniture, and making Tara shiver from more than just nervousness. It felt ghostly, but had a natural origin. Jaide had finally gotten her Gift back.

She tossed the gold card to Jack. "You want the one that looks like two black eyes."

"And then it's our turn?" said Kyle.

"I . . . don't think it works like that. Look around for weapons. Anything will do."

Jack found the symbol Jaide described and swapped his new Gift for the one he had been born with. His confidence returned the moment his shadow sight was restored. This was a Gift he knew. It might be wild and crazy sometimes, but he understood it. It was part of him.

"Here," he said, giving the card to Tara. "Keep hold of it, and it'll protect you like it protected Cornelia. If Kyle's eyes start to glow, give it to him."

"We can share it," she said, offering one edge of it to Kyle, who gripped it tightly between the fingers of his left hand. In his right, he held two pokers that he had found next to the fireplace. He gave one to Tara, and she hefted it with relish. Cornelia launched herself off the curtain rod and landed awkwardly on her shoulder.

"Man the cannons," she squawked.

"I just want to say," said Kyle, "that this is the most fun I have ever had."

Before either Jack or Jaide could reply, the windows smashed in. At the same time, something large and heavy came down the chimney in an explosion of ashen mud.

The four protectors of the golden card instinctively put their backs to one another, facing outward to meet the enemy, equipped with nothing but pokers and their Gifts.

This time The Evil attacked without words, sensing its goal was within reach. The animals were silent, too, not wasting energy on snarling or growling. They just came for the twins and their friends in a silent rush, armed with teeth and claws and all the cold force of the alien intelligence controlling them. There were the two wolf-chimps, plus the other members of the menagerie crossed with all the night creatures The Evil had scared from burrows and nests across the estate. There were at least three owl-lemurs, six deranged possums with eight legs and two heads, and one zebra-warthog that was too horrible to describe.

Behind them all came the stifling will of The Evil, striving to snuff every human thought from those who stood in its way.

Jaide whipped up several whirlwinds that plucked The Evil's creatures and tossed them around the room. The whirlwinds also tipped up furniture and rattled the roof and doors, threatening to tear them from their hinges, but for once this was okay. Jaide wanted her Gift to go crazy, and she found it harder than expected to really let go. She had spent so long trying to control her Gift, it felt wrong to do otherwise.

Jack's struggle was no different. Putting out all the lights wasn't going to help anyone except him, since Tara and Kyle needed to poke their pokers every time an inquisitive snout snapped too close, but apart from that, he was free to do anything. He threw palm-size patches of darkness like shadowy daggers, temporarily blinding his targets. He pushed possessed creatures into the shadows at his feet, where they struggled and flailed until they finally emerged into full solidity and the light. He danced around the room like a ghost, shadow-walking too fast for anything to get a solid grip on him.

But still, despite all their efforts, the twins were nipped and scratched and clawed. Their clothes offered little protection against wild animals filled with the fury of The Evil. Steadily and silently, not caring how *they* were injured, the circle of animals pressed closer and closer to the card.

Jaide decided to risk all on a desperate gambit.

"When I say duck —" she cried.

"We duck?" said Tara, clouting a determined wolf across the snout with her poker.

"Exactly." She took a deep breath, gathering as much air into her lungs as she could. "Okay . . . duck!"

The four of them dropped to the ground — even Cornelia, who adopted a dive-bombing posture and landed in Kyle's lap. Jaide blew upward with her lips pursed as though whistling, but what emerged was a new vortex, one denser and more powerful than any she had created before. It hung above them, sucking all of the smaller hurricanes into itself, dragging all of the animals they held within them, and becoming stronger in the process. The vortex whirled and roared above their heads, pulling in furniture and everything else not fastened down.

Jack grabbed Jaide's wrist and pulled her out from under the base of the vortex. He could tell from the way the funnel was dancing that it wanted to touch down, but was trying to avoid hurting them. Tara pulled Cornelia and Kyle after them.

The moment they were out of the way, the vortex snapped like a living whip, smashing down through the floor and up against the ceiling, flattening out in a spreading mushroom cloud, gaining more strength as it grew.

Even the largest of The Evil's creatures, the hideous zebra-warthog, was pulled steadily into it, no matter how its clawed feet scratched at the floor. It fell sideways with a roar, and they saw it tumbling and flailing in ever-tightening circles, mixed up with the other animals, its white eyes blazing in anger.

The Evil wasn't done yet. Confined to the vortex as they were, it was easy for the animals to merge into the giant monster the kids had seen by the castle. But Jack was ready for it. He stretched the night in through the windows like taffy, winding it around the creature's many heads and blinding it.

The creature roared without words and reached out for them anyway, flailing with hand and hoof and claw.

Every time one of the limbs threatened to come close, Tara and Kyle whacked it with a poker, forcing it to retreat.

The vortex spun. The creature spun with it. For a long minute, nothing else changed.

Slowly, warily, Jaide, Jack, Kyle, and Tara stood up and faced The Evil in its prison of wind and darkness.

They looked at one another, bloodied and soaked through, clothes torn and disheveled, the Card of Translocation gleaming in Tara's hand.

"Is that it?" asked Kyle. "Have we won?"

At that moment, the ceiling burst open and something bright flashed down into the center of the room. An explosive force flung the four children back against the walls, stunning them momentarily. The vortex trembled, and Jaide reached out with both hands to control it. Jack pulled more of the night into the room, winding ropes of deepest black around the creature it contained.

"Wait," said Tara, "I think there's someone in there!"

Jack peered through the roiling wind. A flash of lightning blinded his sensitive sight, but he did glimpse the figure of a man spread-eagled in the tumultuous wind. Lightning flashed again, and the vortex rocked and swayed. Jaide tried to bring it into line, but when lightning flashed a third time, the vortex wriggled like a belly dancer and spat a familiar figure out on the ruined floor.

A man who looked exactly like Hector Shield landed on his hands and knees, spluttering, glasses completely missing, a familiar pitted iron rod raised waveringly in one hand.

Jack and Jaide just stared at him, the echoes of a very loud thunderclap still ringing in their ears. Was this man their father or some Evil impersonation?

Then with a roar, a saber-toothed tiger leaped through the hole in the roof, closely followed by a much smaller, ginger shadow. Custer and Ari took a protective stance between the twins and the vortex as above them all a helicopter swung into view, its downdraft and spotlight only adding to the confusion.

"Keep back," said the man who might or might not be their father. "Let us . . . uh . . . that is . . ."

The vortex had returned to its former state, with The Evil firmly trapped inside. To illustrate the point, Kyle jabbed the snout of a passing possum with his poker, making it retreat back into the swirling mass of mixed-up bodies.

The saber-toothed tiger circled the vortex once, then sat on its haunches at Hector Shield's side.

"We've arrived too late, Hector," it said in Custer's voice.

"Do you think?" added Ari, staring up in awe at Jack and Jaide.

The twins had eyes only for their father. It had to be him now, if Custer said so.

"Come here, troubletwisters," he said, opening his arms as his twin had, and this time they ran to him without hesitation.

Above them, the chopper came low over the ruined roof, swaying from side to side in the vortex's updraft.

"Is anyone harmed?" came Grandma X's voice over the helicopter's loudspeaker.

Hector took his arm from around Jaide's shoulders and gave her an enthusiastic thumbs-up.

"Good work, troubletwisters," said Grandma X, and the twins glowed with pride. "Your mother says that this time the grown-ups will do the cleaning up."

CHAPTER TWENTY-FOUR
NOT ALL TWINS ARE TROUBLETWISTERS. . . .

The helicopter put down behind the porter's lodge, allowing its passengers to step out onto solid ground. Grandma X was wearing a long coat over her hospital gown. Susan Shield raised an umbrella once they were clear of the rotors and steadied the older woman as they crossed to the lodge's back door. Kleo ran with them, keeping close to their heels in order to share the umbrella.

Arrayed around the lodge, next to several incongruous suits of armor frozen in mid-step, were a number of familiar faces: Aleksandr, Roberta Gendry, Phanindranath . . . The Wardens had come when called, but they were keeping well back now. They understood that this was no ordinary attack by The Evil. This was personal.

Custer greeted them inside the lodge, in human form.

"I'm on my way to get him," was all he said.

Grandma X nodded with a weariness that had nothing to do with tranquilizers or other modern drugs.

"Be kind," she said, "but firm. I want to see him."

He nodded. They went inside.

The lodge was ruined, gutted by wind and rain. Everything Young Master Rourke had owned that wasn't already boxed up was now soaked through or torn to shreds. The ceiling sagged. Floorboards curled under sodden carpet. Even the wallpaper was peeling from the walls.

The source of the destructive force stood on either side of their father. Behind them were two more children and a parrot. They should have been shivering in the cold and wet, but their faces said it all. They were beaming, proud of what they had done. Success kept them warm.

Near them, hissing like a fat, bloated snake, was the black-striped vortex containing what remained of The Evil, evidence that they had done very well indeed.

"Grandma!" the troubletwisters cried, interrupting their explanation of what had happened to greet the new arrivals. "And, Mom — what are you doing here?"

"Your grandmother . . . appeared to me," said Susan. "She said you were in danger. The chopper was the fastest means we had of getting here."

"I heard the call of the Living Ward," Grandma X explained. "Custer was summoned by Ari."

The ginger cat looked smug. "He didn't believe me at first, but the smell of wolf on me was a bit of a giveaway."

Susan looked around in amazement and alarm at the damage, at the vortex, and finally at the twins' father.

"*Were* you in danger?" she asked them all. "Because that wasn't why we moved here."

"That discussion can wait," said Grandma X, opening her arms. "Come here and give me that wretched card."

They ran to her and hugged her, and after a moment Susan hugged them, too.

Tara hesitantly approached the huddle, holding the Card of Translocation tightly in one hand. She was reluctant to give it up. She had seen its power and wanted more than just a glimpse of it.

"Here," she said, winning the war within herself and offering it to Grandma X. "I guess you'll know what to do with it."

"Thank you, Tara. So . . . the Gift of Translocation. That's what this is all about."

Grandma X took the card from her and studied it for a long moment.

"Let's see. It must be here somewhere." Symbols flashed by, as mysterious as the Gifts they represented. One appeared, one they had glimpsed before — a square with a straight line drawn through it. "Ah, yes. Butler's Gift, lost for forty years."

Grandma X raised the card, and something changed. Jack and Jaide felt it, although they couldn't have defined how or where they were feeling it.

Then the animals in the vortex started howling in terror, and they knew what had happened. The wards were back, reactivated by the Gift Grandma X had found. With the return of the wards, The Evil was driven out, and that left its creatures behind, afraid and confused.

"Oh," said Jaide, "those poor things."

She clapped her hands as she had seen Grandma X do, and her Gift, weary from so much exertion, relaxed instantly. The vortex collapsed, and the binds of blindness that stopped the animals from seeing unwound, too, as Jack followed Jaide's lead. The animals staggered dizzily free.

Kyle stepped forward. "Hey, Chippy, here."

One of the chimpanzees lurched to him and climbed up into his arms, scratching its head in confusion.

"Flippy?"

The second chimp joined him.

"We'd better get them back in their cages," Kyle said, "and all the others, before they run away again."

"Tara, will you help him?" said Grandma X.

Tara eyed the wolves with wary skepticism. "Will they do as they're told?"

"Sure they will," said Kyle, "if you call them by name. Come, Tasker. Come, Kress. You'll be good for me, won't you?"

"Ari, Kleo," said Grandma X, "go with them. They should be safe, now the wards are back up. I have shifted the boundaries slightly to include the lodge and the rest of the estate."

The wolves shook their furry flanks and followed as Kyle led the animals out of the room in a ragtag line. All except Cornelia, who flapped warily back to her perch as Ari passed by.

"You don't have to worry about me," the cat said as he trailed after the other animals. "I only eat free range."

That left just Grandma X, Susan, Hector, and the twins. Jack and Jaide returned to their father's side, so glad to be near him again but wary of their Gifts playing up. Fortunately, both Gifts were exhausted and content to remain quiescent, for now.

"How did you know to come?" Jaide asked him.

"The Evil was keeping me busy in Bologna," he said. "Much busier than usual, which should have made me suspicious, on top of your grandma's accident. I called a couple of times but kept missing everyone. That was The Evil distracting you, too, I guess. But then I felt you begging me — like I was there talking to you, when I couldn't possibly be. There was only one way that could be happening."

"It was dangerous for you to come here," Grandma X said to him, "but I'm glad you did. We need to be together for what comes next."

"I wish someone would explain what's going on," said Susan in a strangled tone, as though she didn't really want to know at all.

"You're right, dear," said Grandma X. "Some of it the troubletwisters might already have guessed, because they are always so curious . . . so determined to know everything. I can assure you, you won't be any gladder for having the answers, Jack and Jaide. I wasn't. And neither was your father."

There was movement in the doorway. They turned as one to see Rodeo Dave and Custer leading a beaten man into the room. He looked almost but not exactly like Hector Shield. Now that they were face-to-face, the twins could detect subtle differences between them. One had a harder expression, as though he had known more doubt and suffering in his life, while the other — the father they knew and loved, *their* Hector Shield — had laughter lines and kindly eyes, even when directed at the man who had tried to give them up to The Evil.

"This man," Hector said, as though confessing to a terrible crime, "is Harold . . . my twin brother."

Susan gaped at him, and the twins were no less surprised, even though the possibility had occurred to them earlier. Fantastical though it seemed, it was the only explanation that made any sense. But it opened up a whole new world of questions. If their father was a twin just like them, why had he kept that a secret from them all their lives? What had happened between him and his brother to make them hate each other?

"Don't look so appalled, troubletwisters," said the uncle they had never known they had. "Blood is thicker than water. Isn't that what they say?"

"You shouldn't have come here," Hector said in a low, almost dangerous tone that the twins had never heard before. "But I suppose you've wanted this ever since you fell to The Evil."

"*Fell?*" Harold Shield's eyebrows went up into his sopping bangs. "I gave myself up willingly, so you could live! The least you could do is be grateful."

"For putting everyone I love in terrible danger? I'll never forgive you for that. And neither will Mother."

"Oh, yes, take her side, just like you always did."

"Only because she's right, and you know it."

"You never see my side."

Hector took a deep breath, visibly controlling himself. "You pretended to be me. You sent an agent of The Evil into Portland to put Mother in the hospital. You kept Custer and me busy so we would be out of the picture. You stole what wasn't yours."

"*He* gave it away," Harold said, tipping his head at Rodeo Dave. "He hid it so well he even erased his own memory of it, so he couldn't get it back when the old man died. The fool!"

"Killer!" squawked Cornelia from her perch.

"*Did* you kill Young Master Rourke?" asked Jack.

"No! I wanted to ask him what he knew, but his heart was weak. He died before he could tell me anything."

"So you tricked the children instead, my children." Hector Shield had never looked so angry as he did at that moment. "You *used* them."

"I just wanted to know them!"

"You could have known them," Hector said. "You would have been welcome to. But you chose a different path. You chose The Evil."

Harold Shield sagged with a cry of pain and put his hands over his face.

"It chose me," Harold sobbed. A light rain began to fall inside the room. "It knew I was the weak one. But I've tried to hold it back. I honestly tried to save the troubletwisters.

The Evil said it would spare them if I gave the card to it . . . it said . . . it said . . ."

"It deceived you," said Grandma X, looking even older and smaller than she had in the hospital. "That's all it ever does."

He just shook his head.

"What are you going to do with him?" asked Jaide.

"Do?" Grandma X turned to face her, and some of her usual stature returned. "Wardens don't have executioners. We don't have prisons, or even laws, as the rest of the world would understand them. We have only one punishment for those who betray us."

"Please," sobbed Harold. "Please . . . don't . . ."

Grandma X shook her head. Hector turned his back. Susan and the twins watched, unable to look away.

"I'm sorry, Harold," she said, raising the Card of Translocation and pointing it at him, "more sorry than I suppose you can imagine . . . but you brought this upon yourself."

The gold card turned blank for an instant, then revealed a new symbol, a curling raindrop — Harold Shield's Gift.

He hung his head and wept in silence. The gentle rain falling in the porter's lodge turned to mist and faded away.

Grandma X put the card in the pocket of her overcoat.

"I believe I saw some armor outside," she said. "They can hold him while we attend to other business."

She snapped her fingers. Thudding footfalls sounded in the corridor, and two formerly Evil suits of armor entered the room.

"Watch this man," she told them. "Do not let him leave. I will return you to your rest when I come back."

They bowed and took Rodeo Dave's and Custer's places at Harold's side, gripping him with strong metal fingers.

"Now," said Grandma X, "is there anyone we haven't accounted for?"

"Thomas Solomon," said Jack, wondering if the security guard could possibly still be asleep. "And Professor Olafsson."

"Professor who?" asked Custer.

"A rather unique individual," said Rodeo Dave. "He advised me on how to hide my Gift."

"And he helped us find it again," said Jaide. "We left him in Zebediah."

Grandma X nodded. "We'll go get him now, and pick up any other pieces that might reveal what happened here."

"Literally," said Jack, thinking of the broken death mask as well as the bent cross-continuum conduit constructor, abandoned in the library.

They filed outside, leaving Harold Shield slumped in the arms of the suits of armor. The lingering rain lacked the fury of earlier bursts, but the ground remained sodden and treacherous. Jaide hung back to help Rodeo Dave, who she only now realized was wearing slippers instead of proper shoes. He slipped several times on the slick grass before reaching the rougher road surface.

"I'm sorry we crashed Zebediah," she said.

"No matter," he said. "My old companion still has a few tricks. The dents will be gone by tomorrow."

"The car was your Warden Companion?" she asked, amazed.

"Never a finer example," he said with a grin.

She supposed that wasn't the weirdest thing she had learned that night.

"I can't believe my dad's a twin," she said.

"Not all twins are troubletwisters," said Rodeo Dave, as though reciting a riddle, "but all troubletwisters are twins."

Jaide had heard something like that before, from her early days in Portland. *All troubletwisters are twins but not all twins are troubletwisters*, Grandma X had told them, but Jaide hadn't stopped to untangle it, then. There had been more pressing things, like discovering she had Gifts and her father and grandmother were Wardens. She thought about it now, though, and began to understand that it was a thing of great importance.

"So just because someone's born a twin," she said, "that doesn't automatically make them a troubletwister."

"Correct, Jaide."

"But every troubletwister has a twin, like I do. And Dad does. And you do . . . ?"

"And Custer, and your grandmother. All of us do."

"So where's *your* twin?"

"She . . . well, she's dead, Jaide. Her Gift gave her the power of language: She could understand and be understood by anyone. But she didn't understand herself, and that, ultimately, was her undoing."

They curled slowly around the lake, far behind Grandma X and the others. Jack walked between Susan and Hector. Jaide felt a tiny pang of jealousy. She wished she was in his place, standing next to her father and mother like everything was normal.

"The Gift I was born with was the Gift of Translocation," Rodeo Dave said, although Jaide hadn't asked. "It's a great burden, one only a few in every generation bear. It's only ever used on Wardens who have gone bad, as you've seen, so The Evil can't gain their Gifts for its own use, or so their Gifts won't be used against ordinary people, but it's still robbing a Warden of everything they are, leaving them empty. I began to feel like an executioner. It made me hate my Gift, and the way my fellow Wardens made me use it, but I couldn't give it up completely. That's why I made the card and put my own Gift into it, along with all the other Gifts I had taken. Then I hid it in a place I thought it would never be discovered. I put charms to protect it and warn me if it was ever disturbed. I made a bookmark to remind me where it was, if I ever needed it again.

"But everything went wrong," he said with a hangdog look. "I forgot too much. I even lost the bookmark — I guess it went with a book I gave to George. And Harold must have watched me for years, noticing how much time I spent on the estate with my old friend, and guessed that was where my Gift was hidden. When George died, I knew I had to recover the card before it fell into the wrong person's hands — I remembered that much — but I couldn't remember where I had hidden it, of course. I couldn't go back to your grandmother to ask for my memories back, because that memory was hidden with the card. I didn't even remember asking her to take the memories out of my head, along with most of my memories of being a Warden. It was too hard, you see, to live life as an ordinary man, knowing what I had lost."

Jaide couldn't imagine what it would be like to voluntarily give up her Gift, or come to hate it as much as he had. But she had never once thought of Rodeo Dave as *ordinary*.

"We thought the card would just move you somewhere else," she said. "That's why we used it. I'm really sorry about that, too."

He smiled. "No need to apologize. I would have done the same, in your shoes. And you've learned to your cost what it really does, haven't you?"

She nodded gravely, thinking of what had been done to her uncle.

"Somewhere deep inside," Rodeo Dave said, as though reading her mind, "I believe that Harold is still fighting. He has not, and perhaps never will be, totally subsumed by The Evil."

At the head of the group, Hector was answering some of Jack's questions, with Susan listening in, not saying anything for now. Harold had betrayed the Wardens a year before Susan had met Hector. His betrayal had taken place in the Pacific, during a mighty battle Custer had mentioned briefly, once before. He had returned several times since then, during the twins' childhood, but Hector had always managed to keep him at bay.

"The Evil is cunning," he said, "but not as cunning as a person. And Harold was always the smarter of the two of us. I don't know exactly what he was doing, but it is clear he can operate independently of The Evil, at least for a time. He had his own agenda. When Harold fought off The Evil when you left the wards, he was acting to prevent The Evil from jumping the gun, not out of any kindness for your sakes."

But Jack remembered Harold saying that he had wanted to see them. He was sure that part of him wanted to meet his niece and nephew, even as another part planned to betray them in the near future.

"What happens to him now?" asked Jack. "Are you just going to let him go? He could still be dangerous, even without his Gift."

"We'll take his memories," said Hector. "He'll forget being a Warden, like Rodeo Dave did. He'll forget his Gift, The Evil . . . all of us."

"I don't know if that's a mercy," said Susan, "or the cruelest thing of all."

Hector reached around behind Jack's head and took her hand. "You and me both."

Jack looked up at his parents, together again for the first time in months.

"Is Mom going to forget this, too?" he asked.

"Not unless she wants to," said Hector, glancing back at Grandma X. "As events proved, she needs to know what's happening at all times, just in case anything ever happens to your grandmother again."

Susan sighed. "I think you're right. If I had known what was going on . . . if you and Jaide had been able to talk to me about it . . . none of this would have happened. So, yes, I think it's for the best I stay in the loop. For good."

Jack smiled with relief. Keeping secrets was hard. He didn't know how Grandma X did it.

They came up the main drive. The wreckage of the golf cart and Zebediah were to their left, across the sodden lawn. Jack pointed, and they set off through the mud.

They had barely gone five paces when Jack saw a dark figure rise up out of the car and turn to stare at them.

"Hey, look," he said. "There's someone there."

"Who?" said Grandma X. "Tell me what you see, Jack."

"It's not Tara or Kyle, or Custer, or Thomas Solomon. . . ." He squinted, straining his Gift to the utmost. Zebediah was still some distance off and it was very dark. But the figure was faintly familiar. It was small . . . a woman, perhaps . . . with tightly pulled-back hair. . . .

"It's that new doctor," he said.

"Doctor Witworth?" said Susan. "What's she doing here?"

"Don't let her get away!" shouted Grandma X.

Witworth had seen them and was already moving, running around Zebediah and across the lawn with something tucked under her arm. Custer snarled and leaped after her. In tiger form he easily outpaced Hector, who had started running the moment Grandma X had shouted. Jack wanted to follow them, but Susan held him back, and his Gift was still too weak to do anything. The twins could only watch as Doctor Witworth fled across the estate with the Wardens on her heels.

At first, he thought she was running for the castle, and Custer clearly thought so, too, for he ran at an angle to cut her off. But then she suddenly changed direction, and put on an extra burst of speed. She didn't seem to be running anywhere in particular at all. Just running at random, Jack thought.

"The edge of the estate," said Jaide, coming up alongside him, breathing heavily. "She's making for the boundary!"

"It's not where it used to be," said Grandma X, raising the gold card. "But not much farther and it's stretched as far as it can go. There must be *something* I can use in here. . . ."

"Sandler's Quake?" suggested Rodeo Dave.

"Too dangerous."

"What about the Noose of Ceylon?"

"We don't want to kill her, David."

"What about the one I had for a while?" suggested Jack. "Running's impossible when your feet are sinking into the ground."

"Or you could put her to sleep with my other one," said Jaide, wishing her normal Gift wasn't so exhausted. "Quickly! She's almost at the trees!"

Witworth looked behind her, and on seeing Custer closing the gap in a long powerful lope and lightning gathering around Hector Shield's upraised hand, she put her head down and took the final yards in a desperate lunge.

Grandma X pointed the card and the trees ahead of the escaping woman shook and rustled. Their branches came alive and laced together, forming an impenetrable net.

Custer leaped, and so did Witworth, right into the arms of the trees.

"Why'd she do that?" asked Jack. "She can't possibly escape now."

But then, unbelievably, one of the trees changed. Its knots glowed white, and its branches untangled themselves from its neighbors. With a weird, grinding cry, it pulled Witworth up above its crown, so its branches pointed straight up along its trunk. Then suddenly it dropped down into the earth, pulled by its roots into the safety of the soil.

It all happened too quickly for Grandma X, Hector, or Custer to respond. One second Witworth was there; the next she was gone, rescued by The Evil.

Grandma X muttered something about "that wretched woman" under her breath and put the card back into her pocket. The trees returned to normal, while Custer and Hector peered warily over the edge of the hole that was all that remained of the tree. The sides were already falling in, softened by the downpour.

"You need a Warden who can turn into a mole," said Susan.

"Yes, indeed," said Grandma X, putting a hand on her daughter-in-law's shoulder and sharing some of the weight of her suddenly weary body. "But unfortunately she's in Angola."

EPILOGUE

The Legacy of the Dead

"So Doctor Witworth worked for The Evil," said Jaide as they waited by the drawbridge for the police to arrive. Thomas Solomon, currently standing guard by the gates, had called Officer Haigh about a natural disaster at the estate once he had finally woken up, shortly after The Evil was defeated. His memories needed to be rearranged only slightly to erase his recall of the walking armor. The same with the helicopter pilot. Luckily they had needed only a small amount of Grandma X's influence to incorporate what they had seen into a freakish weather event, different only in scale to the one that had destroyed the bridge three days earlier.

"So it seems," said Grandma X.

"But she couldn't have been the sleeper agent," said Jack. "She only just arrived in Portland."

"What makes you think there was a sleeper agent?"

"Well, someone drove you off the road. . . ."

"I got a look at his face," Grandma X said. "He wasn't from Portland."

Jaide knew better than to ask if she was certain she knew everyone in Portland. She probably knew what they'd had for dinner every night, too.

Hector Shield and Custer returned from a thorough inspection of Zebediah.

"No booby traps," Hector announced. "And no Professor Olafsson, either."

Cornelia flew down out of the sky and landed on Jack's shoulder.

"Man overboard," she said.

"Doctor Witworth took him?" Jack said. "Why?"

"Will he be okay?" Jaide asked.

"That depends on what The Evil wants him for," said Grandma X. "He has no Gift, being an echo of himself rather than his true self. He can't be consumed like living things. There seems no obvious reason to kidnap him, apart from his knowledge." She looked around, taking in the night sky, the castle, and the Wardens patrolling the estate, looking for any remaining sign of The Evil. "I wonder if he was what The Evil wanted all along, and everything else was a ruse?"

This was just one more mystery to add to a night full of them.

"Time for some quick final words," Hector Shield said, squatting down to look both his children in the eye. "I know you thought Harold was me, and he told you to keep secrets from your mother and your grandmother, and I think we'd all agree that this put everyone in very grave danger. Never again listen to anyone who tries to drive a wedge between you and your family, no matter how trustworthy he or she might seem."

They nodded very seriously, wishing they could take back everything that had happened since Monday, when they had first come to the castle . . . except for seeing their real father for the first time in weeks.

He opened his arms and embraced them tightly.

"Do you have to go?" Jack asked, muffled by his shoulder.

"I do," he said, "and you know I do. Your Gifts won't stay still much longer. But you also know that I love you and miss you every second of every day. Maybe your mother will let you buy a new SIM card for that phone Harold gave you, so I can tell you so more often."

Susan looked down at them and, after a moment, nodded.

"This time the communication breakdown was not just at the troubletwister end," Hector said, standing and turning to Grandma X. "Harold was always angry at you for keeping secrets. That's a mistake best not repeated, by all of us."

Grandma X's expression became very hard when her second son's name was mentioned.

"That, too," she said, "is a discussion that can wait."

Mother and son embraced briefly in the rain. They separated with shining eyes.

Hector shook hands with Rodeo Dave.

"Thanks for trying to keep the twins out of trouble," he said.

"Ever a challenge, ever a reward." Rodeo Dave winked, stepping back.

Hector turned to Susan. "Are you sure you're okay with this?"

"Nothing you can say will make me feel any better about it," she said, kissing him firmly on the lips. "Just stay alive."

"I will," he said. "I've got a lot to live for."

Susan let Hector go.

"All right," he said, patting his pockets as though looking for his car keys, "yes, now it's definitely time to go. Good-bye, good-bye! Wipe that beer from your eye!"

The twins smiled at the latest of their dad's weird sayings as he walked a safe distance from them and slipped the iron rod out of his coat pocket. He waved it in front of him, and the rain took on an electric smell. Jaide put her fingers in her ears. Last time she had seen Hector do this, her ears had rung for an hour.

Lightning stabbed out of the sky, striking the ground exactly where he was standing. The thunderclap felt like the world ending.

When light and sound had passed, Hector Shield was gone.

"Whoa," said a voice from behind them. "Did you see that?"

"I told you, Kyle. These guys are incredible."

Tara ran to examine the smoking ground where the twins' father had stood, then she looked straight up.

"Gone, just like that! Amazing."

"Are the animals back in their pens?" Grandma X asked in a calming voice.

"All accounted for," said Kyle, "except for Nellie, here."

Cornelia did her best to hide behind Jack's head, but her tail feathers gave her away.

"I don't think she wants to stay here," Jack said. "Can she come home with us, Grandma?"

"If that's what she wants, I don't know how we could stop her. Susan?"

"Sure, but Jack has to feed her, and clean her cage whenever he's told to."

"Easy!"

Cornelia bobbed up and down. "Nellie wants a nut."

Pleased, Jack reached into his pockets to see if he had anything edible in there to give her, but found only a scrap of paper and something round and metallic.

Grandma X waved Tara and Kyle to her. "You two, I

want to have a private chat with you about what you saw tonight."

"No way," Tara said. "This happened last time. I don't want to forget. I want to tell everyone how incredible Jack and Jaide are!"

"That's exactly what we can't have you doing."

Grandma X raised the moonstone ring she wore on her right hand and held it before Tara's eyes.

"Oooh, pretty," Tara said in a distant voice. "So . . . pretty . . ."

Kyle's eyes crossed and his mouth drooped open.

"Very good," said Grandma X. "Now, I can't go erasing your memories every time you see something you shouldn't. It's bad for a young mind to be tampered with too often. Instead, I will silence you. Not completely; on every other subject you can speak as freely as you ever did. But on anything to do with The Evil and the Wardens and my two troubletwisters here, you can say nothing at all — unless it is to one of us. Do you understand?"

The pair nodded with solemnity beyond their years. Then Kyle sneezed with such explosive force that Cornelia took off with a squawk, dispelling the seriousness of the moment.

"Let's head back to the lodge," said Susan. "Much better than standing here, catching colds."

She took Kyle and Tara in her arms and guided them down the hill, tailed closely by Grandma X. The twins and Rodeo Dave lingered a moment, looking up at the castle wall.

"George wants all this to go to the town, you know," said Rodeo Dave, "to be turned into a whaling museum. A memorial to the whales themselves, too."

"Do you think that'll happen?"

"Oh, the mayor will fight the idea of a memorial, and we both know that developers are already itching to get their hands on it, but I figure it will work out how George wanted. He had a stubborn streak, expensive lawyers, and a good heart. That's a rare combination."

He glanced at Jack, who was examining the two things he had found in his pocket. The paper was the scrap of dictionary Cornelia had given him in school earlier that day, with the word *twister* on it. Looking at it again, he saw another word, one that had a whole new significance after the night's revelations.

"Look." He showed Jaide. "Cornelia wasn't telling us that she knew we were troubletwisters at all."

She looked at the word he was indicating. "*Twin*. She was telling us Harold was Dad's brother, and we never realized!"

"Rourke," said the macaw smugly, although now it sounded more like an ordinary squawk than anyone's name.

"Cornelia's been in Portland a long time, and . . . and she belonged to someone else before Rourke," said Rodeo Dave, peering down at Jack's left hand. "She would have met your dad and his brother when they were young, and parrots, like elephants, never forget. What's the other thing in your hand?"

Jack held up the locket he had taken from the painting. He opened it, and the three of them looked inside.

"I thought so," said Rodeo Dave. "Dear me, that takes me back."

"Is that . . . you?" asked Jaide, recognizing in the picture the phantom of a young man that had chased them across the estate. "With *Grandma*?"

"No," he said. "That's your grandmother's sister."

"Her twin?" asked Jaide.

"Of course," said Rodeo Dave. "I didn't even recognize the painting of her until my memories returned."

"Was her name Lottie?" Jack asked.

"How did you . . . ? Ah, the inscription. Yes, that's what we called her."

"That wasn't her real name?"

"No. It was —" He stopped himself. "I know where this is headed. If I tell you, you'll only try to find her in the Portland records, and then you'll be one step closer to finding out the name your grandmother was born with." He shook his head. "Well, that's none of my business. If she wants to tell you about that, she can do it herself. So you can forget about me giving you any help on that front. All right?"

The twins nodded. They hadn't been thinking anything of the sort, but they were now. How many Lotties could there be in one small town?

"What happened to her?" asked Jaide.

His face fell.

"That was a long time ago" was all he would say. "What's done is done, and best put behind us."

"David?"

He looked up when Grandma X called his name, and waved to indicate that he should come over.

"And now I'm going to forget it all over again," he told the twins. "It's a relief, frankly. I feel better knowing that you'll remember — and I'll be grateful to both of you if you say nothing to remind me, afterward."

They stared at him, stunned, and nodded, one at a time.

"Thank you."

He strode heavily to join their grandmother, who whispered into his ear too softly for anyone else to hear.

"Something terrible must have happened to Lottie," whispered Jaide.

"Maybe she died," said Jack. "Or The Evil took her."

"Like Rodeo Dave's sister."

"And Dad's brother."

They stood with their heads together, both struck by the same terrible thought.

All the Wardens they knew had been twins, just like Jack and Jaide. All of them had lost a sibling, too. Now they were all alone.

"What are the odds of that?" Jaide asked.

Jack shook his head, remembering something The Evil had told them when it had killed the last Living Ward.

One always falls. Thus it has always been, and thus it will always be.

Could this have been what it was talking about?

"No more secrets," said Jaide in her most determined voice. "From now on we make Grandma tell us about our family, about The Evil, about being troubletwisters . . . everything."

Jack nodded, although he suspected that convincing Grandma X to do this might be the hardest thing they had ever attempted.

The rain was easing off. Somewhere nearby, a frog was croaking. The flashing lights of a police car were coming up the drive. Together, Jack and Jaide went down the hill to where the others were waiting.

GARTH NIX is the *New York Times* bestselling author of the Seventh Tower series and the Keys to the Kingdom series, as well as the acclaimed novels *Sabriel, Lirael,* and *Abhorsen.* He lives in Sydney, Australia, with his wife and children.

New York Times bestselling author SEAN WILLIAMS lives in Adelaide, South Australia. He is the author of more than seventy-five published short stories and thirty-five novels, and has written several novels in the Star Wars® universe.